Dear Reader,

I'm so pleased to present *What Kind of Mother*, a twisted Southern gothic novel by modern horror master Clay McLeod Chapman. If you're familiar with Clay's previous novels with Quirk—*The Remaking*, *Whisper Down the Lane*, and *Ghost Eaters*—you'll see some of his favorite themes at work in *What Kind of Mother*: the horrors of parenting, the all-consuming nature of grief and loss, the dark side of storytelling. But it's the *way* the story is told that will make Clay's most ardent fans, as well as thriller and horror readers, feel like they're getting something entirely new.

Clay initially pitched this book to me as Nicholas Sparks gone wrong—and that's indeed what it feels like in part one. There's a small town, a farmers market that serves as a gathering place for quirky locals, vivid descriptions of life on the Chesapeake, and a second-chance romance between two former high school sweethearts. You can smell the brine of the bay, taste the freshly shucked oysters, and see the water turning from blue to green to gray as the light changes each day.

But this is a genre-blending read, and I don't think it's much of a spoiler to say: watch out, this is a trap. Soon enough, we enter into domestic suspense territory. At the center of the plot is a long-missing child, whom most people believe must be dead. But our romantic hero—who is also the father of the missing child and a potential suspect in his son's disappearance—is adamant that the child is alive. Our romantic heroine must then adopt a second role herself: amateur investigator.

The mystery of the missing child will be solved, and the roles of our hero and heroine will morph again. And that's where the book truly reveals itself—not as a romance, not as suspense, but as a mind-blowing horror freak show that absolutely no one will be able to predict. There's a monster at the end of the dream, but it's up to you to decide who that is.

This is one of the most uniquely horrifying, absorbing, and emotionally tender novels I've ever had the pleasure of editing and publishing, and I'm so excited to hear what you think about it. I guarantee you'll never look at a crab the same way again.

Happy Reading!

Jhanteigh Kupihea

Jhanteigh Kupihea
SVP, Publisher
Quirk Books

A Novel

CLAY McLEOD CHAPMAN

QUIRK BOOKS
PHILADELPHIA

Copyright © 2023 by Clay McLeod Chapman

Library of Congress Cataloging-in-Publication Data
[TK]
[TK]
[TK]
[TK]
[TK]
[TK]
[TK]

ISBN: 978-1-68369-380-2

Printed in the United States of America

Typeset in Bembo, Brixton, Buckwheat, and Westsac

Designed by Elissa Flanigan
Production management by John J. McGurk

[photography credits TK]

Quirk Books
215 Church Street
Philadelphia, PA 19106
quirkbooks.com

10 9 8 7 6 5 4 3 2 1

for Cormac

the world is your oyster,

let me pry open its jaws

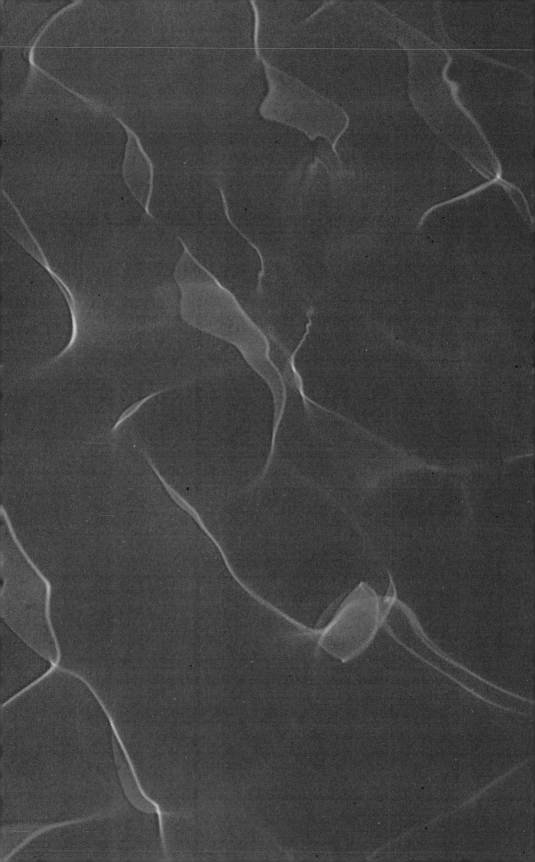

How much I'll strive to please her,

She every hour shall see,

For, should she go away, or die,

What would become of me!

—"My Kind Mother," 1849

ABANDONED BOAT IN CHESAPEAKE CONNECTED TO UNSOLVED MISSING-PERSON CASE

BRANDYWINE, VA.—The Virginia Coast Guard is searching throughout the Chesapeake Bay for a local fisherman after his boat was discovered abandoned on the southern shore of Gwynn's Island.

Henry McCabe, 35, is the owner of the 1974 Chesapeake deadrise. The boat was discovered run aground by a passerby, who noted signs of recent occupancy, including food and children's clothes. Attempts to locate McCabe have been unsuccessful.

Spokesperson Sally Campbell said, "No distress calls were made to our current knowledge, and no hazardous weather was present. So far there are no signs of foul play."

The discovery of the abandoned boat deepens the mystery around McCabe, who was a person of interest in the disappearance of his 8-month-old son, Skyler, in 2018. No charges are being filed at this time.

Matthews County Fire, Poquoson Fire, and the Virginia Resources Commission are aiding in the search.

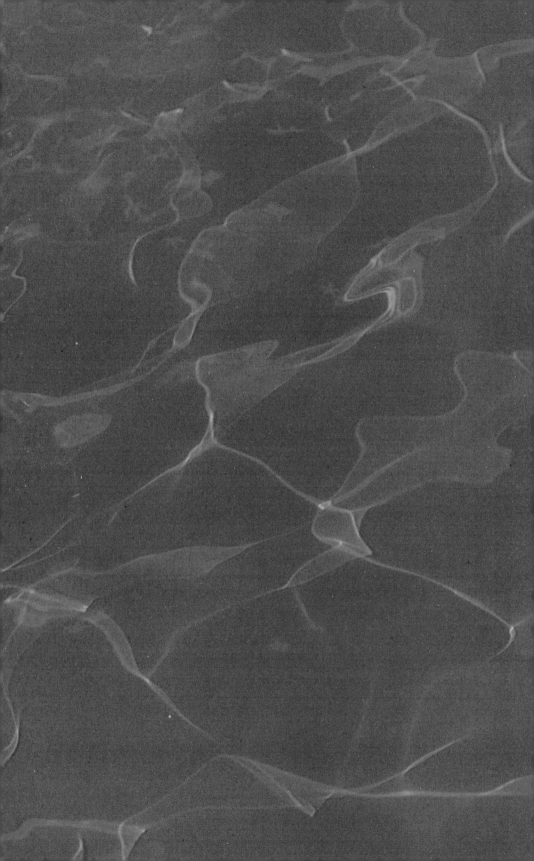

PART ONE

MISSING PERSON

ONE

Give me your hand.

Such a simple invitation. I've asked it many times of many people over the last year. Folks tend to forget how intimate the act is, how vulnerable you become when you surrender your palm to another. Especially to someone like me. The tender flesh of your wrist, the meat of your palm, the peninsulas of your fingers. Their secrets hidden from you but exposed to me.

I'll guide you to there, but first you need to . . .

Give me your hand.

TWO

The Brandywine Farmers Market has been around since I was a little girl leapfrogging over the headstones in the cemetery behind Shiloh Baptist while my mother bought her greens. Even longer than that. Every Saturday at nine on the nose, the church's parking lot is over-taken by elderly entrepreneurs ready to hock their homemade wares.

Each parking space hosts its own stall. Farmers pull in well before the sun even thinks about rising, just so they can snag those hallowed spots up front where the foot traffic flows freely. Truck beds become rusted cornucopias of fresh tomatoes, sweet potatoes, ears of corn sheathed in leathery green husks, cucumbers covered in a fine dust of dirt, broccoli, zucchini, pumpkins, strawberries, and baskets of blueberries. Some even offer jars of pickled okra and peach preserves.

The local fishermen bring their bounty from Chesapeake Bay: blue-shells, oysters, herring, shrimp, mussels, clams, glass-eyed shad—all packed on beds of ice that slowly melt into a briny broth as the hours slip by and the humidity thickens.

Hand-painted signs line the highway for a mile out on either side of the peninsula, luring in passersby with promises of local produce and seafood. People who call Brandywine home still live off the land and water.

I live off your hands. The lines in your skin. The folds in your flesh. A palm reading sets you back twenty bucks. There's tarot, too. I provide a full- or half-deck reading. Aura cleansings.

This is as close to a career as I've got. Long as I can recall, there's always been a palm reader at the farmers market. Used to be my gram. She'd pull out the same tattered tarot deck and let you cut it anyway you liked. I'm not entirely sure why she even did it—wasn't like she was *actually* psychic—other than it got her out of the house on the weekends. I think she simply got a kick out of spinning yarns for a couple quarters, getting the kids all giddy over their destiny— *You'll live a long, happy life, hon . . . You'll meet the fella of your dreams, darling . . . I spot good tidings heading your way, sugar . . .*

It was simple to pick up where she left off after she passed. *Runs in our family*, I'll tell any customer curious about my bona fides. I slip on the same boho tie-back dress with batwing sleeves, armoring myself with enough bracelets that my wrists jangle, *ting-ting*. My work attire, compliments of our local Goodwill. Got to dress the part. I rarely wear makeup nowadays, but when I can afford it, I'll give myself a little smoky eye shadow, just to complete the effect. I'm hoping to grow my hair out, but for now it's trimmed in a bleached crop cut, short on the sides and longer up top, just to give my high cheekbones a fighting chance of catching somebody's eye.

By the time I roll into church, most slots are already full, so I situate my card table at the far end of the lot with the farmers market mafia.

"Morning, Millie. Morning, May. Charlene . . ."

Rain or shine, the biddies of Brandywine come out to sell their jams and freshly baked pies. These three hold court in their lawn chairs, watching over everyone with hawk eyes.

"Was wondering when you'd show." Charlene always sits sweating away in her bowed lawn chair before her stall, selling jams and jarred okra. She cools herself off with her paper fan like some Madame Butterfly in a floral print muumuu hooked up to an oxygen tank on wheels. *My ride*, she calls it, dragging it along with her wherever she goes. The rubber tubes branch out from her nostrils, leaving her looking like she's sprouted a pair of catfish whiskers.

"What did I miss?" I ask as I lay a silk scarf across my table, along with a handwritten sign in flowery font: *PALM AND TAROT READINGS.*

"We were about to give away your spot."

"Don't you worry over li'l ol' me . . ."

"Worried, nothing. You owe me for two weeks now." Charlene serves as the farmers market treasurer, collecting everybody's deposit for the church. "You can't be running a tab."

"Mind spotting me? Just until the end of the day?" I'm not break-ing the bank reading folks' fortunes on a Saturday morning. There certainly isn't a divination 401(k), but it takes the edge off rent. If any of these fine people wish to look further into their future, get them-selves the Madi Price Special, well, I always tell them right where they can find me: *Swing on by the Henley Road Motel, just off Highway 301. I'm in room five. Just look for the neon sign . . .*

"I ain't running a charity," Charlene says.

"Just let me read a few hands first . . ."

"If I let everybody lapse on what they owe, where would we be?"

"I'll pay what I owe, I promise. Hand to God."

"She ain't going nowhere," Mama May mutters. Ever since her stroke, she's been partially paralyzed, only talking out of half of her mouth, slurring her words. "Let her pay later."

Charlene adjusts herself in her lawn chair, grumbling to herself. "End of today. In full."

"You're a lifesaver, Charlene. Thank you."

"Hot one for you today," Auntie Millie says with a sigh. "My face is melting." She's not lying. Millie's mascara clots her eyelashes in charcoal clumps. It looks like she's wearing a pair of melting wax lips, all thanks to that thick shade of crimson she's run over her mouth.

"Weatherman says it's only gonna get hotter," May says. "Well on into the triple digits."

"Don't you start in with that *global warming* nonsense."

"Ain't nobody asking for your opinion, Charlene . . ."

"Then stop listening!" Charlene rests her hand on top of the tank, palming the nozzle as if it were a cane, with a freshly lit Pall Mall nestled between her knuckles. "What'd you predict, Ms. Price? The End Times on their way?"

"Already here, Charlene," I say.

Charlene waves her paper fan at me—*oh hush now*—before moving onto more pressing matters. "Did you hear Loraine Hapkins left her husband?"

Most vegetables are gone by noon, but folks tend to stick around and socialize. Not to mention gossip. Brandywine is small enough that everybody's business belongs to everyone else. If there's anything worth knowing, these three will be chattering on about it.

"I thought they were working things out," I say. Loraine hasn't come to see me for a consultation in over a month. Probably high time I pay a visit, see if I can be of any assistance.

"Tell that to Noah Stetler," Mama May mumbles under her breath.

"What're we talking about?" Auntie Millie asks, leaning in with her good ear.

"Lor-*aine*." Charlene splits the name in half like a wafer.

"Oh, yes," Millie nods. "Loraine's been sneaking off whenever Jesse's outta town."

"Hush your mouth, both of you . . ."

"Everybody knows it's true."

"No thanks to you!" Charlene holds out her sweaty hand to me, palm up, between puffs off her Pall Mall. "I'm long overdue . . ."

"You want a reading? Really?" You'd be surprised how my personal enterprise doesn't sit so well with the Sunday service set, always judgy about my witchy ways. But when push comes to shove, these ladies are just as eager for a peek into their future as everybody else.

"You gonna turn me down?" Charlene asks.

"Take ten dollars off my tab."

"*Five.*"

"Deal. Let's see what we got here . . ." I pore over her palm like a miner sifting for mineral deposits.

"Spot some lottery numbers in there and I'll give you half."

"If I see any winning numbers, you better believe I'm keeping them to myself!" I hear the rasp in her chest, water flooding a phlegmy engine. "How's your health been lately?"

"Why're you asking?"

I run my fingertip along the shallow crease within the left hemisphere of Charlene's palm, as if I'm heading upstream. "Maybe you should schedule yourself an appointment."

"Why? What do you see?"

"I'm no doctor." I try distancing myself from a diagnosis. "Can't x-ray you with my mind, hon, but when I see a line dry up like this, that tends to suggest something needs checking out."

Charlene stews for a spell. "I reckon I'm overdue."

"*Good*. Let's keep you nice and healthy. Who else am I gonna buy my okra from?"

"Lord, you haven't bought okra from me in *ages*." Charlene coughs, then asks, "How's Kendra?"

Hearing her name hits me right in the chest. I'm sure Charlene notices. "Doing just fine."

"She still living with Donny?" Of course she knows. Everyone in town knows Kendra is living with her father after spending nearly all sixteen years of her life with me. That's the whole reason why we moved back to Brandywine. Back to the town where my parents disowned me and my baby daddy made it clear he wanted nothing to do with me.

Charlene's simply testing me, I can tell, digging around for a juicy morsel. Most days I can deflect, but for some reason this morning, it takes all my strength to maintain my smile. I'm not about to give Charlene the satisfaction of knowing she struck a nerve.

"Don't change the subject on me," I manage. "Promise you'll schedule that checkup?"

"Lord above, as I live and breathe." Charlene's eyes widen. Something's caught her attention just over my shoulder. "Look who the cat just dragged in . . ."

"Whose cat?" Auntie Millie leans forward in her lawn chair, straining to pull herself up.

"Over there."

"I don't see—"

"Over there, you blind ol' bat. Is that the McCabe boy?"

"Who?"

"*Henry.*"

I turn to look. Most guys I grew up with lost their hair and gained beer guts, raising a litter of kids in the nearby trailer park. Henry's still got a lion's mane of sandy blond hair.

Lucky him.

He's grown himself a beard, which doesn't look all that bad, to be honest. He's wearing a fleece jacket over a flannel shirt. The stained jeans are a dead giveaway he's living off the river. The Chesapeake raises its fair share of fishermen. He works with his hands, from what I can see.

But it's his eyes that stop me. There's a weight to them.

When's the last time I laid eyes on Henry? Bound to be decades by now. Well before Kendra.

Would he even remember me?

"That poor man," May slurs, shaking her head.

"Poor, poor man," Millie echoes.

"What's he doing here?" Charlene rumbles, offended she wasn't consulted first.

"I hear he's living on his boat," Millie whispers. "After he lost his house, he had no—"

"We'll have none of that talk now." Charlene shuts her down. "You leave Henry alone."

"Just saying what's on everybody's mind . . ."

I can't help but ask. "What's on everybody's mind?"

"Where have you been, child?"

"Not here."

"Their son went missing five years ago," Millie whispers. "Eight months old, *vanished*, just like that."

Did I know Henry had a son? "You mean kidnapped?"

"That's one version goin' 'round." These ladies couldn't mind their own business if they were paid. "His wife had herself an absolutely awful case of baby blues. Nobody saw her for months and—" Millie leans in closer to me and whispers, "She hung herself. *In their house.*"

"Oh God," I say. "That's awful . . ."

"Heartbreaking is what it is," May says.

"Absolutely heartbreaking," Millie echoes, trying to hide a smile, practically pleased with herself for steering the conversation away from Charlene.

"Do they think she had something to do with . . ." I can't finish the thought.

"Depends who you're asking," Millie suggests.

"Ain't nobody asking you, Millie," Charlene says.

"You know just as well as I do—"

"He's one of ours," Charlene chastises them, having heard enough. "Is that how you treat one of our own? A man's got a right to move on. Lord knows he's been through enough."

"Only saying what's been said a dozen times before."

"You wanna cast the first stone?"

Millie sinks into her chair, pouting. "That man's story never made a lick of sense to me."

Charlene straightens her back to let her lungs flex in her chest, easing her wheezing for a spell. "*Henry,*" she belts out across the parking lot. "Get your behind over here, young man!"

Henry does as he's told, making his way over.

Millie pulls out her compact, panicking as he approaches. "How's my face? How is it?"

"Just fine," Mama May says, lying her ass off.

Henry's eyes find me first and won't let go. He smells like a bouquet of Old Bay seasoning and steamed crabs. "Morning."

"Lord, Henry, look how you've grown," Charlene starts. "You're a weed on two feet!"

"Not so young anymore, am I?"

"Hush now." Charlene is all charm. "You'll always be that little boy sitting in the back pew to me. Still got those cheeks I'd pinch every Sunday, even if you're trying to hide them . . ."

"Still got 'em." He smiles, then nods to the other ladies. "Morning, Millie. May."

"Helllooooo," they both coo back.

"You remember Madeleine?"

"I do," he says, nodding at me. "Thought you hightailed it out of here?"

"I did," I say. "For a while. Family brought me home." There's some truth sprinkled in there, somewhere. Nothing would get me kicked out of my own house quicker than a positive Clearblue Easy when I was still under my parents' roof, so the second I saw that plus sign materialize, I knew my fate was sealed. Sure enough, my ass was out the door as soon as my father found out there was a bun in the oven. All seventeen years of myself. *That's not how I raised my girl.* Mom put up a fight, for a while, but she'd never get Dad to change his Methodist mind.

Nobody wanted Kendra. Not my parents, not my so-called boyfriend.

Just me.

The Nova was in my name, so me and my little lima bean hit the road. *We'll make our own future,* I told my tummy, rubbing my stomach like it was a crystal ball and Kendra was a prophecy floating through an amniotic haze. We made a clean break from Brandywine.

For a while, at least.

Henry McCabe. Just look at him. It's like the last sixteen years simply wash away with the tide, swept out to sea, dragging the past back with the undertow. I'm suddenly sent back in time, slipping into high school all over again, thinking about those three months our junior year.

Three months . . . Doesn't seem like much in the grand scheme of things, but back then, lord, it felt like a lifetime. Henry is, heaven help me for saying this, the boy that got away.

The *what-ifs* start stockpiling in my mind: *What if we'd lasted just one more month together? What if I'd stuck with him instead of drifting off with Donny?*

Where would I be now?

Who would I be?

"Wasn't there something between you two back in school?" Charlene prods, even though she damn well knows the answer already. "There was, wasn't there? Now I remember!"

"You selling any beeswax, Charlene?" I ask.

"Always," she says with just a hint of pride.

"Then why don't you mind it?"

That gets a chuckle out of Henry. "It's good to see you."

"You, too," I say. "Didn't recognize you with the beard. You can finally grow one."

"My finest hirsute accomplishment, don't you think?" Henry always tried to hide behind his shoulder-length hair, looking like a pockmarked Eddie Vedder. He'd strum his guitar during lunch, laying low in the school's parking lot where nobody else was listening. But I certainly was.

I'd always sneak out to get stoned in my Nova. Henry set my soundtrack. His voice drifted through the lot, flitting along the parked cars. I went on a mission to find the source of that voice. Sounded so mesmerizing. Lured me in like the tide.

I finally caught him sitting between cars, strumming to himself. *What song is that?*

Henry froze. A long-haired doe.

Sorry. I backed away.

I wrote it. His voice was so small.

For who? He didn't have an answer for that, so I said, *Whoever it's for, she's a lucky gal . . .*

Henry always found himself in the crosshairs of the good ol' boys at school. Anyone who didn't pick up a football with one hand and a can of Coors in the other was bound to be a target. Donny definitely gave him shit. But Henry always seemed destined for better things beyond Brandywine. I believed he could've been somebody. A rock star. He could've taken me with him.

"You're looking just like I remembered," he says, pulling me out of the past. "Haven't changed a bit."

"I got a daughter who'd say otherwise." My fingers find their way to my ear, combing my close-cropped hair back, a reflex from when I wore it longer.

"Kendra, right?"

He remembered. "One and only."

Henry McCabe, I swear . . . What would life have been like if I'd stuck with him instead of Donny Goddamn Watkins? *You wouldn't have Kendra, for one thing,* I say to myself, shooting down this fleeting fantasy before it actually has a chance to take off in my mind.

"You staying out of trouble, Henry?" Charlene asks. "Haven't seen you at services."

"You caught me."

"Never too late to come back . . . Are they still doing that support group on Tuesdays?"

That support group.

"Not enough people signed up," he says without pause. "Closest meeting for families is at Trinity Baptist, but that's a bit far. I'll go every now and then when I feel like I really need it."

"Glad to hear it. What're you doing for work these days?"

"Leave the poor man alone, Charlene," May mumbles out the side of her mouth.

"I don't mind," Henry says. "Little bit of everything, I reckon? Landscaping in the summer, whenever I can find the work. Crab most mornings, but there's not much running."

"Good pickings?"

"Pretty slim, but I'm getting by. Used to sell directly to Haddocks, but they shut down."

"Way of the world," Charlene says. "What're you selling? Those blue-shells I see?"

"Yes, ma'am."

"Any soft-shells?"

"No peelers today, sorry. Maybe in a month. It's been slow this season."

"How much you sellin' them for?" It strikes me that Charlene hasn't harped on Henry for his five-dollar deposit like she did with me, but I figure it's better to let her flirt.

"Twenty a dozen," he says.

"That all?" Charlene lets out an exasperated shout. "Lord, you're simply giving them away! I'll take a dozen off your hands. Been ages since I steamed myself up some blue-shells."

"Very kind of you, ma'am."

"*Ma'am*, nothing. Call me Charlene, you hear?" Her breath catches and, for a moment, I worry one of her air tubes got a kink in it. The oxygen's not reaching her lungs anymore.

"*Madi*." Her expression ignites as she turns toward me. I know where this is all heading before she even breathes a word of it. "Why don't you give Henry here one of your readings?"

"I don't think I should . . ."

"*Nonsense*. If there ever was anyone in need of a forecast for some good weather, it's this young man right here." She lifts her hand and motions to Henry, almost like she's guiding his truck to back into a tight parking spot. "Henry, did you know Madi here is touched?"

"Is she now?" He nods at me, playfully impressed. "I never knew."

Jesus, this is embarrassing. I feel myself blush, all the blood running right to my cheeks. "Gotta put food on the table somehow."

"Go on, Madi," Charlene insists. "See what you can see."

Henry steps back, holding his hands out in a surrendering gesture. This is all a little too rich for his blood. "That's a mighty kind offer, but . . . I'm fine today, thanks."

"I won't hear it." Charlene takes another puff from her Pall Mall, straining to inhale, the smoke spiriting out from her mouth. "First round's on me."

"I've got my own money," he says, a bit defensively.

"Keep your money. I'm paying."

This is only getting more awkward. The two of us are acting like a pair of eighth-graders being forced to dance with each other at the spring formal. "You sure about this?" I ask.

"Doesn't sound like we have much of a choice, do we?"

"Let's get a little privacy." I lead him away from the ladies. I don't want them eavesdropping. Nothing but a bunch of beaming queens giggling on their foldout thrones.

"We don't really have to do this," I whisper as we head to his truck. Lord knows how long he's been driving it. From the rust chewing through its chassis, he should put his Toyota out of its misery before it keels over. There are about five laundry baskets nestled together in the rear truck bed, each one filled to the hilt with blueshells, nothing but a knot of claws.

"I can make something up." I'm still focused on the crabs. "Get Charlene off our backs."

"And miss my chance at peeking into my future?"

"Careful now," I say. "You're giving off one hell of an aura . . ."

"Am I now? You can see all that?"

"Oh yeah, coming from a mile away. A whole lotta dark hues radiating off of you."

He glances over his left shoulder, then his right, checking his personal space for any cumulus clouds gathering around him. "Usually takes longer before the ladies spot my aura."

"I highly doubt that."

Flirting feels so familiar with him, it's easy to slip right back into the habit of it. The tangle of blue-shells shift in their baskets, stirring themselves. Something's agitated them. The wet clicking from their jaws picks up, a froth of air bubbles spuming out from their mandibles.

One crab tries to make a run for it, crawling across the others until it's situated on top. It halts along the basket's handle, inches away from me. It raises its claws over its head.

I can't help but think it's beseeching the heavens.

Henry clasps the crab with his bare hand, unafraid of getting pinched. He tosses it back in the basket. "So how come you don't go by Madame Madi or something like that?"

"Would you trust me if I did, darlin'?" I let my accent linger a little longer. The twang tends to sell the prediction just a bit more. "I'm not gonna glimpse into a crystal ball to sell you on some ham-fisted future. If that's what you're after, try a psychic hotline. They're cheaper."

"You turn away most of your clientele, or just me?"

"Just you."

"Business sure must be booming."

I laugh. "Does it look like I'm hurting?"

"Yeah," he says with the slightest laugh. Or is it a sigh? "I see you're hurting."

"That makes two of us."

Henry goes silent. I can't read him. He's all walled up except around his eyes. There's something buried there, just below the surface.

I glance through the window of his truck. The inside is filled with paperwork. No—not paperwork. *Flyers.* Piles of photocopies occupy the passenger seat, spilling into the footwell.

I lean in and spy a child's blackened eyes peering up from the stack.

The photo of a boy stares back.

It's him.

I hold out my own to Henry, palm up, ready to receive his. "Give me your hand."

Henry suddenly hesitates. His hands are still stuffed in his jacket. "I doubt you'd be able to make much sense of my hands . . . Too many fishhooks."

Why's he stalling on me all of a sudden?

"Either we're doing this or not. You gotta give me your hand so I can do my job."

Does he really want to see? Is he afraid?

"Come on." I give him one last nudge. "What've you got to lose?"

Everything. His eyes pinch and I know I've crossed a line.

"I'm sorry," I backpedal. "I didn't mean to . . ."

"It's all right." Henry hesitates before pulling out his hand. I forgot that he's left-handed. The only southpaw I've ever met other than Kendra. He twists his wrist to expose his palm. The sleeve on his jacket pulls back, exposing thin rivulets winding up along his forearm. *Scars.* I can't see how far they reach, but I can tell these creeks run deep.

"You ready?" I ask, suddenly hesitant myself. What am I so worried about?

"As I'll ever be."

Deep breath. "Let's see what we can—"

I take his hand and there's a sudden rush of water all around me, everything going wet in seconds, a flood rising up from his hand into mine like the high tide and I swear I see a—

duckblind

—I let Henry go and stumble back a step. I hear myself gasp, taking in the air so fast, it's as if I've just burst out from below a body of water.

From the river.

The image persists even after our hands separate. It still feels like I'm in the water. *Where did this river come from?* It's fading now, I'm losing the image, but there, *right there,* just up ahead, I swear I can still glimpse a man-made structure rising up from the water's surface.

A duck blind. Nothing but a freestanding shack on four utility posts, dead center of the river. Do they even make those things anymore? I can't remember the last time I saw one.

Then it's gone. The river recedes all around us, even if I can still feel it.

"What was that?" I hear myself ask, picking up the startled tremor in my own voice.

I'm dripping wet. At first, I think I'm drenched from having fallen into the water—but no. It's simply sweat. The humidity's clinging to my skin, a wet presence, nearly alive. Organic.

I see Henry's sweating, too. Beads of perspiration pebble his temples. "You okay?" he asks as his hand retreats into his pocket, a fiddler crab slipping inside its sandy hovel.

"Yeah, I . . ." I try to gather myself. A dizzy spell has me now in its grip. I can't focus on what's in front of me, my mind still stuck between two places. *What just happened to me?*

I'm thinking heatstroke. I'm thinking I didn't eat anything this morning. I'm thinking seeing Henry after all these years has thrown me off balance. He stares back at me, an anxious expression working its way across his face. "Did you see something?" he asks. "Did you see . . ."

He's about to say his name. It's right there at the tip of his tongue.

"Nothing," I lie. "I didn't see a thing."

THREE

I see him. Just like that.

Skyler.

I'm in sore need of replenishing my Yellow Tail. There's an A&P in the strip mall two stoplights down from the motel, so on my way back home—*home, Christ, since when did I start calling that motel home*—I pull in for a quick pit stop. Seeing Henry—seeing that, I don't know what else to call it, that *vision*—has thrown me off balance. The rest of the day was an absolute bust, slogging through palm readings in a sweltering belch of humidity. All those sweaty hands reaching out for me, slipping across my skin. *Will I find love? Will I find happiness? Gimme gimme gimme.*

I need something to take the edge off. Wash that—

duck blind

—right out of my mind. I've made enough to make rent and still have a little cash left over. Luxuries always come last, after utilities and food. I should put the money away, save it, but after the jolt I just went through with Henry—*what was that, where in the hell did it come from*—I feel like I deserve a little something from the local A&P's wide selection of vintage vino.

I'm still trembling. Even hours later, I can feel the quiver in my wrist. It's in my bones.

What the hell happened? What was that?

Just as the sliding doors part and I step inside the A&P, I hesitate for a second.

Someone's eyes are on me.

I feel them.

Where?

From the corner of my own eyes, I notice someone staring.

A boy.

When I turn, I find Skyler hidden among the flyers for babysitting gigs and guitar lessons. The photo's blown up from its original size, and the image has lost most of its clarity.

Skyler's eyes disintegrate into pixels. He's swaddled in a blanket, covered in hand-stitched animals—a duck, crab, and fish—embroidered along its hem.

Just above his fontanelle, it says: *HAVE YOU SEEN ME?*

The boy's simply been biding his time before I spot him. A game of hide-and-seek. How many times have I passed his flyer and never noticed? How long has he been waiting for me?

Watching me?

I feel the compulsion to take him home. Before I second-guess myself, I slowly peel the flyer from the window and fold it in half, making sure not to crease his cheeks.

Now I see you, Skyler . . .

Now I see.

FOUR

"Give me your hand." I make an empty nest of my fingers, cupping my hands together, ready to receive hers. The young woman sitting across the table from me—Lizzie, I believe she said—offers up her palm. She's eager for me to dive into her skin, but we're not quite there yet. You can't rush these readings. I need to warm up to her. Take her all in. I'm still a bit hungover, opting for the magnum last night instead of the standard bottle. "Ball your fingers into a fist."

"Like . . . this?"

Lizzie's sitting across from me, elbow on the table, palm facing the heavens, her hand and all of its intricate mysteries open to us both, revealing every last facet of her life.

But those cuticles. They're all gnawed.

Let's start there.

"Think of your hand as an egg," I say, "full of life. It's growing, *becoming* something. Soon it's gonna hatch . . . and when it does, we'll see just what kind of future we're dealing with."

I hold her fist for a moment, not saying a word, wrapping my hands around hers and making an enclosure. I gently squeeze, smiling as I do. The parlor settles into its stillness. All that's left to hear is the steady thrum of traffic on 301 purring right outside the window.

"Ready to take a peek?"

She nods, breath held in her lungs. Eyes so wide.

"Let's see what we can see, darling." I crack that egg open. Let her fingers pour into my palms. Now this nest is full of writhing life. Pink skin. A freshly hatched bird.

"My," I marvel, "what a beautiful future you have for yourself . . ."

"You can really see it?"

I see a woman in her early twenties. She's wearing far too much jewelry. Gold hoops. Gold earrings. Gold necklace. Frosted lipstick. Bronze eye shadow. Plucked eyebrows. She's got a metallic complexion, glossy forehead all buffed and polished. She wants to be a sports car, but I can just barely make out the pretty young thing buried beneath the makeup. I'll try to bring that girl back to the surface, if I can. "There's so much to see," I say. "Take a look here . . ."

Lizzie leans in and pores over her own palm, straining to gain some deeper insight from her skin. She's not from around here—but then again, no one really is. Not anymore.

She's never known true heartbreak. I'm sure she's been hurt before, but she hasn't come to me to quell some ache lodged in her chest. Her eyes are too wide for that kind of pain.

She's an impulse shopper. A walk-in. She spotted the neon palm floating in the window as she was driving by and before she could second-guess herself, she pulled her car off 301. That's how I get most of my customers. A neon palm hangs in my window like a beacon, pink and purple bands of fluorescence luring drivers in like the bioluminescent esca on an anglerfish. If traffic is thick enough, the cars all slow down. Folks spot the neon sign, that electrified hand floating by the side of the road, and in that moment, there's a blip in their chest, that urge to pull over. To take a chance on their future.

That's how I catch them. "I'm sensing some anxiety. It's weighing you down, hon."

"How can you tell?"

"The lines never lie." It's not in her palm. It's all right there, on her face. In those milk-saucer eyes that only grow wider the deeper I glance into her hands. I'm clocking all her tells—the myriad of gestures and involuntary microexpressions, the emotions that readily reveal themselves on her face. All the stories she tells about herself without even realizing it.

"See this here?" I trace my index finger across the narrow trench of flesh that branches off from the rest of her palm. It bifurcates a perfectly sturdy love line. "See how it's frayed? Something in your life is causing you unrest. We need to focus on that now. Heal it."

Lizzie's eyes glide side to side. I can tell she's sifting through her own personal history, trying to draw a mental connection. "My mom's been telling me I need to break up with my boyfriend. She *hates* him. They don't get along at all. Could that be it? Is that what you see?"

"This boyfriend. He's new, isn't he?"

". . . Sorta?"

Sorta means not *sorta* at all. But there's a raw nerve here, I can tell. I just have to find my way to the source of this sore subject, see if I can't extract it, like a rotten tooth.

"You and your mother are close, aren't you?" I ask. "You still living at home?"

"Yeah . . ."

"I sense a strain between you two . . ." I close my eyes, as if I'm picking up some bad atmospheric pressure heading our way. Palm readers are like weathermen. We forecast futures. Some predictions may turn out true. Most don't. And if we're wrong? Folks forget. The world moves on to tomorrow's forecast. "This rift's been here for a while, hasn't it?"

Lizzie pulls back on her arm ever so slightly. I can tell she wants her hand back, the two of us playing a game of subconscious tug-of-war. The sleeve of my blouse pulls back, exposing the deep-set tattoo along my wrist—a sun, moon, and star—now nothing but blue lines fading around my forearm. The lines were brighter when Kendra was a girl. She always used to trace her pinkie along the constellation across my skin.

I want a moon, too, Mama . . .

Hold your horses, I'd answer. *You're a little too young for a tattoo, hon . . .*

The star is barely there now, the ink losing its clarity. The sun looks as if it's sinking into my skin. My flesh is now the river and its hazy reflection ripples across the surface of my wrist.

"Did the strain start there?" I ask Lizzie, taking a guess. "With this boyfriend?"

"Yeah." She wipes the corner of her eye with the back of her free hand. *Here it is, here we go . . .* "Jamie—my boyfriend—he borrowed some money from her and . . ."

I definitely don't like the sound of that. "Borrowed?"

Lizzie answers a little too quickly for my taste, "He says he's gonna pay it back . . ."

"Let's focus on your family," I say. "Focus all your thoughts on your mama. Give her your energy. We wanna heal that bond between you two, you hear? That's what's most important."

Lizzie gives me the slightest nod. She wants this. *Needs* this.

"I'm gonna give you some crystals that'll help cleanse you of this guilt you're carrying."

"Crystals . . . ?" Lizzie suddenly senses the upsell. I have to put her pocketbook at ease.

"Amethyst works best," I suggest. "It absorbs any negativity you need to release. Now I'm gonna give you your own stone, free of charge, but you better promise me you'll come back in a month so we can see how things have worked out . . . All you need to do is keep the crystal on you. In your pocket or in your purse. Just have it nearby, so you can connect to its energy."

"Is . . . Is that really gonna help?"

Lizzie needs to release her doubt. She needs to believe she's expelling her insecurities from her body. If a couple crystals can give her a shot of confidence, so be it. Besides, I need more repeat customers if I'm going to get through this rough patch.

"I can already see your aura shifting in its pigments," I say. "You came in here looking like a bruised violet . . . but now I see bands of blue and pink. Healthy colors. *Vibrant* colors."

"Really?" Her voice pinches.

Looking at Lizzie, I can't help but think of myself when I was her age. "Promise me one thing, hon? Boyfriends like Jamie . . . ? They're nothing but ticks. They dig their head in and take whatever they want. Once they're all fattened up, they pull out and cling to the next woman."

And leave you with Lyme disease.

"You deserve better than that, you hear? You are better than that. Say it."

"I'm better," she mumbles.

"Louder now."

"I'm better."

"One more time."

"I'm better!"

I'm giving her peace of mind for twenty bucks. Lizzie will walk out of here, head held high, ready to waltz into her brand-new future a bit more buoyant than when she entered.

Redneck therapy, that's all. People around these parts are more likely to go see a psychic than sit across from a psychiatrist. We don't talk about our problems. We hold them tight, until they weigh us down. We'd rather drown in our insecurities than share them.

What I offer is the same as lying on the couch, only a hell of lot cheaper. The personal matters we discuss in my parlor stay in my parlor. Your secret's safe with me. *Client-clairvoyant confidentiality.* As long as I keep my predictions within the parameters of what's possible, steering clear of any concrete details, everybody gets what they need and nobody gets hurt.

There are worse ways to make a living, don't you think? Lord knows I've slogged through my fair share of shitty positions wherever I ended up: Waitressing at the 3rd Street Diner, stuffing my ass into a tight skirt just for tips. A receptionist at a salon, inhaling nail polish until I felt like I'd faint. Dead-end jobs. No-future jobs. Look at me now. *Moving on up* . . . Right.

"What's wrong?" Lizzie asks, snapping me back to the parlor. For a second, I think she's asking about me—my life—but she leans in, concerned I've spotted a blemish in her destiny.

I'm too distracted. I should call it quits. It's Sunday. *Girls Night.* I'm going to meet up with Kendra and we're gonna have ourselves a tear. I haven't seen her since last weekend—and I'm dying to see my girl.

"Don't you worry. You're gonna live yourself a long, happy life." I offer Lizzie a smile. *You'll meet the man of your dreams . . . You'll come into success soon* . . . Empty prophecies, but we've all given them. I'll be a lucky palm reader if those words never leave my mouth again.

"That'll be twenty dollars, darling . . ."

I see Lizzie out to her Camry. "Promise you'll come back in a month, okay?"

"Okay."

"And don't forget to use that amethyst, you hear? Crystals are game-changers, trust me."

"Yes, ma'am." Lizzie's problems aren't fixed. Far from it. But there's a seed of a belief beginning to sprout. All she needs is a little confidence. The world didn't give her any, so I did.

If somebody had offered me that much when I was seventeen, who knows where I'd be now. Probably not here. Not alone. Nobody opened their doors for me when I needed help.

So I leave my door open for just about everyone else.

Lizzie's gone, just like that. Catch and release. I find myself watching all the cars drift by for a spell, mesmerized by the flow. Highways 5 and 301 dovetail just up the bend, funneling six lanes between the Chesapeake and the Virginia-Maryland border. Traffic is divided by a narrow median of dried scutch. Only lawn I've got. The highway's crumbling asphalt reminds me of those fireworks—a Pharaoh's snake.

Once they're lit, a coiling column of carbon twists out from the flame, wrapping around my home. I'm surrounded by black serpents on all sides.

This place used to be called the Henley Road Motel, back when Brandywine still had its fair share of factories. It only has five rooms. Its faux wood walls flex whenever you lean against them too hard. As soon as the newer highways rerouted traffic, the owner saw the writing on the wall and renovated its rooms into storefronts. Now there's an off-market fireworks store, a Korean mini-mart that never seems to be open, a head shop, and Jimmy's bait and tackle shop.

And me. Brandywine's one and only palm reader. I don't have any set hours. If the neon sign is on, that means I'm open for business. Whenever I head out, I leave my cell phone number taped to a sheet of paper on the front door, telling customers to text me for a consultation. I'm not opposed to making house calls, as long as they're willing to pay for it.

When in the hell did this become my life?

(*Dad says he wants to meet me . . .*)

The motel room is pretty small. Not much space to move around in. Not like I need much. It's just me. There's a bathroom and a closet and that's about it. No television set. The roof must have a few holes in it because whenever it rains there's a leak in the closet. Mildew stains radiate across the ceiling in the far corner. Not that I can complain. Technically, I'm not even supposed to be living here—which is the height of irony: a motel that doesn't allow any residents. But the owner likes me. Takes pity on me. I told him my sob story: how I grew up here, how I'm back because Kendra's biological father found Jesus and finally wants her in his life—how I'm simply trying to do what's right for my girl and find a way to get back on my feet.

As long as rent comes in every month, he looks the other way and I've got myself a home.

Home.

I put up a partition of particle board to separate the domestic from work. A beaded curtain covers the doorway, a mullet made of plastic crystals: *business up front, bedroom in the back.* I've decorated the parlor to give it a little bit of psychic je ne sais quoi. Halved amethyst geodes. Tarot decks. Wilted incense sticks that look like daddy longlegs. I'll light one every now and then when the mildew gets too pungent until the parlor smells like a patchouli factory.

This is only temporary. I'm on the hunt for a permanent residence where Kendra can feel comfortable calling it home. There are a handful of grants for transitional housing. I just have to prove to the state of Virginia that I'm eligible. I can apply for financial counseling, Section 8 housing, rental vouchers . . . Or I can take Donny up on his offer.

A loan, he said, *just until you're back on your feet.* A loan he can hold over my head.

Already I can feel the ennui of Brandywine seeping into my system. All I want to do is pack a bowl and drift for the rest of the day. Watch the traffic pass. The highway is tangled in a web of telephone lines, a spider spinning its threads for miles, tethering the strip malls together—the husks of dead McDonald's, Wawas, Wendy's, and Exxon and Shell stations caught in its web.

I should turn the sign off before I forget. If I leave it on after the sun goes down, the moths gather at my window, battering themselves senseless against the glass. They're desperate for a touch of that flaming hand floating in the dark, yearning for the neon.

Who knows? Maybe there'll be one more customer. I can stay open for a little longer . . .

Just a little while.

I've always had a knack for picking up on what other people want to hear. If you listen closely, you'll learn all there is to know about a person just by what they have to say . . . or don't. It's how people hold themselves. Where their eyes go when they talk. The lilt in their voice.

People just want someone to be honest with them. Palmistry is the sugar sprinkled on top. Makes the medicine go down. Maybe I'm giving these people some comfort. Whatever's weighing them down, I help take away just a little bit of that burden. I show them there's a better future out there for themselves. Somewhere. They just need to reach for it. Grab hold.

Nobody taught me how to do this. I didn't have a book that explains which line in your palm means what. I came up with my own language. My own psychic style. I can tell a story.

Your story.

If I'm going to subject myself to this type of work—*Jesus, a palm reader*—I at least want to make it special. Add some pizzazz. A big ol' bedazzler. I want to tell a story through people's hands, riff on their skin. *Let's go on a journey through your future and see what we can find . . .*

I offer my clients a future they can believe in. Happiness is at hand, so just go on and reach out for it. Grab it. It's yours.

Isn't that what we all want, deep down? A future we can all hold on to? To touch?

Lord knows I do.

I'm thirty-five. I live out of a motel. I'm an outsider in my own hometown, a place I vowed never to return to. I swore up and down nothing could drag me back to this hellhole.

And I came right on back.

For Kendra.

Only her.

Some days it takes all my strength not to break down and cry. I don't know what I'm doing with myself anymore. I don't think I ever really did. *When did this become my life?*

I hear the crumble of gravel under rubber before I look up to see the battered Toyota pulling into the lot. Its engine cuts, the hiss of it sizzling under the hood, metal tinkling like overheated windchimes. Henry finally steps out and takes in the motel. Takes in me.

"Still open?"

FIVE

"Looking for fireworks?" I shield my eyes from the sun so I can take Henry in. If I didn't know better, I'd say he's wearing the same clothes as yesterday. "They're two doors down."

"I came for you."

"You want a reading? Really?" It's women who come to see me. Men tend not to care about their future. Most are firmly entrenched in the present—or running away from their past.

"I need your help." There's no flirtatiousness to him today. None of that sheep-wool warmth from before. There's a lonesomeness about him that he's not trying to hide anymore.

". . . Help?"

"Finding my son." His words are plain, stripped of any charade. He looks exhausted. When was the last time this man got any sleep? "Help me find Skyler."

His son's name pushes against my chest and I reflexively step back. "Henry, I . . ."

"Please." Henry takes a step forward and I see the strain in his eyes, a pair of filaments flooding with desperate electricity, growing brighter by the breath. "You saw something yesterday, didn't you? *Sensed* something? At the farmers market?"

"I don't know what I saw . . ." It's the truth.

"You did, didn't you?" I hear the need weighing down his words.

"Just tell me you did—"

"No." I need to shut this down. *Now.* Put a stop to this conversation before it goes any further. None of this is healthy. "Just get back in your truck and head home, okay?"

"What home?"

Look at the open wounds of his eyes, the grief, the not-knowing simmering within. He'll eat himself alive if someone doesn't stop him. Just not me. "I'm sorry, Henry . . . I can't do this."

"*Please.*" The word spills out suddenly, it silences me. Scares me. He knows he's crossed a line, but there's no turning back now. He has to keep going. Keep falling forward.

"Just hear me out. Please. That's all I ask." He pulls his hand from his jacket and holds it out in front of him, as if he's trying to tell a dog he means no harm. His wrist trembles. He notices it shaking the same time I do, balling his hand into a fist and squeezing the tremors out.

"I couldn't sleep last night," he says. "I kept thinking about—about you."

When was the last time anyone lost sleep over me?

"It can't be chance that we crossed paths . . . can it? Tell me you feel it, too."

I feel dizzy. Numb. Curious. "You really believe that?"

"What else have I got left?" Henry's slowly coming into focus for me. I understand the wall, why he's so closed off. It's not just from me; he's shut himself off from everyone. Himself, even. "I felt something yesterday. I don't know what it was, but for a second, it felt like—like—"

"Water," I say. Water everywhere. A sudden flood in my mind.

"Let me tell you what happened to Skyler," he says. "I'm sure folks have already—"

"I wouldn't listen to them even if—"

"Just let me tell you my side of the story, all right? Please?"

I understand what it's like when everybody whispers behind your back, when people turn your life into a story without your consent.

That's something we have in common.

I at least owe it to Henry to listen. "All right."

Henry takes in as much air as his lungs will allow. "Skyler disappeared five years ago."

I picture Skyler's face. Not flesh and blood, but from his missing-person flyer, that black-and-white baby picture photocopied into oblivion. His pixilated eyes stare back. Two black holes.

"My son came into this world long enough for everyone to fall in love with him. They pinched his feet. Tickled his tummy. If you'd seen him, you would've fallen for him, too . . ."

The words are too heavy. I can feel his hurt, his loss. The man's got nowhere else to go, but down, down, down.

"Grace put him in his crib and kissed him good night . . ."

Grace. His wife.

"The next morning, the crib was empty. Skyler was gone. This world devoured him."

Listen to him. Just *look* at him. Laid bare like this.

"I looked everywhere. Tore through our house. I couldn't find him. He was just . . . *gone.*"

How many times has he told this story? To the police? To reporters? Anyone willing to listen? It has a well-worn feel, like leather, a narrative that's softened itself with each retelling.

It's all he has now. He's wrapped himself up in this story, as if it's a protective blanket.

"What about your wife?"

"I found her body," he says. I see the muscles in his throat constrict, as if the words themselves are getting caught in his throat. He's forcing himself to finish the story he started. "She'd hung herself in our bathroom. No note. No good-bye. Nothing."

"Do the police think she had something to—"

"She wouldn't."

"If she'd been going through postpartum depression or—"

"No matter how many doors I knock on, no matter how many

flyers I hand out, people want to believe she . . ." He doesn't finish. "Grace would never hurt Skyler. *Never*, understand?"

"All right . . ."

"Police started knocking on neighbors' doors," he says. "Search parties cut through the fields, beating down weeds. Nothing. Nobody found a thing. He just . . . just *vanished*."

He's buckling under the memory. His eyes start to well up. He won't cry. He's had years for that. But I can see the pressure building up within him. His pain has nowhere to go, even now, bottled up for so long. It's all about to burst right out from behind his eyes, like a shaken soda can bound to explode. "The police gave up. They still haven't come up with a single goddamn answer. *Five years* and they don't know if he's alive or dead . . . or . . ."

. . . *Or what?* What else is there? Even Henry shakes his head at the absurdity of this, as if he realizes there is no other option. What's between life or death?

"There are no leads," he says. "No one knows a thing."

Now he looks at me, finding my eyes.

"Then I saw you."

I feel as if I stood up too fast. Now the parking lot pitches beneath my feet. I want the ground to flatten itself all over again. I'm afraid of what he's come for. I'm terrified of his need.

He doesn't believe I can find Skyler, does he?

"I've seen psychics on TV helping with missing-person cases."

"No, Henry."

"I've seen them lead police right to—"

"Those are just vultures pecking at people's grief."

"You won't help? Won't look for him?"

"I . . . I just read people's palms, Henry. I'm not actually a psychic—"

"But you *saw* something."

"I didn't."

The sting strikes his eyes. He opens himself up to me and what do

I do? Pour salt right in his wounds. More like Old Bay. He reaches for his wallet. "Is this about money? 'Cause I'll pay . . ."

Now that's a goddamn slap. "I'd never take your money."

"Then why won't you help?"

"*Because I can't.*"

Henry's attention drifts, cut loose from our conversation. Now he's caught in that liminal space between here and there. It doesn't last more than a few seconds, barely a breath, but he's completely lost in it, wherever his mind has gone. "You ever had a memorial service for someone who wasn't there? They buried an empty coffin. Nothing but a hollow pocket of air."

He finally comes back to me. It's like he has just woken up from a deep sleep, discovering there's someone staring back at him. He blinks back to the parlor. To his empty life.

To me.

"Who's that casket for?" he asks. "I didn't ask for that, but everyone from our church just kept insisting it would help. *Closure*, they said. *Healing.* Everyone else moved on, but I won't. *I can't.* How can they do that to him? Don't they see Skyler is still here? *I feel him.*"

I sensed something, too, I want to say. It was there, in our hands, our fingers. I can't explain what happened, but I know if I say anything, it's going to give the man hope . . . and that's not something I feel like I can be responsible for. *Just look at him.* Henry's been torturing himself with his own memories, tapping that raw nerve over and over for the last five years.

There's nothing I can say, nothing I can do, that'll take his pain away. This is where he's lived for so long now. His grief is his home. It's like I'm seeing Henry for the very first time.

"Come inside."

SIX

Henry needs to let go.

I'll give him a reading. Just this once. It'll be open-ended enough to offer him closure. Then I'll close that door between us for good. No more consultations, no more readings. Not even a handshake. I'll simply shine a light toward the end of the tunnel, tell Henry his son is in a better place and that he can finally move on with his own life. Start living again. That's the plan.

Henry peers behind the beaded curtain. "You living here?"

"Temporarily."

He takes in a dusty amethyst geode the size of a basketball perched on the parlor shelf. It's sliced down the center, cobwebs hang off its purple teeth, glimmering in the low light.

"Have a seat," I offer.

Henry waits for me to sit first. How gentlemanly. There's a fresh summer scent to him. Shorn grass. From the sunburn around his neck, I imagine he spends his days in the sweltering heat. A landscaper, he'd said. Crabbing. Odd jobs. Nothing rooting him to one place. He's adrift.

"You still playing guitar?"

"Haven't picked it up since . . ." Henry doesn't finish the thought. He doesn't need to. When he played in the parking lot, he thought nobody was listening. But I was. His voice was always so soft, barely above a whisper. I could never quite make out the words, but I certainly heard his exhales. I caught the breath of those lyrics, the negative space of a song, all sighs.

Sounds beautiful, I said. *Play it again.*

. . . *Now?* His fingers slipped up the metal strings, his skin sending a thin trill through the wires. *I don't know if I can play it anymore . . .*

Why not?

It's different when nobody's around. I don't think it'll sound the same if I know somebody's listening. The song changes when somebody is there . . .

I remember feeling flustered by that, like he was softly rejecting me. Pushing me away.

So much for being a rock star.

I don't wanna be a star. Don't need to when I already got the sun and moon and stars . . .

Henry never knew this, but he was the reason I got the celestial tattoo on my wrist. I tried dragging him out from his shell—for a few months, anyway—but I'd have had better luck wrestling open an oyster with my bare hands. He was in love with someone who wasn't there. A ghost named Grace. She wasn't from around here. Wasn't one of us. He mentioned his summertime crush and I honestly didn't believe she was real. Henry might as well have made her up. A figment of his imagination. There's a part of me that still doesn't believe she's real.

"Just so we get this out of the way," I say, "I don't want your money. We clear on that?"

Henry nods.

I turn off the neon sign so we won't tempt any customers into interrupting our session. Glass tubes fade to a dull bone gray.

Dust motes spiral through the air. The window faces dusk down, sapping the curtains of their color, the faux hickory blanched to a creamy pumpkin hue. The world outside simply fades away. All there is to hear is the steady thrum of traffic from 301. It's just me and Henry now.

And Skyler. The hope of him.

"Before we begin," I say, "I need to ask . . . What're you looking for?"

"The truth." Henry says it so plainly, it pierces me.

"Do you believe your son is still alive?"

If there's any sting to my question, he doesn't show it. "Yes."

"What if the truth is he's gone?"

"I'm willing to accept that."

". . . Are you?"

"That's my cross," he says. "I'll bear it."

I'm trying to read him. His conviction is almost too much, it feels dangerous. There are those folks who'll race right into a burning building without a second's hesitation. Something about Henry's willingness to take a leap of faith worries me that he'll end up hurting himself.

"For this to work," I say, "I'm gonna need you to keep an open mind. Can you do that?"

"Ever heard of fisherman's faith? They go out each morning to catch what they can't see . . . I've put my faith in the police. The church. They all got me nowhere. Now I'm here."

"What's to say I'll be any different?"

"Because I felt it—*felt something*—with you. I haven't felt anything like that in years."

I felt it, too. Felt Henry in all his rawness. I know I shouldn't, but there's something about the need in him, that outright desire, that's drawing me in.

"Focus all your thoughts on your son. Can you do that for me? Nothing else should exist in this room but Skyler."

"Skyler," he repeats. His name is all he has. Saying it out loud, giving it voice, supporting it with the air from his lungs, is as precious a thing as prayer. A tender incantation.

"Okay, then . . ." I reach my arm across the table. "Give me your hand."

I make a nest out of mine.

Henry offers his.

I take a deep breath. I surround his hand with both of my own, sealing off his fist and drawing him in to me. He needs to lean forward. Not much, less than a few inches.

Nothing happens. There's no spark. No vision. I don't know what I was expecting. Lightning? The heavens opening? Frogs falling from the sky? What?

"Okay," I say, a little uncertain of myself. "Focus on your breathing for me. Inhale . . ."

Henry syncs his breathing up with mine.

"Exhale . . ."

I focus on his weathered skin. Tinderstick metacarpals threaten to snap. I feel the veins in his hand shift over bone. His knuckles are so swollen. He's no older than thirty-five but he's got the hands of an elderly man.

Working these rivers has brutalized him. The bay can be unkind.

My eyes stray toward his wrist. To the vertical latticework of scar tissue running up his forearm. Henry notices me looking, staring back. He doesn't hide them. His wounds leave behind a rugged terrain of bitter reminders. There's history here, but I need to look forward.

His hands are a map for me and now we're about to take a journey through his skin.

"Close your eyes."

Henry does as he's told, shutting his eyes. Now it's just me and his hands. Every last wrinkle. All the scars. I have to be careful. There's too much pain at stake. If I want to offer Henry hope for his future, I have to navigate around his past. No one can take that pain away, but Henry has to learn how to forgive himself. Stop burying himself in blame.

"Think of Skyler." I keep my own eyes on him, waiting for the image to settle in his mind. We're stepping onto a frozen river and seeing how far we can go without falling through.

"Can you see him?"

"Yes."

"Good. Now hold on to him. Put all your energy into him, until it's more than just a picture in your mind. Until it's more than just a *thought*. The more you put all of yourself, your energy, into Skyler, the clearer he'll become for both of us. More real. Can you do that for me?"

"Yes," Henry says.

"Thought plus time plus energy. Make him real. Make him whole. Can you?"

"Yes."

"Here we go . . ."

The rivers reaching through Virginia have always looked like the creases in a palm to me, so for my few regulars, I see creeks. I talk about the inlets in their skin. They need to see the land they live off of in their prediction. I tell them to imagine that the meat of their palm is the Chesapeake Bay.

Somehow this relaxes them. Helps them let their guard down. Allows me to poke around without interference.

For the folks who call the middle peninsula their home, whose houses sit on wheels, all of them living beneath the poverty line, simply scraping by just to get to tomorrow, *just one more day . . ,* none of them want to hear about the *rings of Saturn* or *Sagittarius rising* or *your third eye.* These people want a future they can believe in. That they can trust. They need to see it with their own eyes. Hold it with their hands.

We all understand the river. It's fed our families for generations. It's our home. *That's* what I see. The river, all our rivers—the Rappahannock, the Piankatank, the York. The water always gives back. That's a future these folks can trust . . . and I'm their redneck oracle.

"Picture yourself on the water," I tell Henry. "We're in a boat. Just the two of us."

We're heading upriver, into the deeper creases of his hand, where he's never ventured before. There are so many feeder creeks and unexplored inlets in our skin, hidden from sight. You never know where they are until you search for them. That takes patience . . . and a guide.

"It's a clear day," I say. "Not a cloud in sight. Just the sun beating down on our backs."

The water is calm. Smooth as glass.

"Go ahead and run your fingers through the water. Feel it, if you can. How cool it is."

What lies below remains hidden. There are crabs beneath us, scuttling through the mud. The fish follow along. It's all there, in Henry's hand, as long as he can picture it within his mind.

"Can you see it?"

Henry swallows before he answers, eyes still closed. "Yes."

"We're going farther upriver now. Farther than you've ever gone before . . ." The only sound is the gentle lap of the river against the side of our canoe. Our oars slice through the water. "There's no one, not another soul, for miles. We're completely alone. This river is ours."

The waterway suddenly narrows. The trees along the shore reach for us as we paddle on. The surrounding shores close in and we find ourselves covered by a canopy of trees.

"Now that we've come this far, I want you to look around. Tell me . . . What do you see?"

I slowly trace my fingernail through the deepest groove in his palm, making sure Henry takes in the surrounding territory. He needs to see these things for himself. In his mind.

"Tell me," I say, "can you see the—"

Duck blind.

The room constricts. The faux hickory paneling flexes all around us. I swear I heard the word, but I can't tell if it was Henry who said it—or if it just popped into my mind all on its own. It sounded like one word rather than two, *duckblind*, tethered together. Where did that word come from?

"I see . . ." His voice falters, words fail, but something's there, at the tip of his tongue. The knots in each panel of faux wood along the walls now look like leering eyes, peering out from behind a different tree, staring from the fake forest surrounding us.

The beaded curtain at my back suddenly starts rocking on its own, each strand of plastic swaying back and forth, as if the front door just opened, a stray draft sending the crystals swinging. I hear the *clink-clink* just over my shoulder, their faint tinkling filling up the room.

I force the sound out of my mind. I need to focus on Henry. "What do you see, Henry?"

"I . . . I see . . ." Henry keeps hesitating, lost.

"Can you see a duck blind?"

"Yes."

"Where is it?"

"Up ahead."

"Go to it now." The acrid tang of salt water fills the parlor. It stings my nostrils, as if a whiff of the Chesapeake has just drifted in. There's brine in my lungs. "Can you reach it?"

"Yes."

I sense someone else's presence. Someone else is in the room with us. I feel them over my shoulder, closing in. We are not alone. Henry and I and someone else. Someone new.

"Is there someone there? At the duck blind? Who? Who is it? Who do you see?"

"I . . ." He tries again, only to swallow the words before he can go any further. "I see—"

Water. The chill of it rushes up against my ankles. It splashes against my shins so suddenly, I can't help but gasp. It's simply not stopping. The black swell of the river floods through the room. It's at my knees now. My stomach. The tide rises so fast, we can't escape it.

Water splashes across my chest. I'm about to call out to Henry, but the river's surface lifts above my mouth, choking me, while I remain seated at the card table. There's just enough time to tilt my head back and gasp for air, the river rushing over our heads, swallowing us.

We're underwater now. The whole room is flooded with murky, brackish water. I'm still holding my breath, still holding on to Henry's hand from across the table as—

our bodies intertwine . . .

wooden boards buckle under our weight . . .

bending in the dark . . .

but we won't fall can't fall . . .

we're hovering above the water . . .

the river lapping at the posts . . .

there's no telling what's around us . . .

lost in the dark . . .

the night and the river merge into one black chasm . . .

we're lost in the very center of it . . .

all the stars in the sky reflected in the water . . .

there's no telling what's up or down . . .

it's only you and

—Someone pulls me out from the river. I gasp for air the instant I feel fingertips dig into my skin. The tide recedes in a blink. The room comes back into focus as if nothing happened.

We're in the parlor. The trees surrounding us along the shoreline quickly revert back to faux wooden walls, nothing more than flimsy paneling at either side.

There's no river. There are no stars, no night. It's just Henry and me and—

"—*Mom?*"

Kendra looks just as startled as I am. She knows she's not supposed to come inside the parlor when the neon light is turned off. That's our signal that I'm sitting with a customer.

But the sign is on. Pink and purple light bleeds over the walls.

I turned it off, didn't I?

"I didn't know you were . . ." The words fade in her mouth as soon as she sees Henry's hand still in mine. We haven't let go of each other. The only thing rooting us to this room—to this world—is our hands. If I weren't holding on to him, I would be drowning.

"What're you doing here?" I don't mean for it to sound as sharp as it does, but I still haven't found my equilibrium yet. The humidity in the room has only escalated, far too thick.

"It's Sunday," Kendra says, wounded. "Girls Night."

Shit. How did I lose track of time? How long were we in that river? My shirt is so damp, it clings to my skin. It's not the river. I'm simply sweating. I can't stop trembling. My body feels like it's freezing. Half of my mind still feels like it's lying on the—

duck blind

—so I squeeze my eyes shut and try to focus. What just happened? It felt like I was transported to another place. Another time. It wasn't me anymore. I was someone else.

I saw everything through the eyes of someone other than me. *Those weren't my eyes.*

Who was I? It wasn't my body. Wasn't me. *Whose eyes were those?*

Grace. For a moment, just a split second, I was—

"Mom?" Kendra can't look away from Henry, confused by her own intrusion. *Who is this guy?* I don't recognize the outfit she's wearing. It's new. Looks expensive.

Henry rises, face flushed. "I should be heading on."

"Wait." I stand, searching for the words.

"I've taken up enough of your time."

I need to ask, need to know if he saw what I saw, if we felt the same thing. Shared it. But I don't know what to say. How to articulate what I sensed—the warp of wooden boards against our backs, listening to the lap of the river beneath our bodies while we lay there in the dark, marveling up at all the stars above. Together. That just happened, didn't it? That was real?

Henry looks at me and in that moment, his eyes say more than his words ever will.

He saw it, too. Felt it. Whatever it was.

"Thank you." He gives Kendra a nod before stepping out, barely able to meet her eyes.

I don't want him to go. I want him to stay so I can ask—

What happened?

What was that?

What is this?

Kendra turns to me. I'm getting look #42. I've got some explaining to do. She's not saying a word until I do. "Don't be mad," I say. "Time just slipped away from me, I'm sorry . . ."

"Uh-huh . . ." She's not going to let me off the hook. But she breaks out into a grin. "If all my customers looked like him, yeah, I'd probably flake, too."

"He wasn't a customer."

"Oh?" Kendra likes the sound of this. "What is he, then?"

"An old friend." I hear Henry's truck's engine strain to engage in the parking lot, so I wander over to the window. The ignition struggles to turn over once, then twice. Third time's the charm. Just like that, Henry McCabe is gone all over again, entering the stream of traffic.

"You sure that's all he is?" Kendra asks at my shoulder, staring out the window with me.

I sock her in the shoulder. "Get those dirty thoughts right outta your mind, young lady."

"Okay, okay . . . Fine. So what kind of *old friend* is he?"

"He's more like a . . . like a participant." I flip the sign off. No more neon. No more hand.

"You mean client?"

"Christ, Kendra, he's not a client. He came to me for help and I'm offering it."

"So . . . which is it? Is he a friend or a *participant*?"

"Can't he be both?"

SEVEN

We've made our way to the mouth of the Piankatank. There's a boat ramp at Roanes Point, where the salt water blends into fresh. The Chesapeake is near enough that you can see where the river opens into the bay. Most folks around here own a boat—not as a sign of luxury, mind you, but a necessity, just to get around. It's late enough in the day that the water-skiers and casual fishermen have all packed up and left. Now it feels like the river is all ours.

"What do you think?" I ask.

"It's beautiful."

I've scrounged up a modest picnic to have on the dock, just some Ritz and cheddar. Donny always offers to pay for our dinner, but I won't hear it. I don't want to be in his debt any more than I absolutely have to. Besides . . . it's Girls Night, dammit, our night. Nobody's taking it away.

"Used to come out here all the time when I was your age," I say. "There wasn't much to do back then—just sit around and get drunk. Still isn't much to do . . ."

"*My age*," Kendra says.

"Easy now . . ." I give her a grin. "Perfect date spot, though. Anyone you want to bring here?"

"Yeah, right."

"Nobody? Really? Plenty of fish in the sea." I gesture toward the water, sweeping my hand across the vista of the river. "All you gotta do is dive in . . ."

"It's just not a priority for me right now."

"Listen to you. Tell me about these priorities."

"School, mainly. Soccer." I couldn't afford to put her into organized sports when she was a kid. She deserves this. I know that.

"Well, good. The boys around here are a waste of time anyhow . . ."

Henry brought me here. I'd totally forgotten all about it. The memory suddenly resurfaces of the two of us sitting on this very dock where Kendra and I are now, feet dangling over the water, staring out at the exact same view. This is where we first kissed. We'd been dating for about a month by then and I was about to give up on Henry ever working up the nerve to kiss me. Sometimes all it takes is the right view. He slowly leaned in, pressing his mouth against mine. I swear I felt his lips tremble. His whole body shook, he was so nervous.

Was that okay? he asked after he pulled away from me.

Ask me again later, I said as I closed in for another kiss.

I haven't been able to get this river out of my mind ever since I ran into Henry. I sense it, *feel the water,* somehow, even now, as if the tide is flowing through my head.

Is that why I wanted to come here?

There hasn't nearly been enough time to stop and think about what happened this afternoon. The session with Henry opened something up for me. Now I'm asking questions I shouldn't ask, like *What happened to us?* I know I've unlocked something in Henry, too.

My visions are linked to this river somehow, calling to me.

Grace. I swear I saw through her eyes. It had to be her. It's almost like—like she was letting me see this moment in her life. See herself and Henry. What was she trying to tell me?

What am I supposed to see?

A part of me wants to tell Kendra, but I know better than to share any of this with her. If word got back to Donny about any of this, that would be just one more nail in my own coffin. I still have sole custody of Kendra but he'd love to take that away from me if he could. Make our unofficial agreement binding in a court of law.

Kendra tosses a Ritz into the water. A mouth from below rises up from the dark and snatches it, gone before I can make out what kind of fish it is, if it even was a fish.

"When did you become such a bird? You keep pecking at your food."

"Not that hungry, I guess."

"What's Becky feeding you?"

"Mom."

"What? I can't ask?" Becky is fraught conversation for us. I'm not supposed to bring her up. It would take two hands to list all the topics I'm not allowed to mention. Donny's at the top, definitely. The twins. Kendra's first taste at suburban bliss, now that she's living in Greenfield. That land was nothing but Eastern white pines for miles back when I was growing up, before some developer got it in his mind that what this town really needed were some crappy-ass condos. These turnkey houses cropped up like pastel toadstools. Now you got the same prefab preapproved floor plans. Two-car garages. Recycle bins. Year-round lawn care.

"Let me guess." I keep going. "Becky's on that—what's it called— that *keto* diet?"

"Do you even know what keto means?"

"Certainly *sounds* like something Becky'd be on." That gets Kendra laughing.

I used to call Kendra my wild sprite. My little will-o'-the-wisp. People would catch sight of her dancing by herself, a waif with freckles scattered across her pale face. Her hair was always untamed. I practically had to tackle her just to run a brush through that thicket.

Where did that little girl go?

The last bit of sun bounces off the water, striking the faint dusting of freckles across her nose. There's enough of a breeze blowing in from the bay to rustle up her curls. She's gone back to her natural auburn.

"I've been waiting all week for this," I say. "Missed you."

"Missed you, too."

"They treating you okay?" I can't stop myself from asking. "Like family?"

"Yeah."

Donny wanted nothing to do with her for the longest time. I tried for years to get him to help pay for child support and he never sent a goddamn dime.

What changed his tune so suddenly?

Jesus.

Becky started dragging his ass to one of those mega-tabernacles—that big ol' box of a shopping mall chapel they recently built down on Route 17—where services feel more like a rock concert than worship. The pastor's got a backup band and everything. Donny had his ass planted in those padded pews, listening to this particular sermon about the sins of our past. Whatever indiscretions we've made might be in the rearview mirror, but they're always closing in. *Objects are closer than they appear.* Won't be long before our transgressions catch up.

Like a lightning bolt to his soul, Donny allegedly fell to his knees right then and there and begged for forgiveness. He had a child out of wedlock. His little girl was still out there, somewhere in this great big world of ours—in Richmond, that den of iniquity—and she was in dire need of saving.

Donny tracked Kendra down. *More like hunted.* He wanted back in.

"You should come over," Kendra says. "Becky asked if you wanna join us for dinner—"

"Soon," I say. "Just been busy lately."

"Busy." It's not a question.

"Working my ass off," I lie. "But yes, dinner sounds lovely."

"Promise?" Kendra really needs this. Needs to believe everything's going to work out.

That she didn't hurt me.

"Promise," I say. "As long as Becky doesn't keto me at the dinner table."

I know Kendra is carrying all this guilt over what happened. It's got to be up to me to put her at ease. Let her know I don't hold it against her for wanting to live with her father, no matter how much it pains me. I've got to hide that hurt from her. *But it does. It hurts so much.*

"How's the college hunt going?" I'm scrambling for small talk. College is a safe topic.

"Think I've narrowed it down to two. Well . . . one, really. RCU's just a fallback."

"Listen to you. You got options." Kendra's got her whole life ahead of her. A bright future. You don't need to be a psychic to see that. There's such a swell of pride in my chest.

I never went to college. My baby girl is forging ahead without me and I can't help but feel her slipping away, even when she's sitting right here in front of me. Why can't I let go?

"Dad thinks I'll get into Broadleaf, but he says it's smart to have a second choice."

"Well, I *know* you'll get in."

"You can see my future?" It's a dig, I know, but I let it slide. I have to. I'm not entirely sure what Kendra makes of my new business venture. If she approves. She's kept her cards pretty close to the chest, which makes me think she's got some opinions on the matter.

When it comes to my clients, I know exactly how to read them. When it comes to my daughter, my own flesh and blood, I'm at an absolute loss.

"Keep this between you and me?" I ask.

". . . What is it?"

"You gotta promise me first . . ."

"Just tell me!"

I pull out my scrimshaw onesie. It's a whale's tooth with a mermaid carved into the ivory. I've had it for years after finding it in some dusty antique shop. I knew I needed it as soon as I laid eyes on her. I unravel my Ziploc with my last ounce, pulling the pipet and lighter out.

"Ever smoke?"

"No," she says a little too quickly.

"Look, you're going to get offers from your friends before much longer. You probably already have. I'd rather you be responsible about it and know what you're doing than not."

I'm so frazzled after everything that's happened today, I'm dying to unwind. I'm still carrying this image in my mind—*duck blind*—and I just want to let it all go up in a puff of smoke.

"Are you sure it's okay?"

"If you do it responsibly, yeah. *Don't* tell your father."

"Are you for real?"

"Just don't be an idiot about it."

I pack the bowl and take a quick hit, showing her how it's done. I light the bowl for her. She inhales, a little too quickly, and starts coughing. That gets me laughing.

She coughs and laughs along with me. "Dad would definitely kill me."

"I won't tell if you won't."

I remember the first time I took Kendra's hand into my own. Just a few breaths after she was born. Eleven hours of labor later and here was this blissful cinder, toweled off and pressed against my chest. She blindly gripped my index finger with her entire hand and tugged. I couldn't get over how small her fingers were, but she really clamped down on me. I thought she'd never let go. There were no creases in her palm, not a single line to foretell what lay ahead for her. Her future was wide open. The world was her oyster and she was my pearl.

"How come you never mentioned this Henry guy before?" she

asks, coughing.

"Nothing really to tell. He just popped back up." Back into my life. Out of the blue—

water

"I thought you're done dating guys from Brandywine."

"It's not like that." I haven't had much of a love life since high school, before I was pregnant, but that doesn't make me feel any better hearing her say it out loud.

"So . . ." Kendra inhales, holds the smoke in, then lets it all out. "What're you gonna do?"

"Help him." I say it before I even have a chance to consider it. It comes out so quickly.

"With what?"

Tell her what happened.

"He's stuck. Caught in his own mental loophole. He just needs someone to pull him out."

"And you're the just the gal for the job?" she asks.

"Damn straight.

"Just be careful, okay?"

"Yes, Mom," I say.

My attention drifts over the water. I spot the remnants of a long-gone dock reaching up from across the river, these petrified pilings poking out from the surface in a lopsided row, like vertebrae on a malformed animal. The tide is so low, I can see a smattering of sun-dried barnacles clinging to each pole's base.

"You talk to Dad yet?"

". . . About?"

"I've got an away game next week," she says. "It's regionals. If we win, we go to state."

"That's great, hon. Congrats."

Clearly I'm missing something. "We leave after school on Friday . . ."

"Oh."

"I'll see you the following week," she offers. "Dad says we could have the whole weekend."

"Of course," I say as chipper as I can, forcing myself to smile. "The week after works for me." We're just over a year into our new living arrangement and it still feels like a fresh wound. Donny and I are ironing out the kinks in our little agreement, haggling over who gets Kendra on the weekends. Whose holiday is whose. Who pays for what.

When Kendra told me that Donny had tracked her down, contacting her behind my back, she made it sound so matter-of-fact, like the thought just popped into her mind.

I want to meet him. I've given it a lot of thought and I think it's time . . . I didn't say a word, so Kendra kept filling the silence. I barely heard her. The words weren't registering.

I want to know what his life is like . . . and I want him to know about mine.

This is how I lose her, I remember thinking. *This is how she slips away.*

To think, her father—the absence of him, the negative space of that man—made him all the more mesmerizing. Now he's offering her the life I could never give her. Never afford.

Something small wails from farther upriver. Thin reeds, the tiniest vibrations inside a throat. It echoes over the water in a repetitive high-pitched pattern, then fades.

There it is again. Thin, but persistent. Such a lonely vibrato, distorting up and down, up and down. I strain to hear the sound. A baby's wail cuts through the evening humidity.

Just a grackle cackling. The sound of an egret's call almost sounds like a child, echoing across the empty waterway.

"Want another hit?" I ask, holding out the pipe.

"I'm good, thanks . . ."

I know I've got to grow up. I know I'm the one fucking up my life. But Kendra and I were supposed to stay together forever. We'd hit the road whenever we wanted, living the kind of life I wished I had when I was her age. For a while, it was. Fifteen years of scraping by, of *double, double, toil and struggle*, but it was ours alone and nobody could take it away from us. I raised Kendra on my own. There were days when I couldn't eat because there was only enough food for one of us. I never asked for a handout. Never.

Give me your hand, I think, the familiar refrain from work echoing through my head.

I glance down at my reflection across its surface. It's so still, smooth as black glass. The water is calling for me. I can hear it, even now. Can't Kendra hear it, too? It's so loud.

"Let's go for a dip."

". . . Seriously? I don't have a bathing suit."

"So?" I stand up, feeling the dock wobble. "Just us here . . ."

"I don't know . . ."

I slip off each shoe and leave them on the dock. Then I slip out of my pants. "We're going in. You and me. I'm not taking no for an answer."

". . . Why?"

Because I sense a presence. Because I feel something I can't explain. Because there's something out there, I can feel it, calling for me, needing me right now.

"Because it's Girls Night and us girls just wanna have fuuuuun!" My voice carries over the river. A startled egret launches into the air. I want to be that bird. I want to fly.

I take a few steps back, then start running. "Heeey laaaadies!"

I leap off the dock.

I almost do a cannonball. Water crackles all around me as my body ruptures its glassy stillness. A rusted flavor fills my mouth. There's a bit of grit to it, salty and muddy.

I pop through the surface. The water comes up to my waist. Soft mud seeps through my toes.

"Hop in!" I splash the water at Kendra, still standing on the dock.

She's perfected a full-body eye roll, but she's kicking her shoes off and slipping out of her clothes.

"I can't believe you're talking me into this . . ."

"That's the spirit!"

Kendra runs and dive-bombs into the water, squealing all the way through the air. She pops back up from below with a gasp, laughing as she brushes her hair out of her face. *God, she looks happy. So truly happy. Maybe for the first time in her whole life.*

I splash her and she splashes me back. "Warm, isn't it?"

"Feels good," she says.

"Told you so." I kick off from the muddy bottom and float along the surface. The sky is only bleeding out more and more, but all I want is to drift on forever. Watch the—

—stars. The night sky blending in with the river. There's no telling them apart. No separating the sky from the water. Our bodies intertwine on the—

duck

blind

Kendra finally calls it. "That's enough for me," she says, paddling back to the dock.

"But we just got in . . ."

"It's getting dark and I'm pruning up already."

"Come on." I swim farther out, where the river grows deeper. "Just a little longer."

"I should probably head home . . ."

Home. The word stings.

"Where are you going?" she asks when she realizes I'm drifting in the wrong direction.

"I'm going to swim across," I call out.

"*What? Are you crazy?*"

"It's not that far!" It's the strangest sensation. I feel myself get picked up by a current. Something under the surface tugs me along. Not the water. I feel the pull in my chest. This invisible presence from within, not outside, and I'm not resisting. I surrender myself, letting the tide guide me, tied to the moon, its gravitational pull creating a force that draws the water closer to it and here I am, following right along, as if I'm being drawn by the same celestial flow.

"Mom!" Kendra climbs out and stands at the dock's edge. "What if a boat comes by?"

"Better keep an eye out for me!"

There's little sun left at this point. The river has slipped into blackness. What was ashen before is now ink. If a motorboat comes plowing through here, that'll be the last you see of me.

But I can't turn back. Not yet. I take a deep breath, hold the air in my chest and ...

Plunge below the surface.

All I can make out are the vague shapes of leaves and clusters of kelp. The shadowy outlines of freshwater seaweed. The pressure of the water pushes against my ears. I'm in a saltwater womb, the rush of blood swarming all around me. I wonder what kind of child might gestate in a watery prenatal chamber like this. What kind of mother it'd be.

What kind of mother.

I'm waiting. Waiting for something to happen. But there's nothing to see. The air begins to prickle in my lungs. What am I doing? Even I'm beginning to see how silly this all is.

Better head back before Kendra really starts to—

I feel a gentle scrape across the nape of my neck. A soft thread passes over my shoulder. Slick, slippery hair. It could be kelp, I think, just some seaweed—

Something fleshy brushes against my cheek.

Cold skin.

I yank my head back just as the blurred form of a baby floats by.

Only its head. It drifts, inches away from my face.

My lips split to scream but the river slips in. That rusted taste of brackish water, thicker now, pennies and salt, reaches for my throat. I'm trying to hold on to what's left of my breath, the air quickly burning itself out within my lungs.

I see right through it. This transparent phantom. This child has no eyes, just hollow sockets in its translucent skull. It's so close, staring right at me, insisting that I see.

Its hair is long, silken threads drifting up from its scalp and weaving through the water. It looks black and white, drained of color. A photocopy of a child's face.

I know it's not possible, but I can't stop myself from thinking—

(Skyler?)

Another infant's head drifts into view, floating alongside its invisible sibling.

Then another.

So many heads. I can see through them all. What little sunlight—so little—is left pierces their tiny translucent skulls, illuminating their empty eye sockets, setting their heads aglow.

No—those aren't eyes. They're digestive rings.

Jellyfish. The sting rises up from my skin where their tentacles raked over my neck.

Luminous chemtrails drift through the water like the tails of a dozen comets. I can see their pulsing bells fluctuating within the river. Jellyfish have always been in these waters, but I've never seen so many all at once. There's no point counting them. They're everywhere now, enveloping me. Their tentacles tangle into my hair, wrapping around my arms, my legs. They're not going to let go.

I push up from the muddy floor and burst through the surface, gasping. I can feel their bulbous bodies dangling off my arms as I try to paddle toward the dock.

It's full-on night now. The sun has disappeared and I'm stranded in pitch black. How did I get this far out? I was much closer to the dock only a minute ago. I swore I was in shallower waters. Wasn't it at my waist? How did it get so much deeper?

The tide. I was being dragged out by the undertow. Even here in the Piankatank there's a pull to it. There's no telling how far I could've been pulled if I hadn't come back up for air.

"Mom?!" Kendra stands at the end of the dock. She's so much farther away from me now.

"I'm okay," I shout as I keep paddling. The water rushes right in and I spit it back out. I stop long enough to search for the bottom with my feet, tapping my toes for the muddy floor.

"I'm coming back . . ." My toe grazes across the sandy basin, and I feel leaves and branches and bones and all the discarded trash that decomposes into an algae-ridden sludge. There are sharp things poking out from the craggy landscape, coated in a slippery film, but I plant my feet upon it like an astronaut bobbing along the moon's surface, trudging my way back to the dock. I have to lift my feet up higher just to make any progress, knees nearly hitting my waist, marching through the river. I'm hefting lord knows how many jellyfish with me, all of them wrapped around my limbs. I'm on fire now. But I have no choice but to keep on trudging. I need to get back to the dock. Need to reach Kendra before I pass out.

"Almost there," I call to my daughter, even though it's really for my sake.

Something slender slips between my legs. It's cold and muscular, not a jellyfish.

What was that? It moves with a twining intensity that lets me know I don't want to find out. It could be a fish. Easily a fish. There are plenty of fish out here. It whips against my shin before slithering off—and in my mind, I'm imagining an eel weaving between my thighs.

A fish. Just a fish. An eel. A water snake.

A hand.

There it is again. Higher up my thigh this time. It's circled back for me. It takes all my power not to shout. I don't want to alarm Kendra any more than I already have.

What the hell is it? A fish, please let it be a fish, just a fish, just a—

It pinches me with its bony fingers. A shout escapes my mouth.

"What's wrong?" Kendra asks. "Mom, what is it—"

"Nothing," I call out. A lie. "I'm all right."

I pick up my pace. I don't want to be out here. I want to be safely on that dock, out of the water, drying myself off and heading home.

The jellyfish won't stop stinging, their tentacles scraping my skin. I'm burning—

Burning—

"What were you thinking?" Kendra scolds me when I'm finally just a few strides away from the dock. She can mother me all she wants. I'm nearly there. Just a few more steps.

"I thought I"—*sensed*—"saw something."

"In the water?"

"Yeah . . ." Two more strides. The stinging sensation is unbearable. I'm covered in welts already, breaking out in an angry rash.

I reach my hand out to her. I need her to pull me out.

Kendra takes my hand. "Hold on."

I plant my free hand on the edge of the dock. The wooden boards are old enough that I can feel it buckle under my grip. The jellyfish mercifully slink off and drift back into the water.

But that hand clasps my ankle. I can't help but scream now. This tiny fist tightens its grip, digging its serrated nails even deeper into the meat of my foot. It won't let go, no matter how hard I kick. The pain is a thousand times worse than all the jellyfish combined.

"What?" Kendra cries. "What's wrong? What is it?!"

"Pull me out pull me out pull me out . . ."

Kendra wraps both hands around my arm and leans all the way back, falling onto the dock. The momentum hoists me the rest of the way out of the river, reeling in whatever has got my leg. First my shoulder hits the wood. Then the rest of my right arm. I roll onto my back and look down at my leg, cramming my chin into my chest to see what's gripping me.

A crab.

A pissed-off blue-shell has sunk its claw into my Achilles tendon and won't release me. Its free claw is elevated over its head, ready to snap at anything that comes close enough. *Crabs are such assholes.* They don't know when to let go, stubbornly pinching anything they perceive to be a threat, when what they should do is just unlatch and leave.

I kick wildly at the air, pumping my leg in some frantic aerobic exercise, hoping to fling this fucking crustacean off and away from me, but the goddamn thing just won't let go.

"I got it." Kendra spots the crab and rushes to help. She crawls across the dock for my foot, but as soon as she gets near, that blue-shell starts snapping at her. "Jesus—"

"Get it off get it off get—"

I keep pumping my leg through the air, but it only clamps down harder. Its serrated claw has reached all the way to the bone, grinding against the fibula until I swear it's about to snap.

"—it off get it—"

I stomp my bare foot onto the dock. A splinter drives into the sole of my foot, but any other pain feels like absolute bliss compared to this crab's claw sinking deeper into my tendon.

"Hold still!"

But I can't stop. I have to keep stomping, swinging my foot through the air until—

The crab finally releases me. "*Fucking hell,*" I shout.

The crab performs a spiraling skid across the dock. It's only a few feet away from us. It lifts itself back up onto its segmented legs, all six of them, and begins its defensive sidestep. It brings both of its claws into the air, elevating them above its head in a threatening gesture.

Praying. That's what it looks like it's doing. This blue-shell is honoring me.

Hailing me.

Kendra shrinks back. It's unclear what the crab is going to do next, slowly scuttling toward us.

The crab charges. It skitters over the wooden boards at a frantic speed. Its segmented legs peck at the dock, scuttling faster. A froth of bubbles pours freely from its mouth plates, rabidly sputtering the closer and closer it gets until it's right on top of us.

I kick, punting the motherfucker straight off the dock.

Splish! Its hard shell strikes the river's surface and sinks below the water.

Kendra and I take a moment to gather ourselves. Catch our breath.

"Have you ever seen . . . a crab do anything . . . like that before?"

"Never." I lean on my elbows and lift the rest of myself up slowly. My skin is so red that I look like I'm covered in a thin layer of strawberry jam.

"Come on," I say as I turn my back on the Piankatank, slowly limping down the dock. Girls Night feels officially over for this Sunday. "Let's get you home."

EIGHT

I tape Skyler's missing-person flyer to the wall and focus on the flattened dimensions of his face. There are thousands, tens of thousands, maybe a million photocopied dots that come together to form his faint eyebrows, those candy-apple cheeks, the thin bridge of his nose. The dots materializing into his eyes look like a constellation of stars surrounding two black planets.

There's Andromeda . . . There's Orion . . . And here's Skyler, a vast galaxy of pixels.

Grace reached out to me. These visions are hers, not mine. She's trying to guide me to—

Skyler.

I'm drinking directly out of tonight's bottle of Yellow Tail. I realized I've run out of plastic cups but now I'm too tipsy to drive to the store. If the mini-mart were ever open, I could simply knock on my neighbors' door—*mind if I borrow a cup of sugar?*—but they're always closed. The room pitches a bit beneath my feet. I steady myself against the wall.

HAVE YOU SEEN ME? It feels like Skyler is accusing me. *HAVE YOU SEEN ME?*

"Where are you?" I ask out loud, expecting his flyer to answer.

What if I could find him? How wild of a news story would that be?

Local Palm Reader Discovers Missing Child.

No one's around. It's just me and Skyler's flyer. I can't believe I'm even thinking about doing this. If Kendra were here, I'd never hear the end of it. *But what if it's real?* If I'm actually having these visions—these *psychic epiphanies*—maybe I've got what it takes to locate him.

Connect with him.

Let's give it a shot . . .

I close my eyes and clear my head, pushing out all other thoughts, and focus on—

Skyler.

Picture—

Skyler

—in my mind. I give all my thought, all my energy, over to—

Skyler.

I open my eyes. Breathe in deep. Take in his expression. Those pixels forming his face.

HAVE YOU SEEN ME

I close my eyes again. Try manifesting—

Skyler

—in my mind. Focus on—

Skyler.

—his face.

I open my eyes.

HAVE YOU SEEN

See him.

HAVE YOU

See—

Nothing. I can't make myself see anything. There's no revelation, no overwhelming sensation. It's just me in my room staring at a flimsy sheet of paper with a half-empty bottle in my hand. *Well, that was a fucking bust . . .* I feel like an idiot. *What the hell are you doing, Madi?*

I can't help but laugh at myself.

So I guess I'm not psychic. Scratch that off the list. For a second there, just one quick blip in my brain, I thought—I don't know—maybe I actually had it in me. That I really was touched.

Second sight. Right.

I can't help but think of all the folks who come here to see me, hands out, *gimme gimme,* all of them ready to believe that there's something better out there, just waiting for them. And I give it to them. I happily oblige. *Your future's so bright, hon, I gotta wear shades.*

But these visions are different. These visions are real. I can't control them.

HAVE YOU SEEN ME?

"I'm trying . . ."

Just under Skyler's chin, it reads: *IF YOU HAVE ANY INFOR-MATION PLEASE CALL—*

There's a phone number.

Henry picks up on the second ring. "Hello?"

I expected it was his cell phone, but something about hearing him on the other end of the line takes me by surprise. After a moment of finding my nerve, I'm finally able to say, "Hi."

"Madi?"

"Yeah."

"Everything all right?" He sounds like he's been sleeping. I hear a rustle of sheets.

"Yeah. Sorry, I . . ." I don't know what to say. Clearly I didn't think this through. It's too late for Henry to be picking up his phone, anyway. He should've let it go straight to voice mail.

Should've let me off the hook.

"You really feel him?" I ask, the question coming out of nowhere. "Even now?"

The other end of the line is silent for a spell. "All the time."

"How? How do you know it's him?"

"I just know."

I remember calling him back in high school. Henry was never great at phone conversations. Most of the time the line would be silent on either end, but then he'd say something that would make the endless stretch of nothing worth it. Sometimes he'd sing to me.

"I believe you," I say, as if it'll help if he knows at least one person who does.

"Good night, Madi."

"Good night."

Sleep simply isn't coming for me tonight. I can't stop thinking about that boy. I keep repeating his name in my head. *Skyler* . . . Maybe it's an incantation.

Since I struck out contacting Skyler with the power of my mind, I figure it's high time to do it the old-fashioned way: dig through the internet.

I pull out my battered laptop. It's a clunky hand-me-down that's about four generations behind everyone else's, but it still works. The battery is always at ten percent, never fully charging no matter how long it's plugged in. I connect to the mini-mart's Wi-Fi. At least they're good for something. I type in Henry's name and click the first article that pops up—

An Amber Alert has been issued for 8-month-old Skyler Andrew Mc-Cabe, it reads. He has been missing since Thursday. The boy was last seen on July 12 with his family. Police responded to a report of a missing infant on the morning of the 13th. The boy's mother, Grace McCabe, allegedly took her own life at home shortly before it was discovered that Skyler was gone. She was found by her husband, Henry McCabe. The circumstances of the child's disappearance have led authorities to believe the child is in "imminent danger of serious physical harm and/or death." Anyone with information about the location of the boy is asked to contact local authorities at . . .

That's all there is. There simply isn't much information to uncover. I swear, there are more dead ends in Henry's story than the middle peninsula. A few photos float around Facebook. Grace still has an account, inactive for years now. Nobody's thought to shut it down. It feels grim digging through her pictures, trying to piece together her state of mind before she hung herself.

Does Grace want me looking at these pictures?

HAVE YOU SEEN ME?

"What do you want me to do?"

HAVE YOU?

"Where am I supposed to look?"

Most cold cases leave a digital imprint. Not Skyler. His stamp is no bigger than the ink footprint the hospital likely took when he was born. It's supposed to keep babies from getting accidentally swapped in the hospital. Or kidnapped.

I think back to Kendra's tiny toes. Her ink-stained heels after the nurse ran the rolling pin across them. The creases in her feet resembled tree rings radiating out from the sole.

What am I even looking for? This feels pointless. Dead end after goddamn dead end.

I go ahead and Google *postpartum depression*. Looking over the symptoms—insomnia, loss of appetite, difficulty bonding with the baby—I wonder if Grace had slipped into a state of postnatal psychosis that ended in her death. Was she having hallucinations? Delusions about her own child?

Is this what she wants me to see?

I reach for the Yellow Tail and realize it's empty. I should go to sleep. Stop looking for—

Skyler

—information that's not even there. I honestly don't even know what I'm looking for at this point. Something, *anything*, that might help me understand Henry's story.

I come across a two-minute news clip archived on Channel 11's website, cached under local news: *Matthews County PD Holds Press Conference over Missing Baby.*

I click on the video and watch.

The camera is set up in the rear of a boardroom with no windows. The fluorescent lighting makes the walls look like butter left too long in the fridge. A lectern stands alone with a microphone.

An easel holds up a blown-up photo of little Skyler, the same picture as his missing-person flyer, now magnified and mounted on foam core, propped up for all to see.

A smattering of camera flashes go off as the sheriff takes the lectern. I've seen his beaming mug on reelection signs. He clears his throat before speaking into the mic, his bloodhound jowls shaking. "Today, the Matthews County Police Department will provide information relating to the disappearance of Skyler Andrew McCabe . . ."

The camera tilts, revealing half of Henry's face. His cheek. He's standing off to the side, staring into that far-off space.

"Before we begin, Skyler's father has requested to speak." He steps back from the lectern, cuing Henry. The two have a muted exchange. The microphone doesn't pick it up.

"Thank you." Henry looks so much younger, confirming my instinct that the last five years have been unkind to him. Here, he looks like a boy. He nods at the reporters, swallows, then reads from a prepared statement. "I'd like to thank all the volunteers assisting law enforcement agencies, the Gloucester Fire Department, the County Department of Civil Defense, and family and friends . . . You've given your all to help find Skyler."

The paper is shaking in his hands. It takes Henry a second to steady his wrists. Everything's so silent in the clip. The hum of the fluorescent lighting gets picked up by the microphone.

"Skyler was wearing a pair of fleece pajamas. A red one-piece. It had a sailboat sewn on the front. He was . . . was wrapped in a satin blanket his mother had just made for him. The blanket has a duck. A crab. A bee. It seems to have gone missing with Skyler."

I know that blanket. It's in Skyler's missing-person flyer. Did it ever turn up? Did anyone find it?

"I know my wife would've appreciated everything you've all done these last few days, so . . ." He halts, swallowing something down. Even though the words are written right there in front of him, he's struggling to read them out loud. "There have been a lot of whispers going around . . . lies about Grace. I just want to ask every-one, *please*, focus on finding Skyler."

What if it was Henry?

The thought comes to me as a whisper, faint, barely there. But there's no getting around the question now that I've thought it. My Google search disclosed that the authorities cleared him.

But . . . why? Why does everyone automatically assume it was Grace?

Because he's one of ours and she's not.

That's right. She wasn't from Brandywine. Henry had told me he spent summers with her.

"My son is alive," he says in the clip. "I know he's out there some-where. Skyler is—"

Henry looks up. Something stirs within his eyes. He's too far away from the camera, but from where I'm sitting, it looks like tadpoles are swimming through his irises.

I know it's impossible, but it's as if he's looking directly at the camera, staring at me.

Five years ago and here's Henry looking at *me*.

"I just want him back." It takes all his strength to force the words out. This is unscripted. This is Henry speaking from his heart. He's imploring everyone—the folks at the press conference, everyone watching at home, even me all these years later—begging for our help.

"Please just . . . bring Skyler back. Bring him home."

I shut my laptop. Stare at the ceiling. A semitruck hums outside my window, hauling its tonnage through the dead of night.

I start humming to myself. Before long it becomes a song, the words materializing and springing out from my mouth before I re-alize I'm singing it.

"You were born by the water. . ."

Where are these lyrics coming from? I can't say I even recognize the song.

"Raised by this river. . ."

I'm not singing to myself. I'm singing to Skyler. I'm serenading his missing-person flyer, as if he were in the room right now with me and I'm singing him his favorite lullaby at bedtime.

NINE

Henry drives the blade through its brittle lips and twists with his wrist until I hear a hollow pop. He works the knife in deeper, sliding the knife along the jaw before its hinge splits.

"You following me?" he asks me, offering up the oyster in its own half shell.

"Sure seems like one of us is."

"Should I be worried?"

"Don't call the cops on me yet . . ." I bring the shell up to my lips and tilt my head back, letting the oyster slide into my mouth. The briny flavor rushes over my tongue. Tastes just like the Chesapeake. Seaweed and salt. This is as close to taking the sacrament as I'll ever get. Communion with crustaceans.

Henry's right. None of this feels like *chance* anymore. Fate is playing its hand here. You can go nearly your whole life living next to someone and never really see them. People disappear into their own existence here in Brandywine. And then, one day, you suddenly see them everywhere you go.

Henry's *everywhere* now. Not just him . . . Skyler, too. A fresh photocopy of his missing-person flyer is now pinned to the telephone pole in front of the farmers market. I spotted Henry taping one up in the window at the Amoco while I filled up my tank. The A&P's got a new one, too. I can't go a mile along 301 without spotting that boy staring back at me, haunting every last strip mall in Mathews County. I feel like I'm conjuring him up, one flyer at a time.

"You brought the whole fam with you . . ." Henry nods to Kendra, who's doing her best impression of a sulking teenager. She's trapped between me and Donny at the moment.

"Well, I'll be . . ." Donny launches right in, grinning wide, holding out his hand for Henry with all the gusto of a used-car salesman. "Henry McCabe. What're you up to, my man?"

Henry stares at Donny's hand, his own sheathed in gloves covered in oyster juice. "Working."

"On the clock, right." Donny reels his hand back. "Damn, I haven't seen you in ages."

Henry's shucking oysters with two other men. They've got their own assembly line going. The elder man on his left reaches into a bucket crammed full of Atlantic oysters and grabs one, sliding it down. Henry slips his blade through the shell's lip and pops the joint, snapping it back. He tosses the empties at his feet, sliding the half shell to the man working the tabasco and lemon. The mound of shells is up to their shins already. After lunch it'll reach their knees. Maybe their waist by the end of the day. Those shells make for good spat. They'll shovel them into a bucket and toss it all back into the river, seeding the water for the next batch.

"Still livin' 'round here?" Donny asks.

"Still livin'." Henry stops long enough to wipe the sweat from his brow.

I can't tell if Donny is pretending like he doesn't know what's happened to Henry or if he just has his head up his own ass. Either is a firm possibility.

"Look who we got back." Donny's referring to me. "Never thought I'd see the day. How 'bout you?"

"Reckon not." Henry keeps working. He's able to shuck a dozen oysters all while Donny puffs his chest. There's not nearly enough water under the bridge between these two.

"Wanna arm-wrestle over her?"

"*Dad*," Kendra pipes up.

"Only teasing." He slaps Henry on the shoulder. "D'you hear Madi's a psychic now?"

"Dad, stop—"

"Back me up here, Madi . . . You're a fortune-teller, right?"

"That's not what I—"

"Oh?" Donny's playing dumb for his own personal vindication here. He wants to rub my face in my own horseshit in front of Kendra. "So just what exactly are you doing down on 301?"

"I'm just offering a little spiritual guidance to—"

"*Guidance*, right."

"You can go now, Dad," Kendra says.

The grin doesn't leave Donny's face. His lips hold on to it, even as his eyebrows wrinkle, as if he's the only one who gets this joke, bewildered that no one else is laughing along.

"We should grab a beer," Donny suggests to Henry. "Catch up on old times. I can get you out to the club, if you'd like to hit a few balls."

"Golfing's never been my thing."

"Guess not." Maybe Donny can take a hint after all.

"Steer clear of the fried oysters," he tells Kendra. "You got your emergency money?"

"Yeah."

"Love you." Donny kisses Kendra on her cheek, making a show of it, then turns to me, suddenly all business. "Kendra's got practice in the morning, so better not make it a late night."

"How's nine?" I ask.

"Make it eight."

Donny still doesn't leave. He's not receiving the telepathic message we're all clearly sending his way: GO! "All right, I'll get out of your hair." Just as he turns to leave, he slides his eyes over Henry one last time. "Take care of yourself."

Donny slips off into the crowd and I can feel the air on my skin

again, cooler than before. It's almost as if he takes the humidity with
him and I can finally breathe.

"How 'bout a proper introduction this time?" Henry shucks another oyster, effortlessly driving the knife in and cracking it open,
presenting the half shell to Kendra. "I'm Henry."

"Thanks, but . . ." Kendra politely shakes her head, all *P*s and *Q*s.
"I don't like seafood."

"You're lying."

"Sorry . . . Oysters always looked like eyeballs to me."

"I have no idea who this girl is," I say, but now I can't help but
picture them that way, an iris clouded with cataracts.

"How about you?" Henry offers me the half shell. Not even that
disgusting image can ruin my appetite.

"Why, thank you . . ." I take the shell between my fingers. "Down
the hatch."

"Want another?"

"I won't say no."

I watch him drive the oyster knife through the shell's lips and
twist. It's such a violent motion, but he makes it look smooth and
effortless. There's something graceful in the way he does it.

"Got yourself quite an operation going here," I say.

"Dirty work, but somebody's got to do it."

"You don't give a shuck, do you?" God, what an awful joke, but
Henry laughs anyhow.

Henry turns to his coworker, the one handing the oysters to him.
"Mind if I take lunch?"

The man stops long enough to wipe the sweat from his brow,
dripping wet. "Half hour."

Henry yanks off one glove, then the other, tossing both on the
table. He steps out from behind the pile of oyster shells and asks,
"Where are we heading, ladies?"

Everybody descends on Urbana for the Oyster Fest. Two days
full of fried food. The oily odor of funnel cakes drifts through the

air. Main Street is blocked off, filled with food stalls and foot traffic. I remember coming to this as a kid, marveling at all the people. I'd never seen so many strangers. Folks drive in from Richmond to get their fill of fresh oysters and a belly full of beer. Come sundown on Sunday, they're all gone. It's the one time of year where I don't recognize everyone, losing myself in all the unfamiliar faces.

"Can I interest you in a beer?" Henry asks.

"I'll have one," Kendra cuts in.

"Nice try." I shoot her down.

"What a hypocrite," she says. She turns to Henry. "Just the other night she wanted to get high with me."

"Marijuana is organic," I say defensively. "It's natural. Beer is not."

"Mother of the Year over here," Henry hoots.

"Like you didn't smoke when you were sixteen . . ."

"Nope."

"Liar."

"Hand to God." Henry holds his right hand in the air while pressing his left against an invisible Bible. "You always tried to get me to smoke up with you, but I never did."

"Right," I say, suddenly remembering. "Forgot that."

"Did Mom drink when she was my age?"

Henry laughs as he buys two beers. "Definitely remember her being a bit of a hellraiser."

"Don't you start now."

Henry carries a pair of plastic cups, foam dribbling down his fingers. "Here you go." He hands me one, then licks the spillover of foam from his hand. I can't help but drift for a bit, losing myself in his fingers. The shimmer in his skin.

"So you two knew each other back in high school?" Kendra asks.

"Oh, yeah, I knew your mother."

"Knock it off." I elbow Henry, nearly spilling both of our beers. He has to perform a little crablike sidestep, scuttling to the right before I clobber him. "We dated for three months."

"You sure it wasn't four? I could've sworn it was longer . . ."

"You dumped me, remember? You always had your heart set on some other girl."

Other girl.

Henry looks away, distracted, or maybe he just doesn't want us to see him wince.

"You never told me any of this," Kendra says to me.

"What's there to tell?" I'm drinking my beer far too fast. Only she seems to notice. "Not all that long in the grand scheme of things. Blink and you'd miss us."

For a second, just a blip, I'm outside my own body, watching the three of us—me, Henry, and Kendra, walking through the crowd, laughing and jibing at each other. If anyone else were to pass us on the street, they'd see us and probably think we were a family. I can't help but lose myself in this alternate version of our lives. The three of us. That magic number.

"This was before Donny swept your mother off her feet," Henry says, snapping back.

"*Swept?*" I huff. "Hardly."

"So you knew my dad?"

"Oh, yeah—everybody knew Donny. That boy was hell on wheels back then." When Henry notices the look on my face, he adds, "But I'm sure he's leveled out since then."

I'm not proud to admit this, but when it was over between me and Henry—his choice, not mine—I decided to do just about the dumbest goddamn thing I could do, which was get drunk and mess around with Donny. You couldn't get more night and day then Henry and goddamn Donny Watkins. I figured, if you're gonna rebound, might as well make it a fucking earthquake.

Nine months later . . .

There was no whirlwind romance between me and Donny. It wasn't love. It was just Brandywine. The boredom was in our bones. But when I pulled up to his parents' house to deliver the double whammy—knocked up and homeless—Donny wouldn't even let me in.

You aren't gonna keep it, are you? he asked, acting like some kind of cornered animal.

Can I just come in? Please? So we can talk about what we're gonna do?

What do you mean "we"?'

Well, I didn't get pregnant by myself . . .

You can't keep it, he kept repeating. *My parents'll kill me. You gotta get rid of it.*

"Were you friends?" Kendra asks Henry.

"Me and your father? Nah, not really . . . I pretty much kept to myself back then."

"What can you tell me about Mom? She won't share anything about herself from back then."

"What do you wanna know?"

"What was she like?"

Henry considers this. "Pretty much the way she is now. She's always been—"

"Don't you dare," I warn him, taking that tone that tells him I'll cut off his pecker if he says the wrong thing and toss it into the Rappahannock.

"*Confident.* How 'bout that? She knew what she wanted and that's all that mattered."

"What'd she want?"

"You," he says without hesitating. I feel the weight of it, like a blow to my chest.

A cavalcade of cars slowly rolls by as we keep drinking. Little Miss Spat perches herself on the back seat of a convertible, donated by Gentry's Auto just off 301. She's Kendra's age from what I can tell. She waves at the crowd, beaming, her purple-and-pink satin sash draped across her chest. I think of the neon sign back at the motel, that hand levitating in the air, waving in that way that suggests you're royalty even when you're not. Her tiara is decorated in plastic pearls and oyster shells. I remember how all the girls yearned for a chance to be Little Miss Spat when I was growing up. It said something about you, like maybe you were special enough to leave this town one day. I never wore that tiara but I didn't let that stop me.

"You mind holding this? Just for a sec?" Henry hands his cup to me, then reaches into his back pocket. He pulls out a folded wad of flyers. He peels the top one off like a dollar bill.

I look at the flyer and realize it's changed. Skyler's all grown up. It's no longer the baby photo from his old flyer, but a digitally aged version of him. He looks like he's six years old.

"How did you . . . ?"

"They're called age progressions. You send a photo and they digitally age a person up to however old they are now. Increases the chances of someone recognizing him."

Henry swims against the current of the parade, passing through the marching band. He's focused on the telephone pole before him. He grabs a handful of pushpins from his pocket and tacks the corners of the flyer to the pole, as if he's done this a hundred times before. A thousand.

I've energized Henry. Revived his drive. Given him hope. Before our sessions, whatever hope Henry had for finding his son had ebbed into this dull resignation. Now it's burning bright.

Kendra grabs my wrist. "What's going on?"

"What do you mean?"

"With you two?"

"I told you. Henry's an old friend."

"You're not acting just like friends."

"So?" I'm trying to keep myself from getting defensive. "What if we're not?"

"I'm worried about you," Kendra says. "I think you should stop."

I let out an airless laugh. She's deadly serious. "Stop *what*?"

Kendra shakes her head. "You're not psychic."

A swell of anger rises in my chest. I'm losing sight of the people surrounding us.

"You can't walk into this guy's life," she says, "and pretend like you can help him . . ."

"If you ever lost someone that mattered to you, you'd understand." I keep my voice down low, keeping these words between the two of us.

"Who've you ever lost?"

"*You.*"

Henry heads back. He takes his beer. He can sense something has changed since he left. "Everything all right?"

"Just fine," I say. We drink in silence while Kendra stews.

"Uh-oh," Henry says. "Don't look now."

"What?" I turn to see.

"I said don't look . . ."

I find Charlene and the ladies squatting off to the side of the road. Charlene's got herself a new hairdo, her perm practically bulletproof. She's flanked at either side by Aunt Millie and Mama May, the three of them holding court in their lawn chairs. Charlene's waving a miniature American flag along with a Pall Mall. You can't miss her in that bright floral muumuu.

"Better pay our respects to the Godmama."

"Just wave back and keep on walking," Henry suggests.

"Charlene's not gonna like that . . ."

"She'll live."

"You want another beer?" I ask. "This round's on me."

"Easy now," Henry says.

"You keeping an eye out on me?"

"Maybe I am."

Maybe it's the heat and my empty stomach, but everything feels slippery. The humidity thickens, making me sweat. I'm supposed to be here all afternoon, reading folks' fortunes, but the alcohol and vats of boiling oil and powdered sugar leave a greasy layer over my skin.

I can't focus on our conversation, even as Henry and Kendra keep talking. I hear her ask, "Do you really think he's still out there?"

"I know he is."

"Yeah, but . . . how?"

"Sometimes you can just feel these things."

"But you don't know."

"*Kendra*—"

"It's fine," Henry says. "You go about your life, you find someone who brings you happiness, brings you joy, you make a family, a life to share, you put time and energy and pour your heart into this life, and one day, it brings you a baby. A pearl. All that sand and grit and pain leads to *this miracle of nature*. You're connected to that child. Physically, biologically, but . . . something else. Something more. That child is a part of you. You'll always be linked."

Kendra can't bring herself to ask anything more. What else is there? That grain of sand in his chest. That grit. It made a pearl.

Now it's lost. "He's out here," Henry says, then turns to me. "We're going to find him."

We.

TEN

Henry comes back to the motel with me. He's brought a dozen oysters packed in a bucket of ice, as well as a couple lemons pilfered from the food tent. He drags a briny bivalve odor into the parlor with him, the cramped space filling up with the smell of the bay. I'd be lying if I said I didn't like it.

There's enough beer in my belly to leave me feeling like I'm aboard a capsizing boat. The humidity has soaked into my bones. Everything feels thicker than it should be.

"What're you humming?"

"Am I humming?" I hadn't noticed. I must be nervous about having a guest over. Never had one.

Born by the water . . .

"Just got a song caught in my head . . ."

. . . raised by this river . . .

I watch him shuck each oyster with his knife, one after another, with a brutal proficiency that nearly makes me dizzy. Now there's a ring of half shells around the card table, glistening with juices.

Henry plucks one, holding the half shell between his fingers for me. "Down the hatch."

"*Cheers.*" I toast the oyster in Henry's hand.

The oyster slips out from the shell and into my mouth. The meat is nearly sweet, almost buttery, as it goes down my throat in a bath of its own brine.

"I swear, I could eat a hundred of these . . ."

"Better keep me around, then."

"Was that an offer? 'Cause I'll take you up on it."

"We might be competing over who's got the worse living situation."

"Hey now," I say, "this is only temporary. Until I can find something for me and Kendra."

"That's the plan?"

"I'm sticking to it."

After a moment, Henry says, "Seems like she's turned out all right."

"Don't tell her that."

"I'm serious . . . You did a good job raising her."

"Every parent fucks their kid up just a little," I say. "It's a parental rite of passage. Some mess their children up a lot more than others, sure." We've all got some kind of scar tissue. That's just what makes us who we are. The most any parent can hope for is that the damage they've done to their kids doesn't root itself too deep. Make its way to the next generation.

"Kendra will be just fine."

"Think so?"

"Yeah."

"Can I ask you a question?"

"Shoot."

"It's about Grace."

"Okay."

"What was she like?"

"You two would've gotten along."

"You think?"

"She never felt like she belonged here in Brandywine, either."

"I know how hard that can be." *Am I comparing myself to Grace? Is he?*

Henry's silent. I can see he's still grieving, but beyond that grief, there's a loneliness in him. I feel it, too. I've been so focused on the fact that Henry's stuck in the past. The God's honest truth is I'm stuck in it myself and I don't know how to get out of it alone.

"You ever think about all the choices you've made?" I ask. "All the different directions you could've gone in, if you'd just chosen a different fork in the road?"

"If I'd done anything differently, I probably wouldn't be here now."

"Is this where you want to be?"

"Yeah," he says. "The thing about grief is that you've got to be ready to move on."

"Are you?"

"For the longest time, I didn't want to. I felt like I needed to stay in one place. Right here. Felt like I was trying to hold back the tides. But then, I don't know . . . Something changed."

"What?"

"You." I know that look. I feel it, too.

"I don't mean to pry," I say, not ready to take the bait. "Force of habit, I guess. Whenever I'm in this room, I'm always looking for deeper insight into people's lives . . . I'll stop now, promise."

"Is that what you're doing to me? You prying into my mind?" He's teasing me.

"Everybody's born with their own abilities, you know. Even you."

"Be careful," he warns with a warm smile. "Gonna find yourself out of a job."

"You don't think you've got it in you?"

"I highly doubt it."

"It's like any other muscle. You just have to use it. Exercise it. If folks only flexed it now and then, they'd see for themselves."

"Imagine that," he says.

"Never too late," I offer. "You should try."

"You gonna teach me?"

"It'll cost you this time."

Henry leans back. "I'll leave it to the professionals."

"If you ever change your mind, just say the word."

"I'll keep it in my mind's third eye." He's not afraid to make cracks at his own expense. A perfect defense mechanism.

Defense against what?

"How about another round?" Henry offers me another oyster.

"Keep 'em coming, bartender."

I part my lips as I raise the shell, glancing down just in time to see it—

Wriggle.

The gleaming oyster is alive, lurching out from its shell toward my mouth.

What the—

It slips past my lips and crawls across my tongue. I can feel legs—

Pincers.

I gag and spit it back into the shell.

"You all right?"

An albino crab, no larger than a dime, scurries across the shell. Two black orbs hover above the rest of its head. The crab scuttles out of the shell and across my index finger, its slender legs digging into my skin with each sidestep. It raises its minuscule claws up in the air, as if to salute me.

Honor me.

I drop the shell in horror.

"Man down," Henry announces. "I'm cutting you off. No more oysters for you, ma'am."

"Serves me right." I try laughing to play the moment down but, Christ, I'm creeped out. *That crab was staring right at me.* It had invaded an oyster's home, huddled inside.

"You okay?"

"I'm fine." I look down and see the empty shell on the floor. The crab has disappeared, lost somewhere in the shag. "Will you excuse me?"

The floor pitches beneath my feet as I push through the beaded curtain, the long crystal strands like tentacles against my neck. Was there even a crab? Maybe I had too much to drink.

I need a moment to collect myself. I look at my reflection in the bathroom mirror.

Get a grip, Madi.

"You okay in there?" His voice cuts through the bathroom.

"Just a sec."

Henry's standing behind the beaded curtain when I come out, as if he's trapped behind a barrier. "It's getting late," he says. "Guess I should probably head on."

"Where else is there to go?" The crystal strands softly sway between us.

"Are you saying you want me to stay?"

I push through the beaded curtain. "How about a reading?"

"Right now?"

I nod. *Is this my way of keeping him here?*

He stares at me. Into me. I want to know what he sees. How much he can see.

"What do you see?" he asks, his thoughts mirroring my own.

"I see . . ." I step toward him. Before I can second-guess myself, I press my lips against his. I can taste the salt on his skin.

I feel his muscles tensing. I quickly pull away. "I'm sorry."

"Don't be."

"I don't know what came over—"

Now it's *Henry* who's kissing *me.* He closes his eyes, casting himself off. I keep mine open. I just want to take him in. He's so vulnerable right now. I can feel him surrendering himself to me.

I slowly close my eyes and give myself over to the kiss. We're both blind now, defenses down, our bodies pressed together. His hands run through my hair.

I try to guide us to the bedroom backward, but my back abruptly hits the card table and our mouths bump hard together.

"You okay?" he asks.

I laugh before finding his lips again. I close my eyes as I kiss him even harder. His hands run along my waist, fingers working their way over my arms and shoulders until they reach my neck. He cups my jaw.

We don't make it to the bed. We fall to the floor in the parlor, our bodies intertwined. The feel of him takes over all of my senses; all I know is the thickness of his scars, the bristle of his whiskers against my chin, the feel of his skin. I welcome it. All of him. I let myself go, losing myself in his hands, his lips—and then suddenly the floor feels wet, water rising up through the carpet, swallowing our bodies up so quickly, there isn't even time to take a breath before—

water in my lungs . . .

a brackish blend where the river meets the bay . . .

salt and fresh water . . .

silt settles into the fleshy reservoir of gray tissue . . .

sand and sediment gathering in the ruptured sacs beneath my rib cage . . .

a sunken treasure chest . . .

resting along the river bottom . . .

reedy ribs remain submerged in the cold mud . . .

among the fallen branches that reach up from the muck and mire . . .

until there's no telling their twisted limbs apart from my own bones . . .

knotted boughs coated in a ruddy-colored algae . . .

—I bolt upright in bed, gasping for air, like I've just burst through the river's surface.

Where am I?

I'm at the motel. In my room. In bed. I've never lost this much time before. It takes a second for my breath to settle. I could've sworn I was underwater. I'm covered in sweat. No, something thicker than sweat. Filmy, almost like oil. Alive, almost. The air is thick and humid, suffocating my skin, coating my throat. I can taste it now. Algae in the air. I smell the briny odor of the bay on me, but it's wrong somehow. Sulfurous. Dead fish and rotten leaves.

Henry's in bed next to me, fast asleep.

What the hell just happened? *Focus*, I think. Focus on what you saw. *Where was I?*

In the river.

Whose eyes were those?

Not Grace's. These eyes felt different. Cold.

The only illumination comes from the neon hand, casting its pink and purple light across my skin. Moths batter themselves senselessly against the glass, desperate for the hand's light. I can hear their wings beating against the other side of the window.

Why is the sign even on? This is the second time this has happened. Something must be wrong with the wiring—

Clink-clink-clink . . . The beaded curtain starts swaying, as if someone just slipped through. *Clink-clink-clink* . . .

The hairs on the back of my neck bristle against a current of electricity. I can *hear* the neon sign. I glance around the room, taking in every shadow.

We're not alone. Someone else is in the room with us.

There's a boy staring back at me from against the wall. He hasn't blinked, hasn't moved. He's standing in the far corner. I can barely make out his face. The black pits of his eyes.

". . . Skyler?"

His face takes shape now. His features come into focus, pulling away from the faux wooden paneling. The neon sign bathes his pale cheeks in pools of pink.

It's his missing-person flyer. All at once, the air floods out of my chest. *Christ, I was about to have a coronary over a fucking photocopy . . .*

The missing-person flyer has been replaced. It's no longer Skyler's baby picture but the digital rendition of his six-year-old self. *But who put it there?* Did Henry swap it out?

The boy in the photo blinks.

"Henry!" I scream.

He wakes with a start, lifting his head. "What?"

"It's—" I'm about to say *Skyler* but I cut myself off. No one's there. It's not him. The flyer is just a flyer. I swear, for just a second, I felt him. Sensed his presence.

Skyler was here.

ELEVEN

"Nothing brings a community together like a search party. I remember Skyler's was on Thursday," Charlene tells me between puffs from her Pall Mall. "I made a pecan pie."

The best news source in Brandywine is right here at the farmers market. Charlene's much better than the internet. I should've started my search with her. I'd read just about every newspaper article I could find online and still hadn't gotten anywhere.

It's too hot for customers, so we lounge in front of Charlene's stall under a blue tarp tied between two trucks. The sun seeps through the plastic awning, casting a faint baby-blue glow across our skin. The crack of beer cans adds a bit of percussion to business.

"There were over fifty volunteers, all told," she says. A clump of ash rests on her chest. She tries brushing it away but just smears gray sweat across her cleavage.

"The fire department was there, too," Mama May adds.

"Don't forget American Legion Post 83," Auntie Millie chimes in.

"Our whole congregation came out," Charlene says. "I put together a phone tree." The parishioners from Shiloh all held a prayer service in Henry's front yard. Congregants formed a circle with their hands and bowed their heads, believing the power of prayer might lead them to Skyler, wherever he might have been. *Please dear Lord our God, answer our prayers, set these men down the right path that'll lead them to our poor lost lamb, Skyler Andrew McCabe . . .*

"Why're you so curious 'bout all this?" Charlene asks.

Because I know Grace drowned Skyler. It's right there at the tip of my tongue. I want to tell Charlene, tell somebody, *anybody*, what I saw . . . but I can't. She'll think I'm out of my mind. And she'd certainly tell anyone who'd listen. Word would reach Kendra and the door between us would almost certainly slam shut.

"Henry mentioned you were there," I say, tiptoeing around the truth. I need to give her a little bit of gossip to gnaw on. "We've—well, we've been rekindling some old feelings."

"Bless your heart." Charlene's shit-eating grin just about turns my stomach. *Jesus, she lives for this* . . . "I knew there was something brewing between you two. Didn't I say so?"

"Say what now?" Millie asks. "What're we talking about?"

"I swear I spotted that ol' spark."

"Henry's so tied up in knots," I say, "I figured I'd ask you. Save him the heartache."

A theory was taking root in my mind: Henry knows what Grace did to Skyler. He's been hiding the truth all these years because he feels he has to protect her, keeping her secret in hopes of sparing her some posthumous indignity. *What kind of mother drowns her own baby?* He needs to pretend Skyler is still out there, somewhere. Henry's been sticking to this routine, play-acting this search for his son so he can honor Grace's memory. What else could it be?

These visions keep rippling through my mind like a rock dropped in still waters. The images echo in my head. If I close my eyes, I'll see them.

See Skyler.

"You came to the right place," Charlene says, patting my hand in approval.

"What happened the day Skyler disappeared?"

"Such a terrible day."

"Awful," May agrees.

"We all heard Henry wailing from inside his house. Took three police officers to pull him out, and even then, he wouldn't go quietly. After dragging the river, the police moved on to the woods. Had to be over a hundred degrees that day." Charlene readjusts her position in her lawn chair and raps her knuckles across the nozzle of her oxygen tank, *rat-tap-tapping* the gauge. "We're talking dog days. The humidity was so thick, *lord*, everybody was drenched in sweat. Only got hotter the deeper into the day we went."

"Nearly passed out from heatstroke," Millie says. "Thought I was gonna up and croak . . ."

"Oh hush," Charlene pouts. "You weren't even there."

"I most certainly was," Millie protests. "I was helping with the refreshments!"

"You never beat those bushes for that boy!"

"Stop it now," May says.

"Everyone had to watch out for deer hunters," Charlene continues. "Even in the off-season. Wandering onto someone's private property could lead to one of us getting shot . . ."

"Most men took a stick," May says. "There were copperheads where we were wading."

"One fella got bit on the ankle, remember? Had to get carried back by two volunteers!"

"What was Henry doing?" I ask. "Where was he through all this?"

"Searching right alongside us."

"He was leading the charge," May says.

"I thought he was down at the police station giving his statement," Millie dissents.

"That was earlier. Search party came up empty-handed, anyhow. Not even the K-9 unit could track Skyler's scent. All downhill from there. Only twenty volunteers showed up the next week. Then ten the week after that. It wasn't that people were losing interest. Life simply moved on." Folks had their own lives to attend to. They couldn't go on searching forever.

Henry could. He's been searching and searching and . . .

But for what?

A memory.

"Since there was no body to speak of," Charlene says, "no physical evidence suggesting foul play, the sheriff started to think abduction was most likely."

"Brandywine's own Lindbergh baby," May says, more to herself than the rest of us.

"They really believed that?" I ask. "That somebody just crept through the bedroom window and grabbed Skyler right out from his crib? Who would do something like that?"

"Beats believing Henry'd done it."

"But there was no ransom note."

"None."

"Then . . . why? Why take him?"

"Because that boy was simply too beautiful for this world," Charlene sighs. "I reckon somebody laid eyes on that child and just wanted him all for themselves . . ."

"So somebody else is raising Skyler right now?"

"Stranger things have happened."

"Different name, different family? Nobody's recognized him?"

"Happened before, hasn't it?"

"How could no one see Henry's flyers and think, *Oh, that kid in the picture looks an awful lot like the baby down the block* . . ."

"Maybe he was sold and sent overseas," May suggests. "Blond-haired babies command top dollar in other countries . . ."

"Oh hush," Charlene says. "That never happened."

"Well, how do you know?"

"'Cause I just *know*."

Nobody says a word for a spell, until Charlene picks up. "The police set up a hotline. We all took turns manning the phone, volunteering to help take down any useful information . . ."

"*Useful*," May mutters.

"It's true," Charlene says. "When word got around about a reward, Lord have mercy . . ."

"That phone never stopped ringing. Nothing but quacks calling in for cash."

"Shiloh raised the money," Charlene is quick to add. "From our roof repair fund."

"Did anybody offer anything useful up? Any leads or tips or . . ."

May shakes her head. "After a while, the sheriff told us we were likely looking for a body, not a living boy."

Charlene lights a fresh Pall Mall. She exhales and all I hear is the wet roll in her lungs. "He's been heartbroken for far too long. Bring that man back from the brink, Madi."

"Be careful," Millie says.

"And why exactly would you say something like that, Miss Millie?"

"Well . . . We just don't know the whole story about what happened, now, do we?"

There's blood in the water now. "You got some theories of your own that you've been working on, Millie? Is there something you want to share with the rest of us?"

"A boy doesn't just disappear," Millie mutters. "Nobody vanishes like that. Something gets left behind. A clue or evidence or some scrap of DNA or—*or something*."

"That so?" Charlene snipes. "You a member of the FBI now? I didn't realize."

"It's nothing like that . . ."

"Then tell us what little tidbit you're sitting on that the rest of us ain't privy to, detective."

Millie turns to May for help, but May won't stand up to Charlene. "I . . . I just . . ."

"Out with it, Millie. Stop beating around the bush and say what's on your damn mind."

"*I don't trust him,*" she blurts out.

Charlene huffs.

"There's always been something off about that boy . . ." Millie is working herself up now, her cheeks flushed pink. "He was never like the other children 'round here."

Henry was just different, I think.

"Nobody saw her for months. *Months.*"

"Grace?" I ask.

"The two of them were holed up in their house right up until Henry dialed 911. He'd pop up every now and then, but Grace may as well have been held hostage in her own home."

"Nonsense," Charlene mutters.

"You're simply burying your head in the sand, 'cause you've always been soft on—"

Charlene throws up her hands. "Always singing the same ol' song . . ."

"We all know there's something about his story that just doesn't add up!"

"Enough." Charlene starts smacking both hands against the armrests of her lawn chair.

"You don't know what he'd done before he called the police—"

"I said ENOUGH!" Charlene's lungs can't keep up. Her face purples over as she coughs in wet retches.

"Easy now." Momma May gently massages Charlene's back. "Just breathe . . ."

"I'm fine." Charlene bats May's hand away, still coughing. "*I said I'm fine.*"

None of us speak for a while. May tends to Charlene as much as Charlene will let her.

That leaves Millie and me. There's a pleading look in her eyes, a pained expression beneath her melting makeup.

"What about the flyers?" Charlene asks with a hint of petulant one-upmanship. "You gonna tell me that's all for show?"

Millie places her hand on top of mine and squeezes. "When you have nothing in your life to hold on to anymore," she says, "you're bound to fill it up with something. Or someone."

"Like me?" I ask.

Millie sits back in her chair. "Don't let your feelings for that man cloud your mind."

"I'm not letting my—"

A burning sensation pierces my hand. It's sudden and carries all the force of a lightning bolt. I hiss and look down to see a wasp crawling across my skin. *The son of a bitch stung me!* I bring my free hand down and smash it, crushing its body into jam.

Millie starts swatting her hand in front of her face. "Oh, heavens!"

More wasps flit through the air. They gather around Charlene's jarred preserves, swarming over the glass. It's as if an entire hive has cracked open across her card table, their yellow-and-black-banded bodies gathering around the hand-sealed mason jars of okra.

The ladies shriek, ducking for cover under the flimsy blue tarp, but there's just too many of them to find shelter. Swatting only agitates them.

"I'm stung!" Charlene shouts, trapped in her lawn chair. "I'm stung!"

I seize Charlene's arm while May grips the other. It takes all our strength to lift her out from her seat and guide her across the lot. The wasps gather on Charlene's face, crawling across her sweat-streaked cheeks, leaving behind angry red welts wherever they sting her. All she can do is shriek. "Get them off," Charlene pleads, "get them off get them off *get them off* . . ."

TWELVE

Henry's deadrise is tied to the end of the dock. It's a wooden box stern vessel with a center-console wheelhouse. The sharp upturned bow tapers off to a shallow stern. Probably springs more leaks than are worth repairing, but it's all his. His home. A cache of crab traps are bungee-corded at the aft, around ten total. The name painted along the stern is flaking off.

SAVING GRACE

I called Henry after escaping the farmers market. Beyond my hand, not one other wasp stung me. Can't say the same for the ladies. Charlene was practically attacked. Auntie Millie and Mama May, too. A winged blitzkrieg. They were covered in welts, head to toe. I was spared.

We see what we want to see, and what we interpret as signs are often just coincidences. Even I can admit that. But I'm not going to ignore the fact that Mother Nature herself seems to be telling me Skyler wants to be found. I don't care how crazy that sounds. There's a connection between me and that boy—unlike anything I've ever experienced before.

Grace needs me to relieve her of her guilt. She's been leading me to the water over and over again, practically drowning me with her desperation. *Look. See. Find him.*

Henry can't hide the truth for the rest of his life. Look at what it's done to him. His mind is caught in a loophole that he's simply unwilling to cut loose from. He's wrapped up in his head, suffocating in his own grief. He needs relief more than anyone, living or dead.

"Want to tell me what this is about?" he asks as we stand on the dock.

"Do you trust me?"

"I do," he says without hesitation.

"I want to trust you, too."

"You can."

"Then I need you to take a leap of faith with me."

"All right."

The sky has bruised itself into a deep purple that bleeds across the river's surface. There's not much sun left at this hour. Won't be dark before long. I can't shake this sense that I'm being watched, not from another dock or across the river, but under my feet. From within the water.

"You said the police combed these waters?"

"The fire department brought in divers," Henry says. "They dragged the river for three miles in both directions. They didn't find anything but junk. A bedspring. A bicycle."

So much stuff simply gets tossed away out here. People believe it doesn't matter, as long as nobody can see it. *Out of sight, out of mind . . .* But just because we can't see it doesn't mean it ceases to exist. I feel it, even now. Something's in the river.

Henry steps down onto his boat, then extends his hand out for me. "Hop aboard."

We cram into the wheelhouse. The bunk below is no bigger than a cubbyhole. I notice the sleeping bag rolled up in the cabin. Mounds of missing-person flyers are haphazardly stacked on top of one another, toppling down. This is Henry's home. Or what's passing for one these days.

How can anyone live a lie for five years? Has he been lying to everyone for so long now that even he believes it? It's become easier to imagine Skyler's still out there somewhere . . .

But he's not. Skyler is in the river. Now I—*we*—just have to find him.

"Did you bring something of Skyler's?"

Henry ducks his head into the cabin. I watch him rummage around below before he comes back with something wadded up in his hands.

"Here . . ." He passes it to me and I see a pattern of animals embroidered into its hem.

A duck. A crab. A fish. A bee.

Skyler's blanket. The fabric has a pearlescent sheen, like the inside of an oyster's shell. I take it from Henry's hands and the blanket quickly unravels. It's so tiny, meant to hold an even tinier person. To actually hold it in my hands, run my fingers across its soft edges for the first time . . . I swear I feel the warmth of him, as if he had been swaddled inside not long ago.

There's this persistent thought in the back of my mind. A hazy memory that simply won't come into focus. What is it? Something about the blanket.

The video clip. The press conference. Henry stood before all those news cameras and told them *a blanket his mother had just made for him*. Skyler's blankie had gone missing with him.

So why does Henry have it?

For the first time, I wonder if I've made a mistake. Are my visions a plea for help—or are they a warning?

"What're you going to do with it?" he asks softly.

Don't panic.

"Objects have memories." I weave the satin through my fingers, wrapping it around my hand like a bandage. "Sometimes, just by touching an article of clothing, you can feel the vibrations of that person." I read online how clairvoyants track down missing persons through their psychic link with those who have disappeared. Who's to say I can't do the same? If these visions are real, if I truly have a link to Skyler, there's a fighting chance I'll be able to pick something up. I can track him down.

Everything leads back to this river somehow. I know this is where I need to be.

He's here.

"Do you feel him? Right now?" Henry's so willing to believe me, believe in anything, it breaks my heart. Even now, it's like he wants—needs—someone else to play along. Pretend.

"Yes."

Henry starts up the engine to his deadrise. It hacks and sputters before humming to life.

"How far does this river go?"

"There are close to a dozen different feeder creeks just off the Piankatank," he says. "I drop off my traps along the eastern bend. That's where the water tends to be the deepest."

"Take us that way."

"You ever done anything like this before?"

"Never."

"First time for everything," Henry says behind the controls, steering us upriver. There's a sliver of sun still in the sky. I'm watching it sink into the surrounding tree line. What was purple before turns black. There will be no moon tonight. Already I can see stars piercing the twilight.

I glance at the river. It's lost its shimmer, my reflection nothing more than an obsidian silhouette. I think of what's scuttling underneath, the crabs skittering along the muddy bottom. Somewhere below that smooth surface, there are claws reaching out, all the bottom-feeders.

"Police brought in bloodhounds along the coast," he says. "They picked up nothing."

"Well, let's hope I'm better than a bloodhound."

"Which way?"

"Up ahead."

The river bends in nebulous directions. I'm worried we'll run aground the darker it gets, but the river's empty at this hour. No other boats slip through the blackened channel.

It's just us out here. We're the only people out on the water. In the whole world, it feels like . . . but I'm not sensing anything. I haven't picked up a signal since we started. It's silent. Cold.

"You sure this is the way?" Henry asks.

"Just a little farther up."

Each creek is a segmented leg, branching out and clasping at the soil. I ask Henry to steer up each and every last inlet, searching every bend. I need to focus. Find the thread.

Where are you, Skyler? Where are you—

"It's pretty shallow up here," he says. "We should turn around."

"Keep going."

"You sure?"

I'm straining to pick up a sign. A *feeling*. Anything. But there's nothing out here. We've been up and down the same river for the last hour and I still haven't picked up a damn thing.

We're losing the last bit of sunlight with nearly every breath. We'll be in complete darkness before long, but I'm determined to keep looking. I'm getting so frustrated with myself.

Why isn't this working? What am I doing wrong? Why can't I feel him out here?

Where are you where are you where are you where—

"You all right?"

"I'm fine." It comes out more forcefully than I want it to. "Let's try the next creek."

Henry has a searchlight mounted to the wheelhouse. He clicks it on, sending a thin beam across the channel. Even so, it barely cuts through the darkness. There's too much night.

Where are you? Henry's trawler slowly crawls up the creek, barely above a knot, our wake radiating across the surface in inky ripples. *Where are you where are—*

Whump!

The deadrise abruptly halts, pitching us both forward. The engine strains and Henry immediately cuts the throttle. The absence of the running motor allows the surrounding insects to gather in volume, the crickets chirruping along the shore. Cicadas grind away in the dark.

"Sandbar," Henry says.

"What happens now?"

"Either we back up or we're swimming to shore." He starts the engine—the motor shoving the insects' chorus to the side—and puts the boat into reverse.

The heft of the deadrise pitches us back. It takes a couple minutes for us to slip off the sandbar, but Henry's able to steer us clear. He has us back in the riverway before long.

"I'm sorry . . . I'm not getting anything." I thought this would work. Why can't I pick anything up? Every time I've been with Henry, I've felt a connection, but I'm coming up empty.

I'm so mad at myself. I feel like a complete idiot. A fucking fool. I never had any psychic abilities. There were no premonitions. It was all just in my head. I made it up. I wanted it to be real, I wanted to feel like I had something—*just this one goddamn thing*—that made me special.

"What's wrong?"

"I . . . I thought this would work. I'm sorry, I'm just not picking up anything . . ."

I swear I saw Skyler in the water. Why not now? Why has his trail gone cold?

Why can't I see him?

"Let's keep going," Henry says.

"No, Henry . . ."

"Why not?" Henry kills the engine again. The rumble cuts and we're left in the sweltering silence. The crickets come back, their jaws sawing away in the blackness. Henry simply stands there, not saying a word, but I can see him staring back at me through the dark.

"Maybe I can't actually find him." My voice breaks. I wanted this. *Needed* it so badly. I thought we were close, but now I'm getting the sinking feeling that I was wrong.

But I swear I felt it. A current. The tide pulling me in. Leading me. I can't feel anything now.

"You're pushing yourself too hard." Henry places his hand on my shoulders. "You're burning yourself out is all. It's okay to take a breather. We'll try again. Just take a moment."

"Henry . . ."

"I believe in you," he says, and I know he means it.

"Why?"

"Look how far we've come. You feel that, too, don't you?"

I don't know what I feel anymore. "What is it?"

"*Him.*" Henry stares out toward the bay, lost in it. A breeze blows through, pushing his hair back. His eyes drift, cast off into that nebulous space, as if his consciousness has transported him elsewhere, leaving his body behind. He's no longer with me, a million miles away, off to some far spot across the river where only he can go, losing his hold on this world.

I wish I could go with him, wherever he is. *Take me, too . . .*

A crane skims across the surface, snapping him back.

"Been a while since I felt him . . . Since I felt much of anything. Lotta people were quick with advice, telling me the pain goes away. To give it time." After a beat, he says, "Still waiting."

"People sure like to get into each other's business, don't they?"

"Yeah." The faintest hint of a smile tugs at his lips, illuminated by the cabin lights. "Know what you should do? You should take all your customers on a boat tour. Fishermen will pay top dollar if you tell them where all the fish are hiding . . . Bet you'd work better than most sonar."

Why not go fucking further? Really milk this goddamn town. *Bring me something from the river,* I can tell folks living off the Rappahannock. I'll read fish guts as if they're tea leaves. Their intestines will foretell a future these fishermen can believe in, if it's going to be a good season or not, their fate gleaned from within those glistening entrails. What a fraud I am.

"Is that all you think you are to me?" I ask, crestfallen. "Just another customer?"

"You're telling me I'm more?"

More.

"You felt him?" he asks, truly asks, yearning to hear me say the words. "His . . . presence? Out here?" There's a sincerity to the question, like a child asking if he should believe in God.

"I'm not sure what I felt."

"Then we can't stop."

"Why not?"

"Because . . . if I stop, I'm afraid I'll forget him. The moment I quit looking for him, that's when his features are going to fade . . . and that's when I'll know he's gone."

I lean in and find his lips. The boat pitches, bobbing beneath our bodies as we kiss. The world doesn't feel solid. I'm trying to anchor myself to him, but a feeling sweeps over me and—

on the boat . . .

there's no moon . . .

only stars . . .

crab traps rattle against one another . . .

thin spokes of chicken wire humming as the engine climbs up another knot . . .

look at me

just look

before we head out any farther . . .

he's taking me toward the bay . . .

toward the

bottom

—something cuts across the river, just a few yards away from the boat. It slashes at the surface so fast, startling both of us.

I saw—

Saw—

One last vision from Grace.

Of—

Him.

It takes all of my strength not to jump off the boat.

"It was you." I step back. One steps, then two. "You . . . you took him."

Henry doesn't say a word. The silence feels worse.

"Into the water."

"What did you see?" His voice is even. Drained of emotion. He steps forward.

"He's out here, isn't he?"

Another fish's tail, sharp as a knife, slices across the black and glassy surface.

"Did you bring him out here?" I ask. "His body?"

"I woke up and Skyler was gone." The words are steady. Rehearsed.

"Don't lie to me."

"I'm not lying . . ."

Yet another fish slashes at the water. Even now I can feel it. Eyes on me. Somewhere from the river. I scan the water just to see if I can spot anything—*anyone*—out here. But it's far too dark for someone to see me if I need them to. It's just me and Henry. Alone on the boat.

And I'd just seen a vision of him throwing Skyler's body into the water.

"Oh God." I nearly shout. I spin wildly, suddenly very aware of the situation I'm in.

I'm trapped. Alone with him.

Nobody knows I'm out here.

I turn to look for help, for any other boats on the river.

That's when I see it. A freestanding shack in the center of the Piankatank.

The duck blind.

It's so close, as if it's waiting for us to find it.

It's been right there this whole time.

Henry takes the wheel, as if to avoid it. But I grab his arm.

"Take me there."

"Madi . . ."

"*Take me.*"

I feel the boat turn toward the structure. He has no more secrets to hide. There's no more hiding from this. Lord knows how long this duck blind's been out here—decades, from the lopsided look of it. It's hoisted up on four telephone posts, the wood riddled with barnacles, hundreds of crustacean eyes blinking back at me in the dark. All this time. Right here. Waiting.

"Pull up."

Henry cuts the engine a few yards off, and we drift the rest of the way in. The boat's barely come to a halt before I climb onto it, using the two-by-fours as a ladder to reach its roof.

"Madi—"

The sides of the blind are two-by-four planks. I use them like a ladder.

"Madi, wait—"

I have to lift my leg over the top post, like scaling a fence. Henry's not so far behind me, abandoning his boat and climbing the blind.

"Madi, please—"

I scramble the rest of the way up and climb onto the roof.

Everybody talks about the sensation of time stopping, but I don't think I ever truly felt it until now. The world stops spinning. The tide halts. There's no breath, no pulse, no nothing.

Just a child.

A boy.

He's curled in the fetal position, a ball of limbs. His face is buried between his knees, each cheek pressed against a patella. His skin looks so pale, even in the dark. A moon where none shines.

"Hello?" I steel myself. "Are you . . . are you okay?"

The boy looks up, revealing his face to me.

I've seen that face before.

I know that face.

It can't be.

It's—

"Skyler?"

It's not me who says it. It's Henry.

The boy holds our gazes, not saying a word.

Skyler.

Suddenly the child leaps on me. His arms wrap around me so quickly that I don't have time to react. He feels so frail. There's barely any meat on his bones. His ribs run up his bare torso like a sagging ladder. He's shivering. He feels so cold. And wet. Clammy. He tightens his grip and it's stronger than I expected. I have to steady myself.

How? How is this—any of this—possible?

"It's okay." Henry kneels next to me and attempts to disentangle Skyler from around my neck. He keeps his voice at a soft timbre so not to frighten the child. "It's okay . . . I've got you."

The boy releases me. It's a jerky movement. There's nothing graceful about the motion. His hands simply suspend themselves in the air for a moment, empty arms outstretched and open as if he wants, *needs*, a hug from anyone.

Daddy . . .

I swear I hear him say it, but there's something disembodied about his voice. I can't root it to his lips, as if the word came from elsewhere, projected by someone else's mouth.

But it's him. Really him. The boy—*not just any boy, Skyler*—buries his face in the nape of Henry's neck. It's as if he's trying to burrow himself into the flesh of his father.

"It's okay," Henry says. "You're okay . . ."

Henry wraps a hand around the back of his son's head while he looks up at me. I can't make out his expression, can't see his eyes. For a moment, just a brief inhale, I feel afraid.

"You're safe," he says, as if reading my mind. But he's not saying it to me . . .

It's to his son.

Just how long has Henry been hiding Skyler out here?

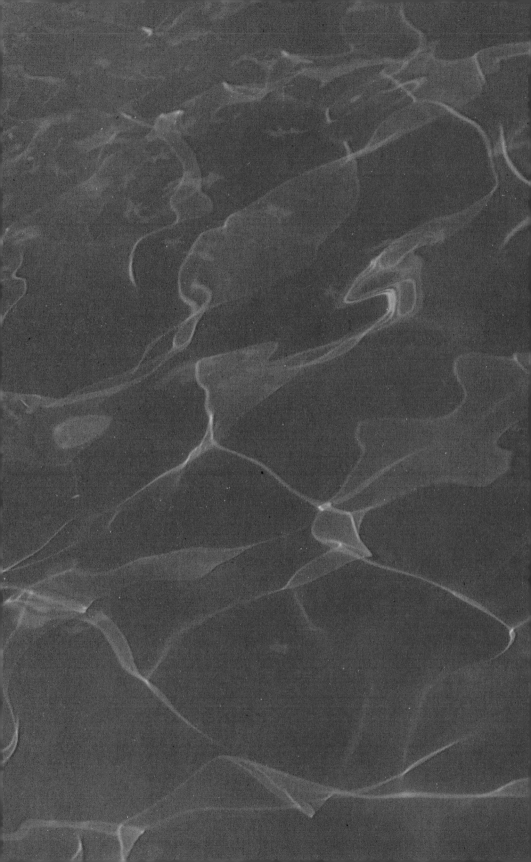

PART TWO

THE STORY
OF SKYLER

You were born out of love, Skyler. It's important for you to know that you were made up of the best parts of your mother and myself. You were nothing short of a miracle, son. A revelation.

When I try to convey the absolute anomaly of you, I always come up short. How am I supposed to tell your story? Where do I even begin?

Once upon a time . . . ?

Words are never going to be enough for you. Believe me—I've tried. Words will always fail. I can't even start this story right. *Your* story. You'd think it'd be simple, that I could just close my eyes, take a breath and begin, but I always get lost somewhere along the way.

Third time's a charm, they say. Let's hope they're right.

———

I first laid eyes on you during Grace's ultrasound. How about we begin your story there? You were never going to be an easy pregnancy. The truth is, you weren't the first. There had been a handful of false starts. We caught brief glimpses of the future we wanted, but fate had a way of intervening. That takes a toll on a person. It did on your mother.

Recurrent pregnancy loss, the doctor said. All I wanted was one of them to look me in the eye and explain in plain English, *Why us? Why our family? Please, just tell me, what have we done to deserve this?*

By the time your mother and I found out you were coming, I hate to say it, but I was afraid. Afraid of *you*, Skyler. I never told Grace this, but I didn't know if I could go through it again. The toll felt too high. She lost a little bit more of herself with every miscarriage. Something fundamental. I was beginning to worry there wouldn't be anything left if we lost you.

But it never stopped us from wanting this life. Wanting a family. Wanting *you*, Skyler.

I spotted you on the monitor—a hazy gray shape swirling over the screen—and I swear, everything changed. I tried not to look. I didn't want to see. You were going to break our hearts, I just knew it. If I didn't look, I thought, you wouldn't be real. Just a figment of my imagination.

Of course I peeked. I was always so powerless against you, Skyler, even back then.

You looked like a ghost in your sonogram. The second I saw the foggy outline of your lima bean body, I remember wondering to myself, *Is this boy gonna end up haunting me?*

Your mother thought you looked more like a hurricane. The ultrasound was a radar scanning the Atlantic and there you were, this swirling storm heading our way, seven months out from making landfall. *Hurricane Skyler.* The fiercest storm this family has ever seen.

———

Was this the beginning of you? Is that where your story starts? Maybe you go even further back than that. How far do I have to go to reach the very root of you, Skyler?

What if we had to get through all these miscarriages just to find you? What if this was all God's way of saying none of these other children would've amounted to you? *Been* you.

No, not this one . . . Sorry, not that one either . . . Nope, not this one or that one.

Then, finally, after everything, He says—*Yes, this is the one! That's the right child.*

This one's all yours . . .

———

You never knew your mother. Her honey-wheat hair always flew into her face when she talked. She had a bad habit of chewing the ends but I found it adorable.

Depending on the light, she had a face full of freckles. When it was cold, they would disappear.

She was elemental, a force of nature. My wild sprite.

You had your mother's eyes.

What did you have of me?

———

The summer when Hurricane Audrey hit, some paper wasps slipped into our attic. They built their hive of masticated wood along the rafters, a honeycombed crib for their queen. The nest swelled over the course of the summer, stretching out from a beam like a bulging belly just above our bedroom.

"Hear that?" Grace asked one night in bed, after turning off the lights. "That buzzing?"

"I don't hear a thing . . ." I was already well on my way to sleep, set adrift.

"There." Grace craned her neck up to the ceiling, pinpointing the hive above our heads.

When I headed up to the attic the very next morning, sure enough, there it was. That buzzing belly was so much louder in the crawl space. It filled the entire attic. *Surround sound.*

I didn't hear those vibrations again until your ultrasound. You sounded like bees to me, buzzing around the womb. When I asked the nurse what it was, she said it was called the *uterine soufflé*, the low murmur of blood circulating through the uterus. All I heard was the flap of a hundred wasp wings.

Were you conceived under that wasp's nest?

Or did your life really start in the duck blind?

———

Find the lighthouse at Stingray Point. If you keep its beam on your starboard, you'll come across the mouth of the Piankatank River. It's not the biggest river, for sure. Nothing more than an estuary whose currents meet the ocean's tide. Its brackish blend of salt and fresh water winds inland, running parallel with the Rappahannock a few miles north. The two rivers create a peninsula that extends from Virginia, like an accusing finger scolding the ocean.

My family's home was on the upper knuckle, less than a few miles from the Chesapeake. Our house was always exposed to the harsher elements. Heavy rains, hurricanes. Whatever weather blew through, we faced it first.

I grew up in this house. I was meant to raise a family of my own within it one day.

Come March, when the weather warms up from winter, the first telltale signs of spring are the ospreys building their nests along the waterways. Fish hawks roost on top of the channel markers. Starlings start chirping, grackles start cackling. Their throats peel back, and they squeal with every flap of their wings.

My mother would start planting in the beginning of spring, sectioning off the soil for every vegetable she could grow within the tight confines of her plot.

The potato says, "If you plant me in March, you're playing a joke on me. If you plant me in April, I'll grow, one, two, three!"

I was raised by this river. Most kids I knew were babysat by their TVs while their parents were off working however many odd jobs, but the water always looked after me.

Never had myself a treehouse, but I sure did have a duck blind. It overlooked our house for half a century, holding up against floodwaters from fifteen different hurricanes, bearing the brunt of heavy winds and harsh winters. The blind is supported by four utility posts, sunk into the river bed and cemented into place, overlaid with a floor of bulkhead boards. Its roof is made with treated oak. Willow thickets cover its frame, camouflaging its man-made veneer for a more natural appearance, as if it were nothing more than a patch of reeds sprouting up from the water.

Daybreak drags mallards out from their nests and sends them flocking overhead. The sun always casts its first light from the rear. Creates a perfect pool of shadow for a hunter to hide within. The blind can house up to three men at a time. They guide their skiff into the watery garage and wait the birds out.

I always knew there were men huddled inside that blind, blending in with the brush and marsh. I could've sworn I felt their eyes on me. Hearing their duck calls, I always thought those hunters were cackling at me. Taunting me.

Every morning, all through hunting season, the crisp thunderclap of shotguns snapped through the cool morning air. Sounded like a storm brewing without the clouds, heavy and resonant. With each crack, I'd watch a duck instantly go limp in midair. They'd land in the water with a heavy *plunk*.

I never picked up a shotgun, favoring the pages of a book over a Remington. Most men sensed that apprehension in me. That made me just as much of a target as these damn ducks. Nobody knew what to do with me. Not my mother. Certainly not my father, wherever he went. None of the fathers in my life. Freaks were always in season, so I had to hide in order to survive.

———

I met your mother on that duck blind.

As soon as the weather's warm enough, the river is overtaken by speedboats. Canoes. Jet-Skis. Some folks swim the width of the Piankatank, shore to shore. The duck blind is smack-dab in the river's center. Makes a perfect spot for people to rest between laps. Kids always climb up on the roof to soak in the sun.

I was fifteen the summer I first tried crossing the Piankatank. I wasn't an Olympic swimmer by any stretch, but I knew I could make it back and forth if I simply set my mind to it.

My favorite time to swim was at night, after the boats left. Never fail, every summer, there was a story of some kid getting their skull fractured from a Jet-Ski barreling straight over their head.

Night was the safest time to go swimming, when I could have the river all to myself. Just me and whatever wildlife called these blackened channels home. I'd sneak out after everyone else had fallen asleep. I'd strip down to my underwear at the end of our dock, sometimes even less, and slip on in. The river always felt as warm as a glass of milk heated over the stove. I'd paddle out to the duck blind and climb up on to its roof. No need to go the whole way across the river. The middle was perfectly fine. I could stay out there for hours. Simply lie on my back, take in the stars, and marvel at the magnitude of the silence surrounding me.

"Occupied," a girl's voice called out from the dark.

Nearly shat my shorts, I was so startled. Where in the hell did she come from?

"Sorry," the girl's voice said, laughing her ass off. "Didn't mean to scare you."

I couldn't see her in the pitch black. All I could make out was the hazy silhouette of a girl—ghostly pale, her shoulders glistening in the moonlight.

"My name's Grace," she said, and in my mind, I could've sworn I thought—

Amazing.

"You're not the first to crack that joke."

Shit. I hadn't realized I'd said it out loud. I thought I'd only said it to myself, in my head.

"So . . . You gonna tell me your name? Or do I have to guess?"

"Sorry. Henry."

"What're you doing out here in the middle of the night, Henry?"

"Same thing you are, I reckon."

"Oh yeah?" She sounded suspicious. "What's that?"

"Hiding." *I once was lost, but now I'm found . . .*

Grace had family upriver. An aunt and uncle and some dumbshit cousins who always ganged up on her. Their house was three creeks down from mine. Her grandparents stranded her here every summer after her parents passed. By the end of August, she'd get dragged back to Charlottesville, but every summer, this river was home. That made us neighbors.

"I was here first," she said, lighting a cigarette. She kept her Camels in a Ziploc to protect the hardpack from getting wet. "How about you head somewhere else?"

"You can't call dibs. I've been coming out here all summer."

The cherry end of her cigarette glowed red in the darkness. "Wanna fight for it?"

"Not particularly . . ."

"Then I think we're at an impasse."

I'm not sure I even knew what that meant, but I was transfixed. *Who is this girl? Where did she come from?* I didn't want her to go—or me to leave. "How about we share?"

She took a drag from her cigarette, mulling it over. "Promise you won't try anything?"

"Promise."

"Lay a hand on me and I'm throwing you overboard."

That was the beginning of us.

Our story.

———

We never saw each other during the day. Only on the duck blind. Only at night. I didn't believe she existed, to be honest. There's no way this girl could've been real. She was some imaginary being, made up in my mind, a mermaid waiting for me in the middle of the river.

Every night, I'd fold my clothes in a pile before slipping off the dock. I'd meet your mother in the middle of the river. We'd swim together in that vast expanse of blackness. The warmth of the dark was all ours. Flipping on our backs, we'd float in the water and marvel at the stars. There were nights when there was no telling where the sky stopped and the river started. Night all around. The porch lights blended with the stars until it looked like there was nothing but sky.

I couldn't tell which way was up anymore.

I'd slowly bring my hands behind your mother's back and pinch her. "Stop it," she'd shout, thinking she'd been nipped by a snapping turtle. It was a dirty trick, but it made her laugh. She'd splash me back. We'd have to keep each other from waking the neighbors. If either of us got caught, there'd be a lot of explaining to do. My mother would've had my hide if she found out.

We'd swim back onto the duck blind and climb out, shivering. We'd hold each other for hours, long enough to dry off, trying to pick out which constellations we liked best.

"If you see where a shooting star lands," she told me, "that's where a baby'll be born."

"You really believe that?"

She never said. We'd wait, our eyes cutting across the sky until we'd see a star drop, like an apple falling off a tree.

Grace pointed toward a cluster of stars above us. "What's that constellation called?"

"That's the, um . . . that's the mighty duck."

"Say *what* now?"

"It's true."

"How about that one?"

"That one? Oh, that one's called . . . the queen bee."

"You're so full of shit."

"You asked . . ."

We'd make up our own myths. There was the catfish constellation, Mr. Mustache, with his big Milky Way whiskers. There was the praying crab, waving his claws overhead, hailing us from outer space. There was the mighty fishing pole cast across the sky.

"How come you haven't kissed me yet?" she once asked.

"'Cause you told me not to."

"That was then."

This is now.

––––––––

Both of us drifted off on the duck blind one night. We didn't wake up until a pair of duck hunters pulled up in their skiff. Nearly lost their breath when they saw us, half naked, fast asleep.

One hunter nudged me with his boot. I woke with a start. As soon as I saw the camo, I froze, thinking I was about to get myself shot and mounted on this man's wall.

Grace bolted upright, snapping out of her sleep. "Shit shit shit," she hissed before diving straight into the water. Her head popped out like a fish cutting through the surface.

"See you later," she shouted before swimming back to the opposite shore.

Your mother left me with these men staring up at me. "Guess I'll be heading off now . . ."

Turns out my mother had woken up early that morning. She found my bed empty. She came across my clothes folded up at the end of our dock. She didn't need to look much farther than the duck blind to know where I was. She simply took my clothes, went back inside, and waited for me to paddle back. When I realized my clothes weren't where I left them, I tiptoed into the house, stark naked and dripping wet.

"Looking for these?" she said from her spot at the kitchen table.

I was banned from the duck blind for the rest of the summer.

I was afraid I'd never see your mother again.

––––––––

I had one final night before summer was over and your mother went back to her grandparents. I crept out of the house as quietly as I could, never waking the warden. I tiptoed all the way down the dock, freezing with every creak of wood, holding my breath until I was positive nobody was listening. I squatted along the end of the dock, slipping off toes first, slowly, *slowly*, dipping into the water, not diving, without as much as a ripple in my wake.

Your mother was waiting for me. "Jesus, Henry, where the hell've you been?"

"I got grounded . . ."

"I thought you didn't want to see me . . ."

"That's not true, that's not true at all."

Neither of us wanted this night to end. We tried so hard to stop the clock from counting down. Dawn began to break over the river, warming up the sky, while we hoped to force the sun back down with nothing but our minds, as if our willpower alone were enough to halt time.

"Will you come back?"

Your mother leaned in, kissing me. "Come back on the Fourth of July next year and we'll see . . ."

———

Somehow I had to survive the school year, alone, cast off on my own again.

Nobody believed your mother existed. I told a few people at school, but they all thought I'd simply whipped up a story to pretend I was cool. I might as well have said your mother was a foreign exchange student from France or something.

It's strange, but the deeper into the school year I went, the more I started to believe it, too. Had any of that really happened? The memory of your mother grew faint around the edges. I was beginning to wonder if I'd imagined everything. Imagined her.

Nine months.

Eight.

I met someone else. Madeleine. We dated during the school year. It didn't last, didn't feel right somehow, almost like I was cheating on your mother before she was even your mother. Madi was always kind, but my mind kept drifting back to the duck blind, even then.

The duck blind. All through school, that was my mantra. *Just get back to the duck blind.*

April. May. June.

July.

———

By the Fourth, I'd nearly gone out of my mind. I'd been counting down the days for weeks now. I held my breath through the grilled picnics and the fireworks display, waiting until everybody else passed out before finally making my way to the end of the dock. Into the water.

Please just be there . . .

I never swam so fast. Like my life depended on it.

Please be there.

The second I reached the blind, I hoisted myself up its planks and scaled the roof.

Please—

A starburst of fire flared up and hissed right in front of me.

A sparkler.

Behind its flickering glint, I saw Grace, her eyes glowing. "You showed."

You came back, I thought. All the pent-up breath I'd held in my lungs for the last year came spilling out, and a wave of relief washed over me. *She's real. I didn't make her up.*

Grace lit another sparkler for me. We waved them wildly through the air as we danced on the duck blind, a pair of comets hissing in the dark, side by side, all that light, that foolish fire, twirling and spiraling just above the water.

———

Every summer after that, I'd swim out to the duck blind and wait for her. And every night, for years, I'd find her out there. That was our space. Our time. Our home away from home.

The rest of the year never mattered. School was simply something to slog through to reach the next summer. Reach Grace. I'd count down the days until your mother would return to this river and we could be together again, picking up our story right where we'd left off.

———

I proposed to her on the blind. More like a promise. We were still kids, but I swore that if she wanted to keep meeting me out here, I'd always come back to the duck blind for her.

"If you're ever looking for me," I said, "if you're ever lost, come here."

Come find me. You know where I'll be.

And she always did.

Always.

———

When your mother was three months pregnant, she was weeding in the garden when a long shadow fell across the lawn.

A wood stork was crossing the river. It was fifty inches tall, and its wingspan stretched as far as her arms could reach, shoulder to shoulder. Its feathers were blinding white, save for its black tail.

Your mother watched it land along the riverbank, stepping through the marsh with its bill buried in the water. With a jab of its neck, the stork brought its beak into the air, a wriggling fish caught inside its mouth.

Your mother smiled, watching the contours of the fish wriggle down the stork's gullet. "You gonna bring me a baby now?"

The stork reeled its head toward your mother, scanning the lawn, and then it opened its wings and took to the air again, shuttling off before it could answer.

Crack! A thunderclap shuddered through the air.

The stork's neck whipped back, wings kinking. Its body halted in the air, suddenly spinning itself into a tangle, falling all the way down to the water. The bird's neck hung limp in the wind, its wings raised upward as it fell.

The stork plunged into the water.

Grace heard a whistle. A golden retriever leapt off the duck blind. It swam for the stork, the bird's tangled body drifting along the surface, already dead by then.

When I went to look for her, your mother was sitting on the duck blind. She'd taken our canoe without telling me.

Something was wrong. I dove right into the water and swam out, paddling as fast as I could. My muscles burned but I didn't slow down. I needed to reach her.

As I approached, I could see her knees pressed against her chest.

"Grace—what is it? What's wrong?"

She wouldn't look at me. Not at first. When she did, there was enough misery brimming in her eyes to push me backward.

"The baby . . ." The rest didn't make its way to her lips, but I understood. I understood completely. There was nothing else to say, nothing we could do but sit there as the river went by, the tide sweeping in, then back out.

It was her first miscarriage.

I'm telling this story all wrong. I'm hopping all over the place. I'm sorry, Skyler . . . It's just difficult to know where to begin. You're there, somewhere, I simply have to keep digging.

Once upon a time . . .

There was a boy.

Once upon . . .

There was you, Skyler.

Once . . .

Am I supposed to go back even further? Roots like yours reach down deep, son. Deeper than any one generation.

Maybe the best way to tell your story, Skyler, is to begin with my own . . .

———

I never knew my father. Your grandfather was a fisherman. Most men around these parts are. The way your grandmother told it to me when I was your age—if she ever felt like talking about the man at all—is that my father was a harvester aboard his own trawler. He hefted herring out of the Chesapeake for a living, if you could even call it a living anymore. He used two-hundred-foot nylon nets, as long as the width of this river. Seeing all those herring underbellies wriggle and shimmer behind that mesh, you'd think he was mining for silver.

He'd be out there all morning, before the sun would rise, hauling in fish. His boat would come back with hundreds of herring, their knife-blade bodies stuffed in tubs full of ice. His crew would get to scaling straightaway, making their own assembly line on shore. One raked the scales right off. Another cut the head and tail off. The next removed the salty nest of roe, orange and perfectly translucent. The next man removed the guts. The last man standing at the end of the line washed the blood away, then salted the fillets. Every herring got dropped into a barrel until it was full.

My father came home smelling like brine and blood—until he

didn't. When my mother told him he was going to be a father, that was all he needed to hear. He hopped onboard his trawler one morning and never came back.

I might've never met my biological father, but I sure knew every other man who drifted in and out of our house. Mom remarried some Pentecostal brute who didn't much care for the sight of me. I'd never met a belt before him, but I can tell you I became intimately familiar with his. I remember the silver-finished buckle, scalloped with filigree twists and turns. Smack-dab in the center was a gold inlaid cross, hand-painted with black trim, held in place by silver studs.

He tried to save my six-year-old soul one lash at a time. *Is this what fathers are for? What they're meant to be?*

I'm going to skip this chapter, if you don't mind. You're too young to hear these parts.

Suffice it to say their marriage didn't last. Three years feels like a blip now, but back then, it sure was an eternity. I thought it'd never end. Somewhere during those three years, I lost a little of myself. Mom never mentioned it to me, but once I overheard her say she felt like the lights had died out in me. If that's why she left him, she wouldn't say, but by then it was too late. That part of me was already gone, I guess. Too late to get that light back, wherever it went.

I barricaded myself behind books while my mother welcomed a steady flow of men into our home. They came and went quicker than their names could sink in, their faces blurring together. Most days I hid within a novel, the thicker the better, always keeping to the corners of our house, trying hard not to make a fuss.

My mother never found happiness in the men she met. That despondency sank past the surface of her skin, deeper than the bone, all the way to the very marrow. When the doctor finally diagnosed her, she barely batted an eye, like she always knew the cancer was coming.

It was the treatment that killed her in the end. Chemo hollowed her out.

"Promise me," she labored to say, "you'll find happiness."

"I have." I told her I'd found Grace, but within her delirium, she thought I meant God. The free and unmerited favor of His heavenly love. I didn't have the heart to tell her otherwise.

Mom wanted her ashes spread across the river. I took her out on my boat, emptying the plastic bag over the Piankatank. The ashes gathered along the surface in a swirling storm cloud.

My mother left our family's home to me. All she asked was that I fill it with family once more. *Let the sound of children's laughter echo through its halls, fill every last room with love.*

———

When I was a boy and no one else was around, I'd have a few minutes to turn on our crummy TV and watch as many afternoon cartoons as I could before someone kicked me out.

There was this one song from *Schoolhouse Rock* I remember the most. *There were three in the family . . . And that's a magic number.*

I remember hearing those simple lyrics and making a vow to myself right then and there: *If I ever become a father, I swear I'll never leave my child . . .* As if words were all it took to be a man. I wanted to believe I was stronger than my father. My stepfather. All these men.

I'd prove them all wrong. There was more to being a dad. I would love my son. Love *you*, Skyler. With all my heart.

All of me.

———

The second miscarriage hit harder.

We were still both pretty numb from the first one, but this hurt reached deeper. It felt endemic somehow. The first could've been a fluke, but this one felt personal. Like fate.

Your mother made her way back to the duck blind once more. She didn't need to say a word this time. I knew what happened as soon as I saw her out there. I swam to her, much like I had the first time, only I didn't go as fast. There was nothing I could do by then. I was too late.

I climbed out of the water and sat next to her on the roof.

A grackle cackled from the shoreline, like a baby crying.

———

I imagine you were conceived during Hurricane Audrey. "Tide's swelling," your mother said, not two days before the first rain. "Looks like a hurricane's coming."

Live alongside this river long enough and you form a rapport with the water. You tell each other things—whisper things. Share secrets, even.

Your mother always had a sixth sense when it came to the weather. Grace could look deep into the water and know when to expect rain, better than any weatherman on the radio. I think she knew about the hurricane even before the meteorologists did. The news kept warning folks to move inland. Steer clear of the shoreline. This hurricane was going to be a bad one.

We never left. Even when the clouds had the white sucked right out of them, leaving behind nothing but ash, we stayed. Looked like someone had taken a drag off their cigarette, burning straight through the sky. When the rain finally started to fall, the droplets were as plump as blackberries, hitting my skin with a splat and a sting.

We weren't about to leave just because of *some storm*. A hurricane might frighten everybody else away, but we weren't about to run.

This was our home. This is where we lived.

Where else could we go?

Puddles quickly became ponds, ponds became lakes, and those lakes were quickly swallowed by the Piankatank, hungry as ever. The river turned into one big tongue, lapping up every runoff. A surge from the Atlantic rolled inland, the heavy winds forcing a roiling swell of seawater our way. It plowed through the tributaries and raised the water level by several feet.

Our lawn was gone. The shore reached our back porch. I dragged our canoe up and tied its line right on the knob of our back door. Inland winds picked up every loose object lying around, pitching flowerpots into the air, hurtling them against the house. I nailed plywood sheets to the windows, sealing us in. Grace packed boxes of food, storing mason jars of preserves and tinned fish in the pantry. She stashed soda crackers and salted ham, mixing together a quick batch of poor man's pudding, along with canned peaches.

We heard the hurricane close in. Trees battered at our house. Rain pelted the roof so hard it sounded like hail. We listened to the gale wheezing in every direction. That hurricane sounded asthmatic to me, all out of breath, the wind whistling through the eaves and rafters.

Grace pried apart a sheet of plywood for a peek, even when I told her not to. She watched the river slither up the bank like some snake coming for our house, closer and closer.

"You're gonna let the devil in," I warned her.

"Is that who's outside?"

"Sure sounds like it."

"So," Grace said, easing up to me, "what're we gonna do with ourselves now?"

"Weather the storm, I reckon."

"Any suggestions on how to while away the time?"

"I can think of a few . . ."

By the time the rain finally stopped, days later, weather reports mentioned that Audrey had reached winds as fast as eighty miles an hour. Some gusts even peaked at over a hundred.

But that was nothing compared to the hurricane inside our house. I'd say the heavens opened within our home.

And there you were. Hurricane Skyler finally made landfall.

When the sun peeked out again, Grace wanted to have a picnic on the roof. We hefted as many jars of jam and peaches as we could hold, crawling across the shingles and rolling out a blanket. We dipped our fingers into the mason jars and licked the preserves right off. We watched the river go by, all sorts of debris drifting along with it. Upturned trees, floating furniture. Whenever Grace saw something she liked, I'd scuttle down to the gutter and reach in.

"Be careful," she said. "Don't fall in."

"Thanks for the support, hon."

I broke off a branch from an uprooted tree, using it to pick up the out-of-reach debris. See if I could fish it out. We found just about everything you could think of. A waterlogged Sears catalog. A child's toy lawn mower. A suitcase. A photo album, the pictures all drenched. Even a water-damaged wedding dress. Its white satin had turned yellow from the sun exposure. The lace looked like a used coffee filter, its pearl buttons the only part to keep their luster.

Bits and pieces of people's lives. The flotsam of their existence. We were having ourselves a reverse yard sale, where everybody's household items were drifting toward us. We set everything out along our roof in even rows so that it could dry out under the sun.

"Holy shit," your mother said. "Is that what I think it is?"

"What?"

"*There.*" Grace pointed to an oblong box drifting downriver. At first I thought it was a coffin. A child's coffin. It was so small, there's absolutely no way it could've fit an adult.

That box didn't belong to a body, though.

It belonged to a guitar.

"Well, I'll be goddamned . . ." I opened the muddy case to discover a Recording King Dirty 30s parlor guitar. Twelve frets. Solid spruce. Bone nut and saddle. Had a dark tobacco sunburst finish and a paddle-style headstock. Still dry. There was barely any water damage. A miracle.

Look how this river provides. "Can't remember the last time I picked one of these up . . ."

"Seems like it was meant to be," Grace said.

"I can't keep it."

"Why not?"

"It belongs to somebody else. What if they come looking for it?"

"Then you can give it back," she said. "Till then, you better play me something."

———

I spotted the first lamb. I thought it was a waterlogged wool sweater. The river had filled in its sleeves as it drifted downstream.

I poked the end of my stick into the fleece, pushing the sleeve deeper into the water. The lamb's head came bobbing back up, its bloated face emerging from the surface. Its legs poked at the air as if it were clamoring for the sky. Its tongue had gone white, hanging out from its open mouth, as pale as the rest of itself. Eyes milked over.

More lambs came. A drowned stampede. The whole flock floated around our roof. Every set of eyes was the same gray-white hue, their irises all fogged up. Grace felt sick to her stomach. I followed the fleet of sheep as they sailed by, heads bobbing in the water like pitching ships.

———

When the river finally receded and the duck blind crested the water's surface once more, Grace found out she was pregnant. Third time. A charm.

And that's the magic number . . .

———————

At night, we'd canoe out to the duck blind. I'd bring my guitar while your mother brought something to sew until the sun went down. Sometimes I'd sing something I wrote, incantations capable of conjuring you. Something to give you strength. A song of sustenance.

A cross stitch is simple, Grace always said. Bring the needle through the bottom and slip it back through the top. Left to right, up and down. When you're finished with the first row, simply flip it over and start stitching in the other direction. Your mother always preferred a herringbone stitch. Slip the needle out at the bottom and bring it back in at the upper right.

Back and forth, just like that.

Moths found a way inside our home and made a meal out of my clothes. They would burrow under the collars of my shirts, tucking themselves in the hems of my sweaters. By the time I slipped them on, they were all covered in holes, the sleeves completely chewed through.

Your mother had to patch up those holes with her needle and thread. She would cut off sections from that salvaged wedding dress, sewing them on, even though I told her not to.

"Why not?" she asked. "It's not like I'll ever wear it." There were thirty buttons running down the back, each one a pearl from the oysters fished up from this very river.

"Ever think what our wedding would've been like if you'd worn a dress like this?"

"It's just a dress," she said.

Waste not, want not. Nothing ever gets thrown away around here.

It's merely a matter of making the most out of the materials you already have. That's how we lived. How we loved.

We never let anything go.

All my pants were held together with white satin patches. I shone
like mother of pearl.

I wish I could've afforded a wedding dress like that for her. She
slipped it on once—just once—walking down the hall as if it were
the aisle. I even strummed "Here Comes the Bride."

All dressed in white . . .

"You want to renew our vows?" I asked, slipping my finger down
your mother's back, pearl by pearl, as if each one were a different
vertebra. "Just you and me?"

"Here? On the blind? What'll the neighbors say?"

"Let them talk," I said.

"Already do."

There wasn't much left of the dress by then. I couldn't tell if
moths were chewing holes through the lace or if your mother had
patched up so many of my pants, it just looked like a ratty old cloth.
We kept what was left of the dress in the closet. Just to be sure, I
sprinkled some cedar sawdust along the closet floor, defending that
dress with the wooden aroma. My mother always told me raw cedar
is just about the best insect repellent you can get.

But Grace had bigger plans for that satin. She was keeping it a
secret, whatever it was. I watched her take her brass-handled fabric
scissors, practically as heavy as an iron skillet, and snip right along the
bottom. She spent her nights working on something special, just for
you.

"You're really not gonna tell me?"

"Hold your horses."

She embroidered the eyelets, careful not to pull the thread too
tightly, keeping the stitches close. Her needle swam through that satin
like a fish working its way through water, breaking the surface, then
diving back down, as smooth as the river right outside our window.

———

Your mother made you a blanket and embroidered it with a fish. A crab. A bee. All the elements of your very beginning.

"For Skyler," she said.

"*Skyler?*" This was the first time I'd heard her say it. "Where'd that name come from?"

"Just came to me . . . Fits, doesn't it?"

"Skyler." I tried it on for size.

"Skyler." The sun, the moon, and Skyler, rolling right off your mother's tongue. The more we said the name, the more it became yours. Became *you. Skyler. Skyler. Skyler* . . .

———

Grace was having trouble drifting off. So many sleepless nights, tossing and turning.

"Count sheep," I suggested, then immediately regretted it, thinking back to all those lambs floating around the roof of our home, their bodies spiraling through the floodwaters.

Grace would wake with the worst stomachaches. She felt seasick all the time, without ever setting foot near the water. But she'd made her pact with the river. She wasn't losing you this time, as if these waters were all she needed to bring you to term. *The river always provides.*

Making deals with Mother Nature never felt quite right. I was weary of it all. We needed every blessing we could get, needed Mama Nature on our side, so I wasn't about to tempt fate.

But I was afraid. Always afraid of doing or saying the wrong thing. The stakes were simply too high. I didn't want to even think what might happen to Grace if we were to lose you.

I still had to get rid of the wasps' nest in our attic. Grace kept complaining she could hear it through the ceiling, their humming keeping her awake at night. Wasps always scout for a suitable home, searching in hollow trees and cavities for the perfect space to build their colony.

But I wasn't about to touch it—not out of some fear of getting stung, but because I simply didn't want to jinx ourselves. I couldn't live with myself if I lost you again.

Everything had to remain *just so*.

Grace and I never had a lot, but we got by. What we had was ours and that was more than enough for us. More than what most folks had around here. We had each other—and you, Skyler. The very belief in you. That hope. You were on your way and that was all that mattered.

It's simple enough to find odd jobs throughout the Chesapeake. You work off the land, either fishing or logging, or you find yourself on the assembly line.

I wasn't about to follow in my father's footsteps. Herring was his work, so crabs were my calling. Our harvest dwindled a little more each year. Too many watermen reaping the same channels. Chicken-neckers clutter up the river, tangling their trotlines in each other.

Me, though—I prefer pots.

I wouldn't be anywhere without my crab traps. A pot is nothing more than a large square trap fashioned out of galvanized chicken wire. Think of it as a heart with separate ventricles. Every trap has two internal chambers. The lower chamber has an entrance funnel called a throat. Once a crab crawls in, that crab can never crawl back out.

At the very center is the bait box, a smaller chamber of fine-mesh wire, filled to the hilt with fish bait. That's what lures your crab in. They shimmy through the throat along the pot's bottom, crawling closer toward that bait box until—*gotcha*—your heart's full of crabs. They think they can escape by swimming up to the water's surface, which leads them to the top ventricle, stranding them in that chamber until you pop open the lid and shake your catch out.

I use eels and bull lips for bait. The fresher, the better. I steer clear of frozen bait. It's never as flavorful as fresh fish, breaking down and decomposing in the water once it thaws.

I've got myself a solid row of pots in the water, anywhere from ten to twenty traps at a time. I'll toss my pots out every thirty yards along the river. Each one's marked by a foam buoy with my initials spray-painted across them so folks know whose traps are whose.

Pickings are pretty slim. I'm barely making back the money I spend on gas to go out every morning, but what other choice do I have? I'll take what the water gives, little as it is.

This river has always provided for our family. So why's it drying up on me now?

The real money is in peelers. A single soft-shell sells for nearly twice the price of a bushel. When a crab molts, its body absorbs water into its circulatory system, swelling its hard shell to the brink of busting. The river eases between its loose skin. Before long, it'll break out from the old, flimsy shell. There's a seam along its rear end where the crab wriggles out from its own skin. Its fresh shell has already formed, but it's soft. Tender. It needs time to solidify itself. In a couple hours that soft shell will start to harden from the calcium in the water.

You can always tell when a crab's ready to peel based on the color of its back fins. Once those blue paddles go pale white, you know they're about to blister, but you must act fast. Crabs are cannibals and they'll devour a peeler if they can get their greedy claws on them. You have to pull those soft-shells out before they stiffen up again. It's in those few hours, the twilight between soft, tender flesh and a thickened shell, where these sweet morsels of meat are at their tastiest. That's where the real money lies. You just have to harvest them. Take care of them.

I could start my own peeler farm. I could squirrel away enough money to put together my own shedding system along our dock. I could set up several water tanks to let my peelers molt in private without worrying about them getting eaten. I could freeze or unload them alive. Sell them for a song.

A song.

I could do it. That future was right there. I could see it. I just had to reach for it. Grab it. Anything was possible, now that you were on your way.

———

I spent my nights after work building your crib out of solid cedar. The bottom boards were spline-joined tightly together. Mitered corners, fastened ribs, sanded flush with the grain. Cedar is the tree of God. *As the valleys are they spread forth, as gardens by the river's side, as the trees of lign aloes which the Lord hath planted, and as cedar trees beside the waters . . .*

It isn't a particularly dense wood. It's porous, like bones. It breathes on its own. The sweet scent drifted throughout our house. I was always covered in sawdust. Wood shavings speckled my hair, like aromatic snow. Grace would pick the trimmings out while we lay in bed.

"How's the crib coming along?"

"Almost finished." Red cedar has a coarse grain, its rusty hue darkening with age. I varnished it with a hand-rubbed oil finish to preserve its color, polishing it off with lemon oil.

"He's gonna love it." Grace brought my hands up to her nose and breathed in deep. The sap had seeped into my skin. All that heartwood, now my heart. "You smell sweet . . ."

Woodworkers worry about epithelial desquamation. The more cedar they breathe in, the more its natural acids start dissolving the lining in their lungs. My mother always attested to cedar's natural ability to deter insects from chewing through our clothes. The concentration of oils in the tree's heartwood is potent enough to asphyxiate moth larvae just as they hatch, their very first breath bringing the cedar's plicatic acid into their lungs.

We were breathing it in, all of us, burning out our lungs whether we knew it or not. There was a part of me, later—much later—in this story that wondered, *Was it the wood?*

Could your crib have done all this? Was it my fault?

———

Did I ever tell you about the day you were born? Better late than never. Let me see if I can tell this story right . . .

It was the middle of winter. I can't say why I went out there, but I found myself at the end of our dock, simply staring out at the water. The river was as smooth and black as obsidian glass. Nothing was stirring under the surface. Crabs lie dormant during the winter months, burrowing down deep in the mud until the temperature rises up again. Just waiting for warmth.

"Henry," your mother called from the house. "It's time, it's time!"

I ran back from the dock, out of breath. "I'll get the truck. You stay put. Don't move."

"Don't forget to bring his blankie," she said.

"He'll have it when we come back . . ."

"I want him wrapped up in it when we bring him home. I want it to be his *first* . . ."

"Fine, fine, I'll grab the damn blankie."

I took your mother by the arm and helped her up into the truck.

"Just hold on, honey," I said, one hand on the wheel, the other gripping Grace's fist. I tried to keep my eyes on the road, resisting the urge to look over my shoulder.

"Almost there."

We had about thirty miles between us and the hospital, but I had to say something.

"We're gonna make it, honey . . . Just hold on tight."

———

It took ten hours but you finally came out. Seven pounds, six ounces. I had never seen a child as beautiful as you, Skyler Andrew McCabe. Never.

When I first laid my eyes on you, I swear I felt the entire world open up. I could *see* it, everything laid out before me, all the infinite possibilities of who you might grow up to be.

Our future, our family, was here. At long last.

Your eyes were as cerulean as the pale underbelly of a blue-shell. Over the next eight months, that cool blue hue would peel away. They became threaded with gold and green. Hazel, like your mother's. Whenever your eyes would find me, I couldn't look away. You hypnotized me.

I'd never say no to you. Never close any doors. I'd fling them all wide open, offer you every opportunity, everything this world had to give—*Yes, Skyler, yes, you can have anything you want.* We didn't have any money, but we were rich beyond our wildest dreams now. I wanted to take you for a ride through the Chesapeake—*Look, Skyler, look, it's all yours.* I wanted you to see the world as it was made—*It's all for you, Skyler, only you.* You would never have a care in this world, not a single one. I'd make sure of it. You'd never go hungry. You'd never grow cold.

The world was your oyster and you were our pearl.

I watched your body learn how to live within the world for eight months. I watched you take it all in with those eyes, always so wide, ready to soak it all in.

I watched you smile in reply to my smile, your entire face lighting up.

I watched you struggle to lift your head on your own, the very weight of your skull too much to hold up—but you never stopped trying, wrestling against the unformed muscles in your neck, until you finally hefted your wobbly head up high, all on your own.

I watched you begin to grip. Watched you reach and swipe. Watched you master your own hands. You would clasp my finger and never let go, so strong even then.

I watched you discover your voice. That burbling babble sounded like your own language, a secret lingo only you and your mother could decipher. You and Grace chatted for hours and never grew tired. Whatever that mother tongue was, it was just between you two.

Your laughter sounded like a summer sunshower, the kind a person wants to dance in.

You had your mother's mouth. I know those lips anywhere.

I'm sorry to say, but . . . you had your father's nose.

Those cheeks looked just like an onion fresh from the garden. You had the tiniest wisp of corn-silk hair, sticking straight up from the stalk. Dimples like a potato's eyes. Thin asparagus fingers.

Taking you all in, every little bit of you, was to witness a miracle of nature. You were of this world and yet so utterly beyond it, a product of the land itself, born from the bay.

I simply couldn't comprehend you, Skyler.

Where did this miracle come from?

I watched you crawl. You *loved* to scuttle. I couldn't keep up with you. Always on the go. If I turned away, even for just a second, you'd be halfway across the room. I'd have to run and catch you before you scurried out the door, heading straight for the riverbank. To the water.

Eight months of bliss. Some folks don't even get that much.

This is it, I thought. *Finally. Our happily-ever-after.*

You were such a sound sleeper. We felt guilty, hearing parents complain about how they never got a wink of sleep those first few months after their baby was born, how exhausted, how spent—and here we were, bedtime bandits, thanks to you sleeping through the night.

After Grace fed you, she'd swaddle you in your satin blanket and carry you around the room. "He's down," she whispered. "Out like a light."

"Want to put him down?"

"Not yet."

I found a rocking chair somebody had thrown away. It was a perfectly fine chair. All it needed was a few repairs. Never ceases to amaze me how people toss things that can easily be fixed.

I'd settle into it, pull out my guitar, and sing you to sleep. Just a little something I wrote.

You were born by the water. . .

Grace and I would sing together, me gently strumming as she placed you in your crib.

Raised by this river . . .

Your eyes would grow heavier, drifting off to sleep, while we'd sing softer and softer.

The ocean your giver . . .

And then the song was gone, fading down to just our breath.

I woke up first, greeted by nothing but silence. You hadn't let out so much as a cry since your last feeding.

I climbed out of bed and made my way to your room, just for a quick peek.

Just to see.

Your shades were drawn, the morning sun seeping through them to cast slate shadows across your body.

It wasn't until I leaned over your crib that I realized you weren't gray with shadow.

You were blue.

I'm seeing things, is all . . .

You weren't moving. Your body was so still.

Sleeping. He's just asleep . . .

Pink froth was already drying at the corners of your lips. Crabs blow bubbles from their mouths to discharge carbon dioxide from their lungs, aerating their gills to keep them moist when they're out of the water. *Were you trying to do the same?*

Your face was mottled reddish-blue.

Please don't see these things, please don't look—

You weren't breathing. There was no rise in your chest, no thrumming pulse at your neck. I never saw you so still. Never saw the absence of you while staring at your body.

An empty shell.

Please—

Something separated inside me. You know when you're telling a story and somehow that story gets away from you? The tale heads in its own direction, even if you don't want it to. You can't get it back, no matter how hard you try reining it in. It's got a life of its own now.

You were breaking away from me, Skyler. The story of your life, the tale I've been trying to tell, it was all slipping through my fingers. That future I saw, all the possibilities that I had divined from your newborn eyes, fractured in a split second. *All the king's horses and all the king's men . . .*

Time broke itself in two.

Standing in the doorway, I found myself caught between two rooms. There was the one where you lay. And then there was the other.

I cleaved myself in half so I could go into both.

One part of me would be left to reckon with what was lying in the crib.

The other would go on living a blissful existence.

That day, I became two fathers.

You still wake up that morning for one of me. I go ahead and change your diaper and feed you with a bottle warmed up on the stove. *We're going to let Mama sleep for a little while longer. She deserves it, doesn't she? The least we can do is let her rest. Just a little while longer.*

Let me take care of you, Skyler. Please, just let me keep this life.

———

Then Grace wakes.

———

Your mother's wailing fills every corner of our house. There's nowhere to hide from it. I just pray the house can contain it. *You'll wake the baby*, I think to myself.

Seeing Grace on the floor, next to your crib, I can't stop my mind from taking this separate path, heading down the road less traveled, where I'm still cradling you, picking out your outfit for the day. My mind simply takes me there, away from here, from all of this.

I see the loss in Grace's eyes. The absolute abyss. Her mouth is so wide, lips wet with tears and spit. A string of saliva runs down her bottom lip and sticks to her chin.

But there's absolutely no sound.

Someone has taken the remote and pressed mute on your mother. I can't hear her. In place of her wailing, I hear this other mother humming a lullaby. It's the same song she always sings when it's time to put you to sleep, the song we always sing as a family.

She's not screaming. She's *singing*. The lyrics drift out from her mouth. Even if her lips are locked in a frozen ring, a hollow grotto, all I hear is the hum of your lullaby. It fills the room.

Floods it.

———

I convince Grace not to call 911. I beg her for this day—*just one day*—where the three of us can still be a family. It's too late to save you, but we can still have one more day. Just one more day to be together. To be with you. Our son, our moon, our Skyler.

"Grace?"

She's not focusing on me. My words must not make any sense to her. Her eyes have a difficult time finding me, even when I'm only a few inches away from her face.

"*Grace.*"

I grip her shoulders and shake, not forcefully, just enough to rattle the recognition back into her. Bring her back. She sees me kneeling before her now, even if it's only for a second.

"We don't have to let go," I say. "Not yet."

Her head lolls away, falling over her shoulder. It looks like it's about to roll clean off. She casts her eyes across the room, seeing but not seeing. Here but not here.

Tomorrow, I promise I'll call the police.

Tomorrow, we'll do what's right.

Tomorrow.

"We can still be a family today . . ."

Grace never says yes, but she doesn't say no. She doesn't say anything. What are words worth anymore, anyhow? What's the value of them? Words fail. They always fail. They are not strong enough to save what you love most. They give shape to those things we cannot see, that we cannot hold, but they don't make them real for us.

I want what's inside those words. The spirit lingering within them.

That's what will bring you back.

———

The three of us climb back into bed together. Your mother and I form a protective barrier around your swaddled body. You're in your blanket, woven in white satin. There's the duck. The crab. The bee. All these cross-stitched animals circling around you.

We lie on our sides with you in the middle. We each place a hand on your blanket, pinning, my hand on top of your mother's and this is our pact. Our promise.

You're still here with us, Skyler. You are still here. Please don't go. Don't leave us. Don't.

———

Every room in this house is a receptacle for sound, vessels for audible memories. I remember hearing you coo in this room, I remember hearing you giggle in this one. The sounds seep into the walls, imprinting on them forever.

Imagine that sound fading away. Imagine the silence. How it suddenly cuts through skin.

To the bone.

———

I carried you around the house, swaddled in your blanket. I rubbed my fingertip along the stitched fish, the crab, the bee, tracing the soft contours of the threadwork, sewn by your mother's loving hand. They're nothing but constellations of dead stars now. A galaxy of graves.

I couldn't put you down. Letting go would break our contact and that might shatter the moment. I needed to hold on. Holding on keeps you here with me. Holding on keeps you real.

The shades were pulled all through the house, sealing us in. The world outside didn't exist. Time didn't exist. There was no night, no day, nothing beyond then and there. The now.

Today. All we had was today.

Tomorrow, I'd call 911. I would let the ambulance take you away.

I'd let you go.

Tomorrow.

You were still here. Still in my hands. I felt you. The heft of you. Your body.

We wandered through the house together, singing lullabies. I was vaguely aware of this other father, the man I separated from, set adrift in our house. I couldn't help but wonder how he was dealing with his own story. I felt this tinge of guilt, realizing I'd abandoned him to suffer alone without me, forcing him to take the path I wasn't strong enough to wander down myself.

I only hoped he was made of sterner stuff than I was. He could handle the pain. He could take it. What other choice was there?

You were still in my hands. The future, right here, in my grip. All I had to do was hold on.

———

Grace never left our bed. You and I would peek in to see if she was awake or asleep. She seemed somewhere in between, here but not here. Her eyes were open, staring at the ceiling but not seeing the ceiling. Whenever I called her name, she never answered.

"Let's let Mommy rest," I whispered, taking you back into the hall.

I put you to bed that night. When I laid you down in your crib, letting you go for the first time since that morning, everything suddenly felt so light. My hands were free and that felt wrong to me. I didn't know what to do with my hands. They didn't belong anywhere. They felt useless. Clumsy. I couldn't touch anything within the house without feeling like it might break.

I hadn't taken my guitar out all day, so I decided to play. I never wanted this day to end. Never wanted tomorrow to come. So I started strumming, singing your song.

One song became two became ten. Twenty. A hundred. I lost count.

I played for you all night. Until my fingers bled. The wires sliced through my fingertips but I wouldn't stop. I'd never get this day back. The seconds were slipping right through my cleaved fingers. I'd never get to sing to you like this again. I needed to play, no matter how much it hurt my hands, no matter how slippery my fingers were, strumming and strumming until the blood dripped right off the wires. Until red handprints covered the wood.

It didn't feel like a guitar anymore. I couldn't tell where the instrument stopped and my body started. The wooden neck flexed and suddenly it was my forearm, my wrists sliced open.

you were born

I'm strumming my own arteries, feeling for the frets along my forearm but only finding tendon. My veins are making music now. I keep on singing, strumming the bloody chords.

by the water

Over and over. This was your song, your vigil. I needed you to hear me calling, Skyler. I needed to hold on, bring you back home, back to your family.

There were just too many chapters of your life left to share, Skyler. Who would tell them now? Your first footsteps? Your first tooth? Your first day of school?

Someone needed to tell those stories. Why couldn't it be me?

I pushed myself to keep singing. I poured everything I had left into you. I'd give it all to you, every last breath, until I was utterly empty.

This may have been your story, Skyler, but I was the one telling it now. I'd steer the narrative. Bend the telling back. I just had to be strong, stronger than I'd ever been. It would take everything I had, but I knew I could do it. I didn't care if it killed me. This was my last chance to steer the story back, steer you back to your family, back to that magic number.

Back to me, Skyler.

Come back.

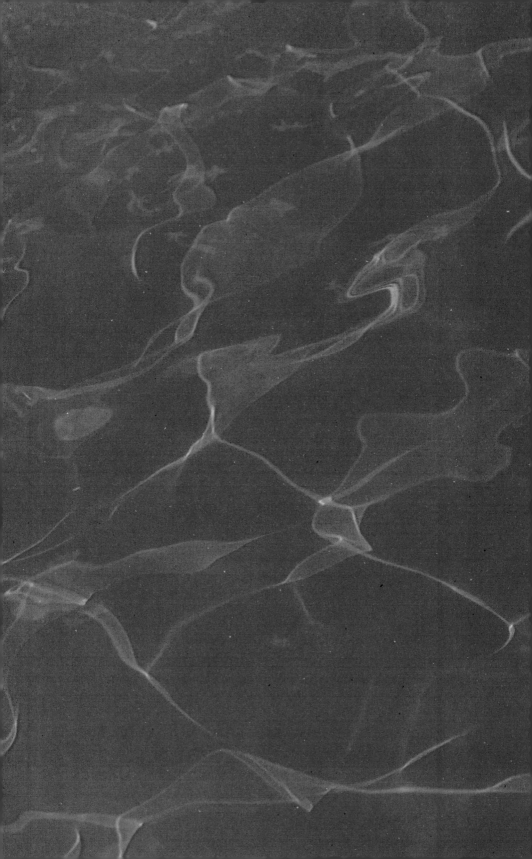

PART THREE

FAMILY MATTERS

ONE

Henry's kidnapped a child.

The question doesn't linger long before a thought surfaces in my mind as we're tearing down the 301. *Henry has lost touch with reality and kidnapped some poor child and now he's pretending it's his son . . .*

What else could be happening here? If Henry didn't abduct this boy, then that means . . .

That means this kid is . . .

That's impossible. I shoot the notion down before it takes root. There's no way this is . . .

Skyler?

Simply thinking his name sends my mind reeling. *It's not him. It can't possibly be him.*

Could it?

The child's likeness is uncanny. Spitting image. I've stared at the boy's missing-person flyer for so long—weeks now—committing his photocopied image to memory. I'd swear this is him.

Skyler, alive and in the flesh.

What if it's him? What if it's actually—

Stop.

I don't know what's easier to believe. Henry losing his mind and abducting a child or . . .

Or the idea that . . .

Skyler's alive.

It's not possible. It's just not possible. I have to force down this feeling of—I don't know what else to call it—*hope? Fear?*

There's this persistent sliver of me that wants to believe it's him. *We found him.* Wouldn't that be incredible?

A miracle?

But who put him in the duck blind?

Henry lifted the boy off the blind and carried him back aboard his deadrise. There weren't many words between us as we sped back to dry land, the hum of the boat's engine filling the void.

Now the child is hunched between us in Henry's Toyota and draped in his fleece jacket, knees pressed against his chest, head burrowed between his patellas. Just like how we found him.

All these bright traffic lights. The fast-food signs suspended in the night sky. The sounds of semis slipping by, horns blaring and the rev of their engines . . . It's too much for him.

He's hiding. Oh, God, does this traumatized child even know what's happening?

I feel him shiver through Henry's oversized sleeves. I bring my arms around Skyler—*stop calling him that*—and hold on, hoping to warm him while Henry runs every red light along 301.

"You're okay," I lean over and whisper. "Everything's gonna be okay."

This poor child, I think—and just like that, a cascade of questions tumble through my mind and I can't quiet them down. *Where did he come from? Who is he?* He must have a name. A family. His parents are probably searching for him as we speak . . . *Where did Henry find him? How long has Henry been hiding him out there in the duck blind?*

What the hell was this boy doing out there?

The nearest hospital is in Gloucester. The second I realize Henry's heading in the wrong direction, it dawns on me that we're bringing Skyler—*don't call him that*—back to the motel.

"Your place is closer," he says when I ask him where we're going.

My place. I don't want this motel to be mine. "We've got to take him to the hospital."

"No hospitals."

"Henry, look at him—"

"They'll take him away from me." He says it with such finality—*end of the goddamn discussion*—that I'm stunned back into silence, left to stare out my window at the swarm of angry red brake lights gathering along the highway. *This is fucked. So absolutely fucked. Everything's moving too fast . . .* I need a moment to think. To breathe. To figure out what in the hell is going on here. *What am I supposed to do?* I could open the truck door and leap out onto the shoulder of the road. Wait for the next red light, when the truck's at a complete stop, then grab Skyler—*it's not Skyler so stop calling him that*—run to the nearest gas station and call 911.

"I can't lose him again," Henry says to the windshield, not to me.

Again? How many times has Henry lost his son?

I didn't know how far he had slipped. I had absolutely no earthly idea how far he'd gone into his own grief. *Did I do this to him?* I enabled his delirious need to believe Skyler was still out there. All our sessions must've stirred something up in him and it pushed him over the edge.

This is my fault, isn't it?

But a *child*? How can Henry believe he could pass off some other boy as his son?

What if . . . ? An insistent whisper reaches out from my mind. *What if it's really him?*

There's no way this could be . . .

Say his name . . .

I can't . . .

Go on, say it . . .

No.

You know you want to believe . . .

Boys don't come back from the dead. They don't materialize out of the blue. That duck blind isn't some little island and that child sure as shit isn't some six-year-old Robinson Crusoe. Somebody had to have put him there. Left him there. Waiting to be discovered.

If Henry's been hiding him all this time . . . then where the fuck has he been? My mind resists the thought but doesn't reject it. This whole town was combed over when Skyler went missing. Charlene said as much. He didn't even have a house to hide him in. And if he *did* stash him, what would be the point of that? Why fake his son's disappearance?

Henry could never get away with something like that. Someone would find out that he was harboring a child. Somebody would *know*.

Henry, all broken. Henry, out of his mind. Henry, hiding a child.

Or . . .

Gravel crumbles under rubber as we pull into the motel parking lot. Henry leaps out from the truck and scoops Skyler—*stop it, just stop*—into his arms, rushing him to my room.

I follow after, just a few steps behind them. The boy glances back at me from over Henry's shoulder and my heart just about halts. I stop. I watch them slip inside while I'm stuck in the parking lot, unable to move my feet any further. What am I doing? I need to—need to—

Go. Now. Just turn around and run away from all this. I could call the cops. The police would be here in seconds and that would put an end to this whole clusterfuck. They'd arrest Henry, that boy would be reunited with his real parents, and my life could go back to normal.

Normal. I'd be right back where I started. Stranded in this shitty motel. Begging for scraps of Kendra's time. I'd have nothing, absolutely nothing, to show for myself.

I'd be all alone.

That boy needs my help. *Henry needs help.* I can't leave.

I find them in the bathroom. The boy is trembling in the tub as Henry cranks the hot water all the way to its hilt. He just can't stop shivering, his lips a muted blue. He's all skin and bones, barely any meat on him, like a hatchling flapping its featherless wings.

Who are you? I silently ask him. *Where could you have come from?*

The boy only stares back. I've never seen the color of Skyler's eyes before. They've always been black and white to me, a cluster of pixels. This boy's eyes are hazel. Bands of brackish brown and green, just like the river we fished him out of.

"Let's warm you up." Henry kneels beside the tub as if he's praying at some mildewed altar. The motel's bathroom barely fits the three of us. The frosted-glass window is so small, barely bigger than my head, sliding open from the top. Even then, it only offers three inches' worth of ventilation. *Can't crawl through there . . .* The sun never reaches this room. The bulb above our heads hardly illuminates the ceiling, let alone the bruised-avocado-green tiles, which look like rotten guacamole in the dim lighting. The shower curtain is a transparent plastic sheet that's the same flimsy material as rubber dish gloves, covered in white patches of dried soap scum.

"How's that feel?" Henry asks. "Not too hot?"

The boy doesn't respond. I kneel next to Henry. "You're okay." I keep saying *okay* as if it means something, but there's no weight to the word. What an empty expression, *okay*, a Band-Aid on a bullet wound. How's any of this *okay*? How's Skyler—

Stop. Calling. Him. That.

But . . . what if? What's if it's really him?

It's not. It can't be.

Say his name . . . Just try it . . . Just once . . .

No, I can't. I won't.

Give it breath . . .

No . . .

Give him life . . .

NO.

If it's Skyler, truly Skyler, then I can't even begin to imagine what he's gone through. What the last few years of his life have been like. Nothing but an absolute nightmare.

Could it really be him?

Henry said he believed his son was still alive after all this time. He held on to that desperate thread for so long . . . What if he's right?

Or what if he's the one who's been hiding him?

The tub is about to flood. Both Henry and I seem to realize it at the same time, simultaneously reaching for the faucet. Our fingers graze over each other and I give a start. He reels back, holding his hands up—*sorry*, his expression says—letting me turn off the water.

A hush settles over us. The frantic lap of bathwater against the sides of the tub settles into gentle waves.

"You okay?"

Takes me a moment to realize Henry's asking *me*. I give him a quick nod. No matter how deep I inhale, I can't keep the air in my lungs. I feel dizzy, the tiles spinning along with my thoughts. Henry wants to know if I'm *okay*. But none of this is okay. We were getting so close, weren't we? I lowered my guard. Brought him into my world. I told him about Kendra. I shared what little life I had with him. Was there ever going to be a future for us? Were we always destined to arrive at this point? Here? Now? *Jesus, was Henry just waiting for the right moment to introduce me to this kidnapped proxy of his long-dead son? What was he expecting to happen? That we could all be some kind of happy family together? Is that it?*

I don't believe that. I read people all the goddamn time. People come to me in need, desperate for a better future for themselves. I saw into Henry's hands, his skin, and I saw none of this. Henry told me he believed in me. If that was all just a crock of shit to get me to go along and play his little head games, why would he hide a child out in the middle of the river?

What about the visions? The things I've seen? The dreams I've had?

Where did they come from?

This kid?

I found that boy, didn't I? *Sensed* him somehow? Even when

Henry avoided heading in the duck blind's direction, it was like I knew he was near. The tide tugged me toward that boy . . .

How is that even possible?

What if . . . ?

What if Henry's ready to reintroduce Skyler to Brandywine?

Ta-da . . . Skyler's back!

He'd need someone else to discover him. Someone other than himself. Someone who specializes in this sort of stuff, who could cover for his abduction without even knowing it . . .

He needed me.

I can see the headline already: *Palm Reader Discovers Missing Child*.

Wouldn't that make for one hell of a family reunion? Fit for prime time. Here come the news crews, cameras clustering to get a good look at the boy who defied the odds just by surviving.

Henry said so himself: *I've seen psychics on TV helping with missing-person cases . . .*

But I'm just some stupid goddamn palm reader. I'm not one of those clairvoyant vultures you read about helping in missing-person cases. I just tell fortunes for twenty bucks . . .

It's not real. None of this is real. *But Henry believes it, doesn't he?* Believes in me?

"You feeling better?" Henry massages the boy's shoulder, as if to stimulate his circulation. Get the blood flowing again. He's leapt into action without hesitation, never second-guessing himself, all reflex, doing everything to protect his boy.

Except take him to the hospital . . .

The bathroom's hazy light illuminates the veins branching across the boy's back. I can see them just below the surface of his anemic skin. Jellyfish tentacles spreading through water.

There's something else. I lean over the tub and hear myself ask, "What is that?"

The faintest trace of diamondlike abrasions on his shoulders. Xs all over his back.

"Are those . . ." I gasp. Pull back from the boy. "Are those *scars?*"

Someone sliced this child. Over and over. Who would do something like that? To a *boy?*

Henry would never.

Never.

There's no way he'd hurt his *son, his moon, his Skyler.*

But those scars . . . Just look at them. A scabbed patchwork. It's as if his body has been wrapped in . . . in chicken wire?

"Madi," Henry says.

Those scars aren't fresh. They look as if they've been there for years. *Years.*

"*Madi.*"

I snap back. "Yeah?"

"Help me." Henry points to the towel rack.

I yank the threadbare white cloth and hand it to him. He drapes the towel over the boy, covering the latticework of scars crisscrossing his arms and shoulders.

"We need to call the police."

Henry hoists the boy up to his feet, toweling him off. "No police."

"He needs help."

"*Please.*" The need in Henry's voice presses against my chest. "They'll think I did this . . ."

Did you?

"You know how the police pull families apart," he says. Yeah, I do. Folks around here prefer to handle personal matters—*family matters*—in private. Nobody wants a stranger stepping in.

But it isn't him, I keep reminding myself. *That's not Henry's son. He isn't kin.*

"So what do we do?" I manage to ask, hoping to keep Henry calm. Placate him. If he's capable of injuring this kid, there's no telling what else he might do.

"Can we stay here?" he asks.

"Someone might see him," I say. *That's it,* I think, *try to reason with him.* "Too much traffic. A customer might call it in. What if we take him to—"

The boy leaps out from his towel. His arms find their way around my shoulders. I have to plant a hand on the tile floor behind me to stop from tipping over. He hugs me so tightly, I gasp.

He buries his face in the nape of my neck. His breath feels hot against my skin. There's a surprising amount of heat radiating from him. Does he have a fever? Is he sick?

Henry places a hand on the child's shoulder. "Easy now, easy . . ."

The boy's grip loosens. He doesn't let go, not yet, assessing Henry's open arms by peering out from my neck, his head still buried against me.

"I got you," Henry says.

"*Daddy.*"

I hear it. The boy hasn't said a single word since we found him, remaining mute until now, and his first word is—

Daddy.

What the fuck is going on here?

The boy pushes off from me and crawls into Henry's lap.

"That's it, I got you . . ." Henry embraces him. One arm wraps around his shoulders while he plants his other hand against the slope of the child's skull. "You're okay now, you're okay . . ."

Okay. We all keep repeating the same goddamn empty word. *Okay.*

Nothing will ever feel *okay* again.

Henry buries his mouth into the boy's hair. He breathes deeply, taking in the scent of him. The two gently sway back and forth, as if they're sitting in an invisible rocking chair.

"You're safe now. Nobody's taking you away."

This game Henry's playing, pretending he's found—

I found

—his son is *insane.* He's so far gone. There's no getting Henry back, whoever that might've been. I need to focus on the boy, get him out of here, as far away from Henry as possible, before he hurts him again. Or me.

I have to play along. Pretend this child is who Henry says he is. Just for a little while. Until Henry lowers his guard. Goes to sleep.

Then we escape.

Henry runs his hand through the boy's hair in a moment of parental ecstasy. I see it. Practically feel it myself. There's simply no other sensation quite like taking in your child.

Henry *believes*. He genuinely believes this boy is his son . . .

"Just give me one night," he says to me. "Just one, just to be with him . . ."

I don't say anything.

"I'll call the police tomorrow, I swear."

"Tomorrow," I finally say. A plan's already percolating in my head. Once we slip out, we'll flag down the first car that passes us on the road and we'll get as far away from—

"*Daddy.*" The boy's voice remains faint. Henry's eyelids flicker shut, as if the word alone is enough to heal every ache he's felt for the last five years of his life.

"I'm never letting you go," Henry says. "Never again, I promise."

"You're going to be okay, Skyler," I say—*that's it, say his name, go along with it*—placing my hand on the boy's shoulder. "You're safe now."

I can't abandon this boy. He needs someone to rescue him from this nightmare.

From Henry.

TWO

The three of us share my bed. Henry and I fashion a valley between us for the boy to nestle within. I still have some of Kendra's clothes lying around; you never know when you might need a *Dora the Explorer* T-shirt. It's a few sizes too big for the boy, reaching his knees, but it'll have to do. The boy is on his back, staring at the ceiling. His eyes are wide open, taking in the world around him and all of its shadows, as if it's the first time he's laid eyes on anything.

"There," Henry says. "How's that? All cozy?"

The boy doesn't say a word.

Before the three of us climbed into bed, I found him standing before the window, transfixed by the neon sign. The boy ran his finger along the hand's gray glass tubes.

"Watch this," I said like I was about to perform a magic trick, simply flipping the switch.

Purple and pink light instantly filled the room. The boy leapt back, eyes wide with a mixture of wonder and fear, startled and marveling at the winding gaseous colors. He reached out and pressed his own palm flat against the sign's, his skin bathed in amethyst hues.

"That's enough for now." I turned the sign back off. I took the boy by his shoulders—*gently*—and tried guiding him away from the window. He didn't want to go, refusing to move.

"You must be sleepy. Come on. Let's get you into bed—"

The low hum of electricity zapped back to life over my shoulder. I turned around and saw that the neon sign had flipped itself back on. No one else was standing anywhere near it.

I unplugged the sign this time.

Just to be sure.

The motel came with a double bed. I'd never shared it with anyone before. Until Henry.

Now there's three of us.

That magic number.

The boy climbed in first, crawling across the top on all fours. He doesn't seem to trust the softness of the mattress, acting like he's on a raft about to capsize. "It's okay. Make yourself—"

at home

"—comfortable."

"We'll get out of your hair tomorrow," Henry whispers to me over the boy's head. He's huddled against Henry's chest.

Just look at them, I think. How well their bodies fit together, almost as if this boy were molded from the man himself. "Where are you gonna go?"

"Back to the boat, I reckon."

"After you go to the police station?"

Henry pauses. "That's right."

I pretend to believe him. "The boat is no place for a boy. You can stay here."

"Sure about that?"

"You got somewhere better in mind?"

"Well, it isn't the Four Seasons . . ."

"Watch it . . . I'll start charging you by the night, if you're not careful."

"Better than by the hour." He's so affable. So . . . *happy.* Henry's got his son back. He can play house now. The thought sends a shiver up my spine.

"We should all get some rest." I slip out from under the covers. I'll sit in the parlor until Henry passes out, and then we'll run. "You two can have the bed. I'll sleep on the floor."

Henry's hand finds mine, weaving around the boy and taking hold. "Stay."

"Henry . . ."

"Please?"

Henry's need unnerves me. It seems so genuine. *So real.* He looks exhausted. I know it's simply the shadows hooding his eyes, but they look as if they've sunk into their sockets.

"You feeling okay?" I whisper—why, I'm not sure. It's not like the boy can't hear us. He's wide awake, nestled between our bodies. Hopefully he'll drift off soon. Let the adults talk as he sleeps.

"Pretty much running on empty," he says.

"Get some rest."

Henry and I stare at each other, our faces only inches away. The breath between us drifts through the boy's hair, rustling his curls.

"You want to talk about . . ." I look down. The boy is staring at me. Those hazel eyes look amber now. There's the faintest glow. Sprigs of gold. Does he understand what we're saying?

Why won't he talk? What's wrong with him?

"In the morning, okay?"

I can't let it go. I know I should let sleeping dogs lie, but I can't help myself. If I can just get him to snap out of it, maybe we wouldn't have to run. "People are gonna start sniffing around. You need to get in front of the gossip. Let everyone know he's—"

"Tomorrow." Henry tries to keep himself from coughing. There's some grit in his voice. Sounds like sandpaper. I have to imagine his whole body is bound to collapse before long, all that adrenaline burning itself out.

"Good night," Henry whispers to the boy, kissing his blond crown. "Sleep tight . . ."

Don't let the motel's bedbugs bite.

The boy turns, nestling his face in the slope of Henry's neck.

They look so peaceful together. This kid isn't afraid of Henry at all. He wants to be here, huddled against his abductor.

A few minutes later, he glances up from the nook of Henry's body and stares at me. I can't help but think this kid is assessing me, trying to figure out just who the hell I am.

Where did you come from, lady? I bet he's thinking right now. *You're not my mom . . .*

I should say something. "It's okay to close your eyes, sweetie. You're safe, I promise."

I still can't get over how much he looks like the age progression of Skyler. I imagine a time-lapse video of the last five years of his life, watching him grow. It begins with his black-and-white baby picture, then speeds through the years, one now two then three, burning all the way through ages four and five, until reaching his six-year-old self, this spoke-limbed kid in bed before me. He's so frail, like a newborn. When Kendra was this age I couldn't get her to sit still for five minutes.

I feel myself start to drift against my will. The undertow of exhaustion drags at my eyelids. I'm ready to let go, simply let myself get pulled below and fall asleep. Just before I do, I turn toward the boy. He's wide awake, lying on his side, back pressed against Henry's chest.

Does this boy ever sleep? He's still watching me. His face is mere inches from mine, eyes glistening in the dark. He looks like he's on the verge of tears.

"You okay, hon?"

My heart breaks. No—breaking's not the right sensation. This feels more like a squeeze. Simply staring into the endless depth of this poor boy's eyes puts my heart into a vise. I can feel the clamp getting tighter.

"This must be pretty frightening," I say, "but I want you to know you're gonna be okay."

Okay. How many times am I going toss out that empty word?

It's so humid in the bedroom. I should crank up the poor excuse for an air conditioner, but it clunks and chugs, eclipsing every other sound until I can't think straight. I don't want to wake Henry. I hear the soft drag in his throat. That leaves me and the kid. I'll give it a few minutes, just to be sure, until I know for certain that Henry has slipped deep into his sleep.

Then we're gone.

"I haven't introduced myself, have I? You must be wondering who I am . . ."

The boy doesn't say a word.

"I'm Madi."

"*Mmmm.*"

"That's right. Madi. You want to tell me your name, hon?"

Silence.

"Your real name?"

I take in a deep breath through my nose and I'm met with the faint scent of wet wood. Cedar. There's a hint of salt water in the air, too. Where is that smell coming from?

"It's okay, you can talk to me . . ." I reach out and run my fingers along his shoulder. "You're safe with me, you hear? I'm going to get you out of here. I'll take you back to your—"

"*Maaa . . .*"

The word is weak. Faint. I swear I hear it, but there's no intonation.

The boy's hands slither across the mattress. His arms wrap around me.

"*Maaa . . .*"

There it is again. That word, warm now. There's a sudden comfort to it, a balm that soothes me. Aloe on sunburn. It reminds me of the first time I heard Kendra call me *Ma*.

You forget how words hold their own potency. Something as simple as *Ma*.

"*Meeee . . .*"

Is he trying to say Mommy?

This feels wrong. "No, hon," I say. "I'm not your mommy. Your real mommy—"

hanged herself

"—isn't here right now."

But that's not true either, now, is it? Grace isn't his mother. Not this mystery boy, whoever he is. If I could just get him to talk to me, tell me his name, I could find out who his real parents are.

He inches closer, rummaging around the sheets until he finds my shoulder, where he digs his nose in like a rutting piglet. I don't know what to do. I feel like I should push him away. I don't want to confuse him. That might make matters worse.

"*Mmmmooooommmmmmmy . . .*"

"Okay, that's enough." This boy simply won't let go. "You're squeezing too hard . . ."

I have to grab both of his thin wrists and pry him off. He's surprisingly strong for his age.

"*Enough.*"

The room goes silent and I'm suddenly worried I've woken Henry.

Nothing.

I flip myself over in bed so I'm facing away from them both. I give the kid my back and immediately regret it, but I need to set up some personal boundaries with this boy.

I'm not his mother . . .

I feel like I've just damaged this kid even more than he was before. He's got nobody looking out for him, no one protecting him from Henry. He's all alone, terrified. He's just—

Skyler?

—a boy, that's all. A frightened, traumatized boy. He needs someone to look after him. Protect him. Get him the hell out of this endless nightmare.

I've read stories about sick individuals kidnapping little children and brainwashing them into believing they're completely different people. New names, new families. Is that what Henry's done? How long has he been conditioning this kid, scrubbing his real identity away until the boy began to believe he was Skyler? That Henry is his father?

He doesn't belong to Henry. But he belongs to someone.

"*Mama.*" His voice drifts through my thoughts, lighter than air, but there's a force to it, as if the boy were somehow pushing my thoughts to the side to make way for his own.

I don't say anything back, pretending to be asleep. Who knows if the boy buys it.

"*Mama.*" His voice is more forceful this time.

I don't move a muscle. I just lie there on my side, facing the far wall, my back to him.

He wraps his arms around my waist, pressing his face against my shoulder blade. His heartbeat thrums against my spine. What a strange sensation it is, feeling someone else's pulse against your skin. The tension in my muscles ebbs as he clings to me. I hadn't realized how exhausted I was. Fatigue sweeps over me in a dull wave.

We'll just lie here for a little while. Just until I know Henry won't wake up.

Just a few minutes to rest and then we'll . . .

We'll . . .

"*Mommy.*" The boy sounds so much older now. His voice gains depth, giving me just the gentlest nudge, sending me right off to sleep.

the currents drag at my skin . . .

loosening the flesh until it slides right off the bone . . .

flapping through the water like kelp . . .

feel the gentle tug of the tides for so long now . . .

can't move . . .

something pinning me in place . . .

the thinnest grid presses against my arms . . .

my back . . .

even against my skull . . .

trapped . . .

the wire slices into my skin . . .

branding my body diamonds . . .

cubes of skin tissue push through . . .

feeding the fish my flesh

THREE

I snap out of my dream. For a brief moment, I don't know where I am. It feels like I'm out on the river. No, not on it—but below, trapped beneath its black surface. The drowning dream lingers at the back of my brain, dragging at my consciousness.

A haziness hangs over the room. My gaze settles on a jellyfish floating freely through the air. It's there, *right there*, plunging toward the floor, tentacles shimmering pink and purple.

Wait, that's not a jellyfish. *It's the sign.* The neon hand in the window. The boy must've turned it on while we were asleep . . .

But I unplugged it, didn't I?

How did it get so hot in here? Feels like the thermostat's been cranked up to its hilt. I'm sweating through the top sheet. It clings to my skin so I try kicking it away, the fabric peeling off my legs with a tacky drag.

Shit, shit. How long was I out?

It's still dark outside. Moths beat themselves senseless against the other side of the window, desperate to reach the neon hand. I hear their wings softly hammer at the glass.

Henry's fast asleep, jaw slack. *It's not too late. We can still make a break for it.* I just have to pry the boy away from him and crawl out of bed. I run my hand along the sheets and—

The boy's not here.

The bed is wet where the boy should be, soaked straight through the sheets. I catch an acrid tang. *Did he have an accident?*

Where did he go?

"Skyler?" I whisper, hoping not to wake Henry.

Where is he hiding?

I reach deeper under the sheet, rummaging blindly across the mattress. "Skyler—"

My fingers graze over something moist.

A piece of fabric. It's cold, flimsy. But the texture is all wrong. It's not cotton. It's more like . . . rubber? Soft plastic?

I pinch it and pull it out from beneath the sheets. I hold it up. It's nearly transparent, the neon sign shining through it. I make out the shape of tiny fingers.

It's some sort of . . . thin glove?

Where did this come from?

"Henry . . ."

He doesn't stir, dead to the world. I have to shake him by his shoulders but he just won't come to. I heft him into an upright sitting position. His head lolls over his shoulders.

"Henry!"

His eyes fly open and he immediately looks to the center of the bed. To the wet stain where the boy should be. "Where's Skyler?"

"He's not here."

Henry springs right out of bed. "Skyler?" He flips on the bathroom lights. "Skyler!?"

Empty.

He heads for the closet, peering in.

"Skyler?"

I peer underneath the bed, just to make sure.

"Skyler?"

Nothing but dust. He's vanished. Where could he have gone?

"What about the other rooms?"

The other rooms. Henry's already rushing for the front door when he asks, not waiting for an answer. He pushes past the beaded curtain, the strands skittering against the walls.

"Skyler!" Henry calls out into the night.

I follow him through the door. Cool air hits my skin. Much cooler than inside the room.

"Skyler!"

The highway is still alive with traffic, even though it's thinned out at this hour. Just thinking about the boy wandering out into the middle of the road sends a chill through me.

He couldn't have gone far, I say to myself, but I'm not sure I believe it. It's close to three in the morning. He could've walked halfway to Deltaville by now. We've got to find him.

Henry makes his way down the corridor of storefronts. I can hear the soft slap of his bare feet against the concrete. First up is the mini-mart. He peers into the window.

"Skyler?"

Nothing there, so Henry moves on to the fireworks shop.

"Skyler!"

Henry stops before the bait and tackle shop.

"Door's open." He glances at me before slipping inside, disappearing into the darkness.

I follow him in, calling out, "Skyler?"

A hush suspends itself over the shop, save for the faint hum of electricity emanating from the refrigerated units of live bait and energy drinks at the rear of the store. This might've been the honeymoon suite back in the day. Now it's full of fishing equipment. Three separate aisles.

"Skyler?" I call out. Maybe he's just scared. Maybe he needs a voice he can trust.

"Skyler, are you in here?"

I spot the boy's blackened eyes peering out from behind the reels and nearly scream.

It's an old missing-person flyer covered in a veil of cobwebs. The one that's been photocopied into oblivion, stapled to nearly every telephone pole for miles, collecting dust with the rods.

Calm down, Madi. Get a hold of yourself . . .

Henry starts at the farthest aisle while I head down the center. Rows of fishing rods stand upright on the shelves. In the dark, the slender graphite stems—the *blank*, they're called—look like the segmented legs of a spider. Any second now, I'm convinced they'll start twitching. All those fishing poles will spring to life and scuttle off, just like everything else has.

"Skyler?"

No sign of him down this aisle. I make my way to the end and turn.

"Sky—"

A severed finger the color of a plum squirms over the floor.

The only light on in the shop is a fiberglass bass promoting a special brand of lure. Its glow isn't strong enough to make out the digit crawling across the linoleum, so I crouch down to get a better look.

A bloodworm.

Not just one, but several, making their way across the floor, wriggling in every direction.

I look around to see if a plastic tub of live bait has been left open and find the boy squatting on the floor. He leans against the white tub, its lid pried off and abandoned at his feet. I hear the faintest squelch of the bloodworms' bodies moving around inside the bucket.

His cheeks look like they're covered in blackberry jam.

". . . Skyler?"

His fists are full of worms wrestling against his grip. He brings his hand to his lips and shoves them into his mouth.

My stomach turns. "Skyler, hon?" I hear myself, the words barely there. "Don't do that . . ."

The wriggling ends of their purple bodies squirm against his lips, desperate to escape.

I take hold of his hands by the wrists, forcing him to let the bloodworms go. I think I'm going to be sick, but I've got to push the nausea down.

"Skyler, please, don't—"

In a sickening slurp, he sucks the mouthful down. The worms quickly flicker and disappear into his mouth, like strands of spaghetti. I think of watching *Lady and the Tramp* with Kendra when she was a little girl. I start to gag.

"There you are!" Henry swoops in, practically pushing me to the side. "Oh, thank God . . ."

He picks the boy up from the floor and brings him to his chest, pressing him against his body. Holding on tight.

The boy's hands unravel and bits of bloodworms plop onto the floor. He squeezes Henry tight.

"I thought I lost you," Henry says and I can't help but think *again. Lost you again.*

"Don't you run away like that again, you hear?" It's an admonishment, but the words sound so broken, as if Henry can't bring himself to scold him. "Don't you leave me . . ."

I notice the other buckets of bait. Four separate lids are pried off and tossed to the floor, exposing writhing masses of bait. Mealworms. Tobacco worms. Butterworms. Nightcrawlers. Grubs. The boy had made his way through each of them, reaching in and gorging himself, lazily dropping loose chunks of insects through his fingers. *Just how much did he eat?*

I lost Kendra in the supermarket once. We were ambling down the aisle together and I turned my back for a second, just one, but when I looked back, Kendra was gone. I called her name over and over again but she never responded. I ditched my shopping cart and raced up every last aisle, shouting her name louder and louder. When I found her by herself in the cereal section, reaching for the Cap'n Crunch, I hugged her so tight, relief washing over me. Then I shook the living shit out of her. *Don't you ever do that to me again! I thought I'd lost you!*

Happens to parents all the time. Children disappear. Children vanish.

Just not quite like this boy. *What kind of boy are you?* He stares at me, then smiles—just for me—so happy that we're all together. I can see chunks of worms stuck between his teeth.

FOUR

Henry set up watch in the parlor and brought in his guitar. The worn wood finish is covered in pick marks, as if a cat once used it as a scratching post. It was in the rear bed of his truck among all the other junk from his house, untouched—until now.

Henry starts plucking mindlessly at the strings.

"Are we gonna talk about what just happened?"

"Tomorrow." He's focused on his fingers. A tune starts to emerge. *You were born by the water. . .*

He loses himself in the song. I see it happen, witness the exact moment when he leaves this world behind and enters a separate level of consciousness, drifting off without me.

Raised by this river. . .

I haven't heard him play since high school. I can't help but think of who he was back then. Who he is now? A kidnapper? Does he even know what he's done?

I realize how much the guitar is holding Henry up, not the other way around. *How exhausted is he?* He's keeping an eye on the front door, camping out at the card table, making sure the boy doesn't sneak out again. Or maybe it's me he's worried about. *Did he figure it out?* I wonder if he knows I was planning to make a run for it. *Stop being paranoid.*

I'd feel a lot safer if I had my hands on my phone, but I can't seem to find it. "You seen my cell?" I ask, poking around the parlor. "Thought I left it on the nightstand . . ."

Henry doesn't look up from his guitar. "Haven't seen it."

I decide to address the pint-sized elephant in the bedroom. "The boy's not well, Henry."

"He'll be fine."

"Did you see—" I cut myself off. I can't bring myself to say what happened. *What I saw.* All those bloodworms wriggling around in his mouth.

"He's just feeding."

Feeding. That's an odd way of putting it. A boy doesn't *feed*. Not like that, not like—

Skyler.

"What are we gonna do now?"

He won't look at me, focusing on his fingers as they skim across the copper-twined wires. Why is he being so nonchalant?

"*Henry.* You need to tell me what you're thinking, 'cause I'm sure as hell not some—"

"Mind reader?"

That stings. *Let him play his goddamn guitar alone until his fingers fucking bleed for all I care.* I turn on my heel and go to check on the boy. See if he's feeling any better.

He's resting on the bed, his eyes wide open and alert. *Why doesn't he ever sleep?* His cheeks are covered in a fine purple crust. Worm jam. It's even in his hair.

How many times have I turned that goddamn sign off? Why does he keep turning it on?

"How're you doing, hon?"

It's so hot in here. The humidity makes it hard to think straight. I crank up the A/C but it simply can't compete with the heat. I swear it's hotter inside my room than it is outside. It's a downright oven in here, set to sweltering. I'm sweating even when I sit perfectly still.

"Your boy needs a bath," I call out to Henry. "Somebody should clean off the . . ."

He's just feeding, Henry said, as if that was all the explanation I'd need.

Just feeding.

What the hell does that mean?

Feeding.

The song pauses, but Henry doesn't say a word. Everybody is holding their breath, waiting to see who folds first. I feel like I'm trapped in my own motel room. Like I'm being held hostage.

Maybe you are.

". . . Henry?"

He starts strumming away again, struggling to hum his lullaby without coughing.

You were born. . .

Something wet loosens itself in his chest. No hospital for him, either. He won't hear it. Just family. As if a little love is all he needs to heal.

By the water. . .

"Guess it's just you and me then, Sky . . ."

It's astounding how fast we all fall into familiar habits. It's been so long since I had a kid to care for. Turns out it's just like riding a bike.

I draw the boy a bath.

He brings his knees to his chest and dips his chin between his legs, assuming his preferred position. A hermit crab without a home.

"How's that? Not too hot for you?" I hold my hand under the water, trying to gauge the temperature against my skin. *God, what I wouldn't give to crawl into a cold bath right now . . .*

"Let's clean you up." I'm trying to keep things light for the boy's sake. Mine too, maybe. I've barely slept all night. None of us have. The delirium seeps in around the edges of my eyes.

Keep it together, Madi. Just a little longer.

"I'm gonna start with your back, okay?"

I run the sponge over his shoulders. His wet skin glistens in the low light and almost appears translucent. His veins are a phosphorescent blue. It reminds me of those science documentaries of deep-sea life that have never seen sunlight.

The boy's shoulders seem broader than they were just hours ago. I continue to quietly scrub him, shaking the thought off. *You're just tired.*

His scars have moved. The diamond pattern that laced his shoulders has unraveled, unspooling into . . . what is that? *What is going on here?* The thickened tissue shifted, altering its pattern somehow, becoming something else. I don't know how it's possible, but I swear I see . . .

A fish.

I can just barely make out the blistered embroidery of fish. Just like from his satin blanket. The scars have come together to form a cross-stitched menagerie along his shoulder.

The boy's been branded. That's what this is, right? I didn't know how else to explain it. Translucent tattoos of suppurated flesh. His body was a canvas someone had taken a needle to—*Henry?*—sewing these blistered beasts across his skin *just like the animals from his blankie.*

"You feeling okay, Skyler?" No response. The boy is a brick wall when he wants to be.

Just like his father.

It's not Skyler, I scold myself. *Henry is not his father. You know that . . . How many times do you have to remind yourself? Don't fall for this fucked-up fantasy and get this kid out of here!*

Henry's song carries into the bathroom.

you were born

I need to keep it together. Maintain my calm.

by the water

Act like everything is fine.

"Time to wash your hair." I squeeze a dollop of shampoo in my hand before running it through his hair. I just need to focus on what I'm doing to keep from panicking. If I can cling to this simple ritual, *just wash this kid's hair*, I'll have something anchoring me to reality. I just need something stable to hold on to. Rational. Anything that'll keep me from feeling like I'm losing my mind.

raised by this river

I didn't even realize I was singing along until the boy starts humming with me. Just how many times is Henry going to play the same damn song over and over again? He's worse than a broken record, repeating the same refrain . . .

After lathering the boy's hair into a sudsy blond bouffant, I rinse the shampoo out. "Close your eyes, hon. This stuff stings."

He turns his head toward me, resting his chin on a kneecap. The look of love in his eyes blindsides me. So full of wonder. Of downright need. Where is all that love coming from?

I look into those amber eyes—and feel myself drowning in them.

"*Mommy* . . ."

Everything within me wants to let go.

"*Mommy*," he says, and I feel my heart ache. He holds a smile on his face, never blinking.

How is this boy getting in my head?

"I'm not your mother. You know that, right?" It pains me to say it. "I promise we'll get you back to your real—"

"*Mommy* . . ."

"No, hon, you have to stop calling me that." I lean over into the tub to pull the plug. I'm not looking where I'm reaching, keeping my eyes on the boy as I dip my fingers into the water, blindly searching for the rubber stopper tethered to its rusted chain. It's time to get this boy out. Just look at him: he's pruning already. His pale skin puckers, all wrinkled. Blistered.

"*Mommmmmmmy* . . ."

"I'm *not* your mother—"

Something squishes between my fingers in the tub. My hand grazes against a soft bundle of flexing jelly. It feels like a peeled tomato.

I peer into the tub.

At first, I don't see it. Can't see it, really. There's nothing to look at. But my eyes slowly take in the translucent shadow caught in the whirlpool of water slipping down the drain.

There's a jellyfish in the bathtub. Just the tiniest comb jelly. No tentacles. These don't sting, but during the summer, they cluster in the Chesapeake and clot up your crab traps.

How in the hell did that get in there?

I count three bobbing in the tub, all smaller than my hand. Faintly pink. The ridged contours of their cloudlike bodies drift and swirl in the water by the boy's feet.

Where did they come from? The faucet? Could they have slipped through the pipes?

"Let's dry you off," I say, pushing back any panic. "Stand up for me."

He does as he's told. I've got the towel over his head now, rubbing it through his hair. He can't see me peering into the tub as one tiny jellyfish after another slips down the pipe. Some of them are too big and collect near the drain, forming a dam.

How many are there?

"Let's get a good look at you," I say. I turn him around, running my fingers through his corn-silk hair, searching for patches, any rashes or stings. "There. All clean and good as new—"

Wait. Something is behind his ear.

"Looks like I missed a spot." *Keep it together, Madi, don't panic—*

Something clings to his earlobe. "Found a potato." I tilt the boy's head forward so I can get a better look. He doesn't resist. Doesn't squirm. "Let me . . ."

Then I see it.

A barnacle.

I know right away. Its acorn-shaped shell has embedded itself behind his ear, no larger than a dime.

"Hold still for me, hon." I slowly reach for it, wrist trembling. The carapace opens to expose the feathery antenna, blindly reaching out in hopes of finding food.

"That's it, hold still . . ." The boy doesn't flinch as I pinch the barnacle between my fingers and pluck it off. It peels away from his pale skin, leaving behind the tiniest pink welt.

"Got it." I hold it up to the light. The barnacle's lacelike whisker reaches out from its shell, a tongue lapping at the air. A chill spreads over me. *How could it grow . . .*

I toss the barnacle into the toilet—its shell *tnk-tnk*ing against the porcelain—and flush.

"*Mommy.*" His lips aren't moving.

"Please . . . Don't call me that."

"*Mommy.*" Why are his lips not moving?

"Stop it."

"*Mommy.*" How can I hear him if his lips aren't—

"Henry!"

"What," he says right behind my back, standing in the bathroom doorway, using the frame to prop himself up. How long has he been there? Just watching us?

I open my mouth but the words won't come. I have to force myself to say something. *Anything.* "Something's wrong with Skyler. The boy . . . He's sick." *You're sick, too*, I nearly add.

"Looks fine to me."

"Are you looking?"

"What am I supposed to see?" To prove his point, he asks, "How are you feeling, Sky?"

"*Daaddy.*"

"See?"

"What about you?" He can barely focus on me, eyes half open, as if fatigue has seeped into his very marrow. "You look like you're about to pass out."

"Parenting just tuckers you out." *Damn straight it does. Just not like this.*

"How would you know?" I instantly regret it the second the words leave my mouth.

Henry's eyelids droop, a slow-motion blink that seems more attuned to bone-deep fatigue than feeling stung. "Skyler's just not like other kids."

"That's it," I say, standing. "If you're not gonna do it, I'll take him to the hospital myself."

Henry doesn't move from the doorframe, blocking my way. "Skyler doesn't need a doctor. He needs his family."

It's practically impossible to have an argument with Henry. He's become un-fucking-movable. I don't know what else to say. "How long do you think you can hide him?"

"I'm not hiding him."

"People are going to start asking questions," I say. "Is that what you're afraid of?"

"People always *talk*. I don't give a damn what they say."

"They're going to find out . . ."

"Find out *what*?" He practically spits it out.

"What you've done."

Henry stares a hole right through me. Suddenly he looks very awake. I've touched a nerve. "Everybody told me—*you* told me—to believe Skyler was dead. But I wouldn't do it. I never let go. I held on to him for years. *Years.*"

"Henry . . ."

"Now that we've brought him back, you want to take him away from me again?"

Brought him back? "That boy's not—"

"Come here, Sky," Henry says, holding out his hand. "Come on."

The boy does as he's told and takes it. *Jesus, the two of them . . . It's like they're in this fantasy together, hand in hand.* I can't tell if this is Stockholm syndrome or something worse.

The boy guides Henry to bed. The man's balance is off. *Maybe I can take him,* I think. *Overpower him. All I have to do is wait until Henry's back is turned and I can . . .*

What? Knock him out?

I head for the neon sign and turn it off. The dark will help me. Henry won't see me coming if the light is off. Now I just have to find something heavy enough to—

The boy tucks Henry into bed, not the other way around.

"Good night," Henry says, already adrift, a wave of weariness sweeping over him so fast, eyes fluttering shut like moth wings. "Sleep tight . . . Don't let . . ."

Just like that, Henry's out.

Now! Now's our chance! Now we can go go go go—

The boy climbs on top of Henry.

What is he doing?

He wraps his arms and legs around Henry, and he splays himself over his father's frame. He lies there like that, his eyes never leaving me.

Something shifts along his scapula. It's hard for me to make it out in the dark, but I swear I can see the blackened silhouette of a spider—no, not a spider.

A crab. The tiniest crab crawls across the length of Skyler's arm.

One claw is larger than the other. A fiddler crab. You find them all along the shoreline at low tide. They burrow their little hovels deep in the sand, creeping out only when they sense that no predators are around. It's slowly working its way along the boy's neck, but he doesn't flinch.

". . . Skyler?"

The fiddler crab lifts its claws up in the air, raising them over its head as it scuttles along the boy's cheek. I watch it wander along the length of his jaw, reaching his ear.

What the fuck what the fuck what the—

The fiddler crab compresses its body and crawls into the fleshy canal of the boy's ear, vanishing from sight and *holy Jesus did I just see what I think I just saw—*

There are more. Shadows shift until I realize they're not shadows at all, but more crabs. Dozens of fiddler crabs slip out from every darkened corner of the bed, from every fold in the sheets.

They're crawling toward the boy. Crawling *into* him. His eyes stay fixed on me. Glowing fish roe, burning bright.

Mommy

I run out of the room. Race through the parlor. Out the door. The cool air hits me and I feel like I'm free from the humidity for the first time in days. I just need to get in my car and—

Mommy mommy mommy

Gravel crunches under my feet as I skid to a halt.

Mommy mommy mommmy mommmy mommmy

What the fuck am I doing? It's just a—

not a

—boy. He needs me. I can't leave him. I *can't.*

Whatever he is.

the crabs came for me first . . .

blue-shells skittered through the chicken wire . . .

lured in by the scent of flesh drifting throughout the water . . .

my body was bait . . .

their claws pinched at my skin . . .

tearing my flesh free and plucking the meat off me . . .

making a meal out of my body . . .

FIVE

Something bony pokes me while I'm still half asleep and for a second I swear it's a crab scuttling up my stomach. I feel its nimble pincers skitter across my skin, jabbing as it crawls.

But it's not a crab. It's a finger. A child's finger.

I'm still in bed, not at the bottom of the river. I'm climbing my way back to consciousness, lifting further up from the water in my dreams.

Mommy . . .

"Not now, Kendra," I mumble into my pillow. I barely got any sleep last night. The weight of exhaustion only seeps deeper into my body. I don't understand how I can feel this . . .

Spent. Like all my energy has been sapped from my bones. It's a sauna in here. It's difficult to breathe. My lungs feel gummy. I need to level my breath before I can pick myself up.

Kendra won't stop *poke-poke*-poking.

Mommy mommy . . .

"I'm up, I'm up . . ." I can barely open my eyes. A haziness hangs over the room. I find a fuzzy form standing next to the bed, hovering above me as it prods its finger into my side.

Mommy mommy mommy . . .

That's not Kendra.

The night before comes crashing back in a cold wave. I lift my head to find—

"Skyler?"

A rusted full moon looms above the bed.

A horseshoe crab.

The dorsal broadside of its sleek, brown shell is only inches away from my face. Its hinged abdomen, along with every movable spiny segment of its exoskeleton, flexes in and out with a wet *click click click*.

The shout that erupts from me fills the entire room. I push back, tangled in the sweaty bedsheet like a fish trapped in a net with no hope of shimmying free.

Now I see him.

Skyler.

The boy's body is right there, but not his head. Somehow he's placed a horseshoe crab on his shoulders. The crab has taken the place of his face, its carapace completely eclipsing his features. *A mask. Jesus, that's all it is.* The boy is wearing the crab like a Halloween disguise.

But *how*? String? There must be holes punched through its hollowed-out husk.

A memory resurfaces of Kendra coming across a horseshoe crab along the beach when she was a girl. She picked it up with both hands, marveling at its size.

But she didn't wear the crab like a fucking mask. The fiddler crabs. The jellyfish. The barnacle. *The worms.* I've been so focused on *who* the boy is. I never stopped to think about *what*.

"You startled me." I try to collect myself. *How afraid should I be?* "You really shouldn't do that . . ."

Mommy mommy mommy . . .

Henry's not in bed. He's not standing guard in the parlor. I call out his name but he doesn't answer. I'm all alone.

With the boy.

His head tilts to one side, a curious gesture that sends the full-moon shell of the horseshoe crab slipping across his face. Its spiny tail points to the floor, twelve inches at least, a bony pendulum on a grandfather clock. The telson flexes, as sharp as a serrated spear. And then I swear I see the crab's eyes—

blink

It's alive. *The horseshoe crab is still alive.* On the child's face.

"Where's your father, hon?" My voice remains even. Calm. Dare I say maternal. I slowly reach out for him, to grab that crab mask *and yank the awful thing off.* "Do you know if he—"

The boy senses my intentions and reels back. His head turns just enough to one side that I can see what's really going on.

All five pairs of legs are wrapped around his head, digging into the boy's cheeks. Its pincers grip his ears. His hair.

How is that even possible? How can it be doing that to him?

"Skyler, can you . . . take that off for me, please?"

The boy's head turns slowly back toward me and I swear I see the crab's eyes take me in. *Consider* me. He grabs hold of the crab's shell. Its claws release his face, each segmented leg letting him go, one at a time. They cycle through the air, snapping at nothing.

The boy slowly lowers the horseshoe crab. There's fear in his eyes.

"What is it? What's wrong—"

A breeze pushes against the beaded curtain.

Someone is here.

A stranger.

"Hello?" A young woman's voice cuts through the parlor. The first thought that pops into my mind is that it's Kendra—*she's can't be here, she can't see this*—but no, that's not her voice.

A customer. A goddamn customer. At this hour?

What time is it?

I glance at the clock on the nightstand table and realize it's already one in the afternoon. *How did I sleep in for that long?* It feels like I just closed my eyes only minutes ago . . .

I couldn't have slept that long. I never sleep—

He never sleeps

—that long. *What in the hell is going on here? What's happening to me?*

"You open or not?"

"Coming!" I call out. To the boy, I say in hushed tone, "Stay here."

He doesn't nod. Doesn't do much of anything other than stare back at me. He seems nervous, anxious somehow, as if the presence of someone else in the room terrifies him.

Maybe they can help us? There's not enough time to process what's going on. How can I explain this? How can I make it sound like I'm not an accomplice to kidnapping? How can I—

"*Hello?* You back there?"

"One sec!"

I have to do something. I can't just leave him here.

The bathroom.

I pick the boy up—*he's heavier, how did he get so heavy*—and quickly carry him into the bathroom. I lower him into the tub and the boy immediately assumes his compressed position, bringing his knees up to his chest and wrapping his arms around his shins.

"I'll be just in the other room . . . You'll be safe here, okay?"

I get one last look at the child before I slip out the door.

"Sorry to keep you waiting," I announce, pushing through the beaded curtain with a halfhearted flourish. "You're gonna have to forgive me, but now's really not a good—"

"Your sign was on," the young woman says in a dull voice. "Must be open for business . . . or you just don't wanna see me?"

I recognize her. Where do I know her from?

Lizzie. She's come back. She's not wearing jewelry now. All that cheap gold is gone. No more makeup. She's stripped down to her skin. Her eyes are bloodshot. I can tell she's been crying. Whatever's happened, she's brought that pain with her.

"I must've left it on by accident." I try chiding myself, but it comes out all wrong. Dry. Nothing but husk in my voice. "Sorry, I'm just spent is all. I don't think I have it in me for a—"

"You lied." Her spite takes the air out of the room. The last time she was here, she was all wide-eyed and naïve, but whatever's happened in the last few weeks of her life has peeled all that away. "I did everything just like you said. I used those stupid fucking crystals but . . ."

The words crumble. She can't finish her own thought.

"Oh, hon," I start. "It's all right . . ."

Lizzie's face wilts. Tears run down her cheeks and she tries wiping them away.

"It's okay." *Okay.* Christ, even with her, I'm tossing the word out there.

I reach out, but Lizzie bats my hand away. "Don't you *touch* me."

I step back. Her emotions are all over the place. I can't get a lock on her.

"My mom kicked me out." There's a grain of pain lodged in her throat. "My boyfriend won't let me stay with him. I don't have anywhere to go. I'm living out of my car . . ."

I glance toward the front door. *Where is Henry? Shouldn't he be here?*

"These things take a turn sometimes," I offer. "I'm sure they'll come around soon—"

Lizzie looks like she's about to spit in my face. Her jaw tightens. "You told me *everything* would be *fine* as long as I did what you *said.* You said you *saw* it in my *palm* and I *believed* you."

I peer over my shoulder, toward the back room, praying the boy doesn't hear any of this. *I have to get this girl out of here. Now.* "These readings are never an exact science . . ."

"Oh, so now you're saying they don't work?"

"I never said—"

"I *trusted* you and now everything I had is *gone and it's all your fault!*"

"I need you to lower your voice."

"I should've seen you coming from a fucking mile away. You're a goddamn con—"

"I can't help you if you're gonna shout—"

"You want to help me now, huh? You gonna *fix* everything?"

"I don't think I—"

Lizzie flings her hand out, palm up. "Go on, then. *Read* it."

"Excuse me?"

"Take another look. Tell me what you see for me now."

"That's not how—"

"*I don't give a shit,*" she hisses. "I'm not leaving until you read my palm! Let's see what my future holds now, you fucking—"

"Hold on—"

"*Read my fucking palm!*"

The room goes silent. The girl just won't go. I can't get rid of her. The quickest way to get her the hell out of my motel room—*away from Skyler*—is to simply do what she wants. If she wants her fucking palm read, *fine*, I'll give her a fucking reading and then *kick her ass out*.

"All right." I guide her to the table. "Have a seat."

Lizzie won't take her eyes off me.

"Give me your hand." The words are ash in my mouth.

Lizzie drops her hand onto the table. "Don't you think about lying to me this time. I'll fucking know if you're lying."

I take her hand into both of my own, pulling her closer to me. I lean in and study the fractures in her skin. Her fingernails are chewed on through, welcoming infection. The gnawing has gotten worse since the last time I saw her, the cuticles all raw and red now.

"What do you expect me to see?"

"Where am I supposed to go now, huh? Show me what kinda future I have left."

"That's not how this—"

"I listened to you," she shouts. "I trusted you! Now I want you to fix my fucking future!"

"I can't change any—"

"Yes, you can! You better find a way to—"

A pair of hands—a child's hands—reach out from behind Lizzie.

I watch them slowly snake their way around her shoulders, rising up past her neck . . . her cheeks . . .

A gasp escapes her mouth—or maybe it's mine—the moment those hands cover her eyes. A surprise game of peek-a-boo.

Skyler—

Lizzie screams.

Where did he come from—

Lizzie instinctively pushes back from the table, her chair skidding across the floor until she collides into the child's chest. His hands remain wrapped around her eyes from behind.

He's holding on to her head. Clutching her.

How did he—

Lizzie's shriek catches in her throat. Her jaw abruptly juts out, as if something is caught in her esophagus. Her tongue pushes past her lips as she chokes.

How—

Lizzie lets out an abrupt sputter and everything across my face goes wet. I shut my eyes at the sudden spray of mist across my cheeks.

When I open my eyes again, I see—

Blood.

Lizzie's tongue surges further out from her mouth, the entire muscle forcing its way into the open air, as if it's about to tumble free. The tip sticks out to a sharpened point, far too barbed for it to be her tongue. It simply keeps coming and coming and coming, three inches, now five, then ten, reaching across the table toward me.

It's not her tongue.

It's a tail.

The horseshoe crab's barbed prehensile telson erupts from the back of Lizzie's throat and continues to extend its way past her mandibles, stabbing at the air. The girl keeps gagging, hacking and sputtering in wet breaths. Blood pools in her mouth. It sprays across the room with every scream. It spills down her chin as she tries to catch a breath.

In that moment I know, in the deepest part of my soul, that I'm never getting out of this. My last chance at separating myself from Henry and protecting—

Skyler

—this boy are gone. *I'm part of this now.* The life I've been struggling to hold on to slips through my fingers. It's gone. All hope is gone in a blink. Just like that. *They'll take Kendra away. Donny will have all the evidence he needs to prove I'm an unfit mother and he'll get full custody and I'll never see my daughter again.*

This is how I lose her.

Lizzie's eyes remain on me, imploring me to help. *Do something. Please.* Her lips continue to move, yearning to form words, but the sounds coming from her mouth are just . . . *all wrong.*

She's drowning in her own blood.

The boy stands directly behind her. I see him now. His mask is back in place. The horseshoe crab's carapace shields his features from me *but I can see his eyes, the crab has his amber eyes, but how oh how is the boy looking at me through its eyes. . . ?*

The crab's barbed telson extends from the boy's chin. The serrated lance is rammed through the back of Lizzie's neck, now branching out from her open mouth. The slender spike reaches a full foot from her reddened lips. Blood continues to drip off the tip, while she remains pinned in this upright position, still sitting at the card table, unable to move.

Her hand is still in mine, her palm facing upward.

I haven't moved. Haven't screamed. All I can think to say is . . .

"Oh, Skyler . . . What have you done?"

The boy steps back and the crab's tail retreats through Lizzie's mouth. Driving its way in must've been easier than pulling itself free. The serrated barbs cut raggedly across Lizzie's tongue and inner cheeks before finally slipping free from her throat. Her body slumps over the second its tail releases her, a ventriloquist's puppet free from its master's hand. Her wet fingers slip through my grip as her body sinks deeper and deeper into her seat in a limp descent.

Whatever breath is still left in Lizzie's lungs comes sputtering out in one last deflated gasp. Then she's gone. Just like that.

Mommy . . .

I hear the boy's whimper, mewling like a congested lamb. It's a frightened sound. A needy sound. His hands pitifully reach out for me, his pace picking up until he's charging—with that mask still on—and in that split second of panic, I swear he's going to attack me, too.

Mommy mommy . . .

He's coming for me. He's going to—

To—

I shield my face with my arms. The second before the boy is on top of me, my elbow gets jammed between us and strikes the horseshoe crab carapace dead center. There's a sickening *SPLKK*, like when a machete cracks into a coconut. I hear the crab's shell shatter, splitting straight down its dome.

Something squeals. Either the horseshoe crab or the boy, I can't tell.

Every last claw releases from the boy's face, now spinning through the air. It lands on its fractured back, legs tearing at the air, at nothing.

The boy falls to the floor, clutching his own face. I hit him. Oh God, I hit the—

he's not a

—boy. I've never hit a child. Never laid a hand on a kid in my entire life. I didn't—

Didn't mean to—

What've *I* done?

Even now, he's reaching out for me as he sobs. He raises his piti-fully thin arms as if he wants me to pick him up and hold on.

daddy

What kind of mother strikes a child? What kind of mother am I? What kind of mother?

daaddy daaaddy

Henry races into the room. *Daddy to the fucking rescue.* Where was he five minutes ago? His arms are full of paper bags, I can't even count how many, but they all go toppling to the floor at his feet the second he sees the boy crying. There's something so intuitive about the way he swoops in and scoops the child into his arms, operating on some utterly instinctual level that feels more animal than man. A primal father. My attention drifts to the grease-stained bags now littering the parlor floor. McDonald's. Burger King. Hardee's. Henry must have stopped at every drive-thru between here and Kilmarnock. I've never seen such a greasy feast before.

There's more. I spot a Dollar General bag stuffed full of rolls of crepe paper streamers. Cone-shaped cardboard party hats. Even a chain of segmented letters, all in different colors.

BIRTH is all I can read.

It's for the boy. All for the boy. Henry must've wanted this to be his welcome home party.

A birthday for his boy.

"What happened?" Henry asks. Who, I'm not sure.

"I . . ." I start. "He . . . he just . . ."

"It's okay." Henry rushes the boy into the bathroom. I hear his voice as he tries to calm him down. "You're going to be okay. I'm here now . . ."

I'm alone in the parlor with Lizzie's body. A thick, red foam slowly bubbles out from her mouth, even through the hole in the back of her neck where the horseshoe crab's tail gored her.

It's so hot in here. So humid. Coats my throat, my lungs.

Where's Henry? What're they doing in the bathroom? What's taking him so long?

I spot a clunky Nokia on the floor, partially buried beneath a Burger King bag.

My cell phone. Henry had it this whole time.

I crawl over the floor to reach for it. I pick it up. *Why did Henry have my cell?* My thumb's ready to dial, but I hesitate. *Who am I going to call? Who's left? Who'll help me now?*

Just get it over with. The police will have to understand. You have to try to explain. It wasn't my fault. None of this was my fault. It was Henry. It was the boy. It was . . .

Skyler.

9 . . .

Skyler did it.

1 . . .

It was . . .

Henry grabs the phone from my hand before I can finish dialing and pockets it.

Henry just . . .

He . . .

Henry now kneels before me, his sunken eyes staring back. He's saying something, but I can't hear the words. Not at first. I'm still focused on the red foam emanating from Lizzie's neck and staining the shag carpet.

"Madi? *Madi.*"

Henry snaps his fingers before my eyes. I follow the sound, waking up to his face.

"It's okay," he says. "I'm gonna handle this, but we need to keep this between us. No phone calls for now, okay? Not until I figure out what to do next."

I don't understand. *Between us.* "Why did you leave me?"

"Madi, listen," he says. "*Listen to me.* It was an accident, okay? Just an accident."

"Accident," I echo. I let the word rattle around my skull. *Accident. Accident.* It could've been an accident, couldn't it? Accidents happen all the time. Especially with children. Kids don't understand their own actions, that their movements might have unintended consequences.

An accident. Skyler could've been running to Lizzie for a hug.

Or to play a game.

Peek-a-boo.

Right before stabbing her in the back of the throat.

Impaling her.

An accident. That's all. Just an *accident accident accident.* Lizzie had been shouting. Threatening me. "He was defending me," I hear myself say. "He just wanted to protect his . . ."

mommy

All he wanted was to keep this woman from yelling at me and I hit him. *Hurt him.*

An accident.

"I . . . I didn't mean to . . ."

"I'll deal with this," Henry says. "You just need to stay here with Skyler while I—"

"No no noooo . . ." Once the moan starts within me, I can't make it stop. *I don't want to be alone with that . . . that . . . whatever he is. Please don't leave me with it. Please I can't I CAN'T—*

Henry grabs both shoulders and shakes so hard my neck nearly cracks. "Listen to me, Madi. *Listen.* You need to do this, okay? If you don't, they're going to take him away . . ."

Please don't leave me please don't leave me please—

"We're going to make it through this," he says. "You just have to trust me, okay?"

"Where are you going?"

"To the river." He doesn't finish the thought. Doesn't need to. "You just need to stay here and keep an eye on Skyler and then we'll figure out what we—"

"*It's not Skyler.*" I don't know where the sudden burst of energy comes from, but I force the sentence out, release it from within my head, where it's been percolating since last night.

"Yes, he is," Henry says without missing a beat. "We brought him back."

"You . . . you kidnapped him."

He stops. Takes me in. He looks wounded. "You really think that?"

"It . . . it's not your son."

"*He's ours.* All that time we—all our thought, our feelings, it brought him back."

I step back. "What are you trying to tell me?"

Henry sighs. "The truth."

"What is he?" I feel like I'm going to fracture into a million pieces. "*What is Skyler?*"

Henry looks me in the eyes and holds my gaze.

"A peeler."

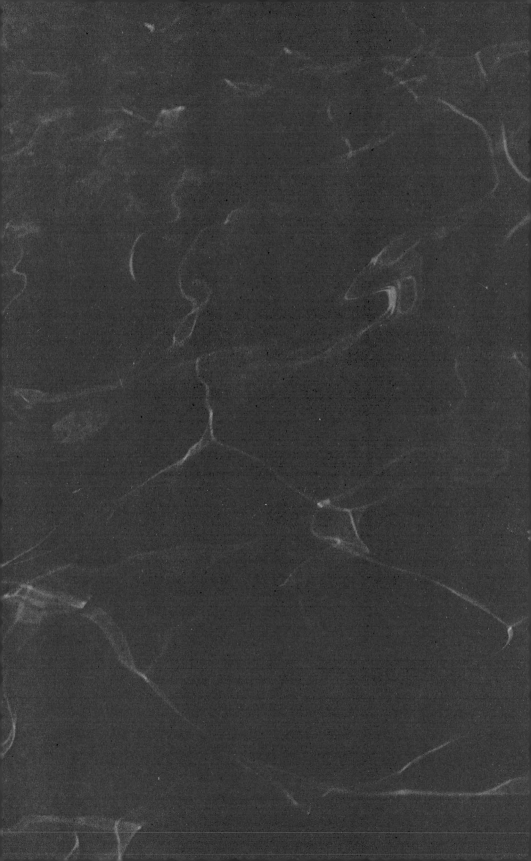

PART FOUR

BIRTHDAY BOY

Your story's not over, now, is it? Just when you think you've reached the end, there's always a little more to be told. Why do you think they call it a *tale*? It winds around *the end*, coiling out from the rest of itself, an extension of the spine, before it tapers off to a fine point.

No, Sky, your story was just beginning. I simply needed to keep telling it. And telling it.

How'd that story go again?

———

I had laid you down in your crib, swaddled in your mother's hand-made blanket.

I picked up my guitar.

I sang to you—*of you*—pouring everything I had into that last lullaby. I knew I'd never sing for you again, so I put my whole heart into it. My goddamned soul. All I had to give was yours, until I was empty. Bled dry. And still I kept singing. I need to keep the song alive and in the air, because I knew the moment I stopped singing, as soon as that song stopped, it would all be over and I'd never serenade my son again.

I would not let it end. I refused to let go.

Take me with you, Skyler.

Take me . . .

———

I must've fallen asleep next to your crib. I can't remember passing out, but I came to as soon as I heard the cry. In that delirious moment, still half asleep, I'd forgotten all about the last twenty-four hours. In that liminal space between sleeping and waking, everything felt normal.

You were crying, Skyler.

I heard you crying.

I was still gripping the guitar. My hands ached from all the hours of playing, the low thrum of my pulse pushing its way past my fingertips, raw and sliced open.

The crying was coming from under your blanket. *That's not possible. How is that . . . ?*

I lifted your blanket.

It took me a moment to focus, to pull my head together and bring myself to look. To take you in. Even then, I couldn't quite comprehend what I was seeing. It didn't make sense.

There are two of you.

Right there, in your crib, next to your blanket, is another baby. Two babies for two fathers. Same size, same weight, same everything. Same eyes. Same expression.

It was you. It had to be you. In every sense of the word.

You.

You were on your back, head lolling this way and that, taking in the room.

Then your eyes locked onto mine.

You made a sound. Or maybe it was me. This pressure unbuckled in my chest, a chunk of ice cracking along the river's surface, now free to float with the current.

It was a miracle. What else could this be? You were right there. It was you.

You, Skyler, *you*.

Alive.

You must've been cold. Your skin had a soft cerulean tint to it, like a blue-shell crab. On instinct, I reached for the blanket—your blanket—to wrap you up, and realized it was already wrapped around some other child. This inert version of you. The story I had left behind.

This was the fork in the road. Two paths. Two stories.

Which one was I going to tell?

It was still early. The sun wouldn't come up for a few hours. Without second-guessing myself, I took the story of you—this version, at least—wrapped in your blanket, and brought it to the dock. I'd need to hurry if I wanted to finish before Grace woke up.

———

The moon was full. That made it simple enough to motor out into the water without the need for a spotlight. As long as I kept an eye on the river, I didn't have to worry about any other boats. No one else was out at this hour anyhow. The only crabbers who got a leg up this early were the poachers, and they prefer to keep a low profile. If they saw me, they'd steer clear.

I had the whole river to myself.

The air was cool. I sailed past the duck blind and didn't look back. A stubborn wind coming in from the east kept pushing me, as if to blow me back, but no, this needed to be done.

Nothing was going to stop me, Skyler. There was still too much story to be told.

Your first step. Your first tooth.

Your first word.

Your first . . .

You.

The vibrations from the motor loosened your blankie. I spotted your hand. Your tiny hand. The length of your arm. The baby fat still wrapped around the bone. The moon cast a deeper hue of blue over your skin and suddenly the story skipped in my head for a second.

Now I can't remember which tale I'm trying to tell. What am I even doing out here?

Oh God, what am I about to do?

Then I remember you at home. Lying in your crib. Eyes so wide. You were waiting for me, Sky . . . All I needed to do was yoke these two stories back together. Simply tie up loose ends.

Two stories need to become one again.

The autumn air gave way to a grinding sound, a mechanical rustling that stretched out from the forest. Cicadas lay in wait in these trees. Their mottled bodies would eventually break out from their skins, peeling free and starting new, leaving their old bodies behind, the husks still clinging to the bark.

Nature is everywhere. It was within you, too. A blending of the elements.

A miracle.

I took the deadrise as far out as I could, where the river opened up into the Chesapeake, then cut the engine. I needed to reach deep water, where the bottom was a murky grave of mud and sand. Where no one's feet would ever touch.

The crab pot might as well have been a birdcage, and the old version of you its swaddled occupant. All I had to do was open the upper compartment, slip the body in the parlor, seal it back up, and toss it overboard. I've baited so many traps over the years, stuffing the bait cage with bull lips and menhaden and chicken necks. What difference was this? This was just a story I was telling myself that I'd soon forget. None of this was real. You were waiting for me back at home.

I unraveled the blankie from around your body. The satin was slippery. Cold. It shimmered under the moonlight. I'd bring it back home. You—the you waiting in your crib—would need it to keep you warm. But it didn't seem right to leave this version of you without something to protect you.

So I tore the blanket in half. Ripped it right down the middle.

One for you, and one for you . . . Everybody would be happy. Everybody'd be warm.

I needed something to weigh the body down. Didn't have a brick. There was one back at the dock, but I wasn't about to turn the boat around now. The body would anchor the trap down enough, I reckoned, so I took my knife and severed the line tied to the marker buoy.

This crab trap had to stay at the bottom. I didn't want anyone finding it—finding you—thinking it was full of blue-shells.

An image suddenly fluttered into my mind: You in the bait cage. All those blue-shells swarming around you, lured in and now trapped, their jagged claws grabbing at your pudgy arms, as if they were some auntie trying to pinch your cheeks. *You're just good enough to eat . . .*

Stop. I squeezed my eyes and tried forcing the image out of my head. *Please, stop.*

The currents might come for the crab trap eventually. The tide would drag the pot farther out into the Chesapeake and nobody would ever find it and that would be the end of that. No one would find you out here in the water. This was my secret and nobody else's.

Not even Grace would know.

The closer I got to home, the further away that old story faded into the back of my mind. The tide dragged that story away from me, out to sea, like it never even happened.

How'd that story go?

———————

Dawn broke just as I pulled up to our dock. The sky seethed in a neon pink. Walking down the dock, crossing our lawn, then entering our house, I felt like stepping back into my previous life. The last twenty-four hours never happened. I had barely slept. The weight of exhaustion dragged my body down. Pulled on my eyelids. All I wanted was to collapse in bed next to Grace and wake up from this whole nightmare, wake up and realize it never happened.

I passed your bedroom door and . . .

I heard you.

Something in me at that moment didn't want to look. I think I was afraid that if I turned, I'd realize it wasn't real. That I'd made it all up in my head. But what choice did I have?

What choice did I ever have?

Of course I looked.

You were awake. Eyes so wide.

It was you. Had to be you.

Our son and moon and Skyler.

The future I saw for my family was still in the cards, as long as Grace and I were willing to accept that nothing had changed, that these last twenty-four hours never existed.

Yesterday came and went and now it was gone. Just a momentary skip of the record playing a sad song. How'd that tune even go? *You were born . . . ?* Something-something. I can't remember. I try humming it to myself now and then but the melody is never there. Never was.

The three of us could still be a family.

I needed to believe with all my heart that it was you. Our Skyler. What else was there?

Who else could you be?

When Grace woke, she pulled herself out of bed and wandered down the hall. Something lured her our way.

She must've heard me humming.

She found us in your bedroom.

I was in the rocker next to your crib, holding you in my arms, wrapped in your blankie—half of it, at least—gently rocking my heels, the chair swaying forward and backward.

She took you in.

She saw you.

All of you.

Your wide eyes.

Your runny nose.

It was you.

Had to be you.

Her baby boy.

Her Skyler.

"Look who's up," I said. "Wanna say hi to Mama?"

———————

There were no answers, so it was better not to ask any questions. What else could this be but a miracle? Our prayers answered. Like the last twenty-four hours never happened.

Never happened. I kept repeating that to your mother. "It never happened, Grace . . ."

Your mother wouldn't let me touch her. I had to reach her with my words, echoing the same promises I'd made to myself and hope they simply sank in. She felt so far away from me. She was in the room but she might as well have been miles away.

"Look at him," I said. "Please, Grace, just look at your son."

She couldn't bring herself to glance down at you. She looked everywhere else *but* you.

"He needs you right now. He needs his mama . . ."

She'd aim her eyes at me. I'd never seen that look before, as if she didn't recognize me. It was a wounded expression, brought on by the kind of pain you feel when you realize the person you love isn't who you thought they were. She's looking at me like I'm some stranger.

"Grace, it's him . . . I swear it is. It's Skyler."

It would take some convincing, but we had time. Nothing but time.

Time and energy.

———————

I'd need to keep a close eye on your mother. She didn't trust the touch of you anymore.

I wouldn't say I was worried she might . . . do something . . . to you . . . but I figured it would be wise if I stuck around the house whenever I could. Just in case she might try and . . .

And . . .

Never mind. That's not how this story goes. I take that all back.

Your mother was fine.

She would be fine.

We didn't see many folks after you came back. Neither of us had much family left, anyhow. Besides, it simply felt safer to keep close to home. As a family. Just the three of us.

That magic number.

———————

You never slept now.

———————

The river had gone gray. The marsh grass began to yellow before fading to rust.

There was no noise. Nothing budged within the woods.

Sound has a different way of traveling through the air, depending on what season it is. The cold winter air is a much better amplifier for noise than the summer's humidity.

Once the temperature drops down into the thirties, the atmosphere turns crisp, sharpening itself like a knife against a whetstone.

A simple cackle from an egret can cut through miles' worth of frigid air, reaching distances it couldn't in the summertime. Sounds like a baby wailing away along the waterfront.

You were always crying. Always hungry. Always wailing for more of your mother.

You craved Grace in ways that felt different than before. Your tiny hands clasped at the air as soon as she came in the room. Your pudgy arms would turn in her direction, wherever she went, as if she were the sun and your hands were flowers desperate for more nourishment. More of that warmth only a mother can give. I tried to provide, but you always wanted her.

"Grace, please—just hold him."

She'd never answer me.

Never look.

"Would you at least try? Just for a little while? You might like it ..."

You only seemed sated when we held you. There needed to be contact between you and us at all times. When you would finally quiet down and I believed you were asleep, I'd begin the arduous process of disentangling from you, peeling you out of my arms and placing you as gently as humanly possible into your crib ... but the second I let you go, you'd begin wailing all over again.

All that crying.

You were a teakettle at full boil, spewing hot steam. All the blood would rush to your head, your cheeks turning a deep purple. I thought you'd burst like a tick bloated on too much blood, ready to pop at the simplest pinch. We had no choice but to hold you.

We lost so much sleep. Grace most of all. You needed her in ways I couldn't quite understand, but don't all babies need their mother? Why would you be any different?

I watched her eyes sink into her sockets. Watched her cheeks wither against her teeth. Watched her gums recede. She looked so exhausted. So ... *spent.* Her skin dry as parchment. I tried buying lotions from the grocery store but the bottles simply went unopened, stacking up.

All I wanted was to help. How could I fix this? Make things go back to the way they were?

How'd that story go again?

Grace and I weren't speaking much by then. The only sound in our house came from you, wailing for one of us to hold you. Your mother would never say your name. Not out loud.

But you were on our minds.

Always on our mind.

———

Now she'd let you wail for hours.

"Can't you just take him?" I'd ask, practically imploring. "Just until he calms down?"

She would turn her head toward me and just stare back without ever saying a word. When she looked at me like that, I'd always feel a chill.

What did she see? In me? Who was she even looking at in those moments?

———

It was up to me to figure out what you needed. I slowly grew accustomed to the different kinds of crying, learning how to determine which pitch meant what.

A shotgun blast was hunger.

A wailing siren was a soiled diaper.

A kettle whistle was loneliness.

Carrying you always calmed you down. I had no other choice. I'd take you into my arms and the two of us would just walk through the halls of our house for hours, back and forth.

I'd try soothing you to sleep by singing. You sure loved a lullaby.

"As I walked by myself, and talked to myself, myself said unto me: Look to thyself, take care of thyself, for nobody cares for thee . . ."

Sometimes, the things we think we're only thinking suddenly creep out, finding their way outside our mind. These thoughts escape through our mouths, air bubbles slipping past our lips underwater. I'd sing you a lullaby around the house, thinking no one else was listening.

"I answered myself, and said to myself, in the self-same repartee: Look to thyself, or not look to thyself, the self-same thing will be!"

Grace would catch a nursery rhyme as it drifted through the hallway, listening in as if the song were a piece of debris drifting downriver.

"What are you doing?" It sounded like an accusation to me. How long had it been since I'd last heard your mother's voice? I missed it so much.

"Just singing." I held you out for her. "You want to take him for a little—"

Your mother turned, leaving us behind.

"Once there was a little boy, he lives in his skin. When he pops out, you may pop in!"

Time moved so much slower in our house. The days tended to blend together. It could've been weeks, months, since your birthday. But we had to hold on. We needed to maintain our connection.

We needed to be three, that magic number.

So I made up excuses. *Skyler's come down with a cold. Some bug's going around . . . Grace just isn't feeling like herself lately. She needs to rest . . .* No one ever questioned or judged us.

Nobody doubted.

But this house . . . The air never stirred anymore. When you grow up around here, you get accustomed to the humidity. It's simply a part of life down South. But this was a different kind of swelter. I'd never felt the air thicken like this, like gravy made with too much cornstarch.

If I didn't know any better, I'd say the humidity was radiating from you, Skyler . . .

———

My peeler farm hadn't amounted to much. Most of my soft-shells ended up dead. They ate each other. As soon as they began to molt, the others would pounce, ripping the peelers apart with their claws and devouring the soft-shells until there were none left.

I just hadn't been paying enough attention. Guess my dreams of a shedding facility in my backyard would have to wait another day. Besides, I had bigger fish to fry. I had you, son.

Taking care of you was a full-time job.

———

You never wanted to play with any of your old toys. Whenever I'd put you down and give my weary arms a rest, I'd hand you a plastic rattle or one of your plushies. "How about this?"

You'd pitch them all across the room and just start wailing
wailing
wailing

———

Teething was tough. The eruption from your gums must've been painful, from the wail of it. I tried everything. Benzocaine. Frozen teething rings.

I slipped my index finger in your mouth and slid it along that rubbery ridge, hoping to massage your gums. Maybe see if I could feel any teeth budding up from below.

All the baby books say the first tooth to emerge is usually one of the lower central incisors, so I was a bit taken aback by the bony rim along your upper gum.

Hadn't really expected to cut myself on it, either, but—

Surprise.

———

First fertilizer, then prayer.

A knot of catfish entrails were tangled up on the cutting board, the bones in a pile next to them. I would sweep them all into a bucket, hefting the mess of parts out to your mother's garden. Taking a spade, I'd dig a hole big enough for a single fish and plant its parts in the soil. I'd shuffle down a few steps and dig up another, dropping the remnants of another fish in. By the time I was done, the entire garden was sewn together with fish bones.

"Sure could use your help out here, hon," I'd say to your mother. "The garden won't tend to itself."

Grace's head would swivel toward me, always without a word, and she'd simply stare back. Her teeth looked loose now, the gums receding all the way to her roots. Her eyes looked like comb jellies washed up on the shore, shriveling under the unforgiving sun.

What's happening to her? Where's her body going?

Whenever I caught a catfish, I'd heft it back home in a cardboard box. The cardboard would soak up so much water that the box would sag at its center. I'd use both arms to carry it. I'd open the box in the kitchen and the catfish would slither out. They'd huff and puff so hard, I could see all the way down their throats.

Your wailing reached out from those fishes' mouths. I couldn't escape the sound of you. Always in my head. There was no blotting out your cries.

I'd grab each fish by the neck and bring it over to the cutting board. Its gills would brush over my thumb, tickling me. Sometimes

I'd lose my grip and it would slip to the floor.

"You come back here, Mr. Mustache," I'd say, bending over to pick it up.

I'd gut the fish to fry, the knife separating the meat from the bone. One by one, I'd pluck off each rib—*she loves me, she loves me not, she loves me, she loves me not*—until I was left with a spine and a head. Then I'd lay it out in the sun until the whiskers shriveled.

I'd slip a handful of peppercorns into the catfish's mouth. Once it was full, I'd take a needle and thread and sew the catfish's lips together, sealing the peppercorns inside.

Holding it by the spine, I'd shake my hand. The peppercorns would rattle inside the catfish's mouth, shuddering against its shriveled skin. Will you look at that! Daddy made you a rattle . . .

You loved it. I finally found a toy you wanted to play with.

———

Grace showed me the bite marks on her breast.

At first, I didn't understand what I was looking at. "What did you do?"

"It wasn't me."

I noticed the row of red trenches on either side of her chest. They looked like claw marks more than anything else.

Not you. Not our Skyler. You would never hurt your mother. She fed you. *Loved you.*

"Do you see now?" she asked, her voice like sandpaper. "Do you?"

It was the most I'd heard your mother speak in days.

Weeks.

———

You never slept. So we never slept.

Always awake. Always hungry. Always in need. I held on to you until my arms ached. I cradled you, carried you until I felt like I was falling apart. I gave over all of myself to you, Skyler.

I could never let you go.

You never let me.

———

I took a bucketful of fresh cedar sawdust and carried it up into the attic. I placed it directly underneath the wasps' nest, humming along to the sound of their wings.

Lighting a match, I stoked a smoldering fire inside the bucket. The sawdust was too wet to flare up. A thick tuft of smoke rose up, enveloping the nest with its sweet smell. The frantic activity inside the hive slackened, the vibration of wings downshifting into a lower register. Wasps started dropping along the attic floor, stumbling drunkenly around.

I carefully plucked the nest from the rafter, holding it at arm's length down the steps and out through the door, rushing into the yard and placing it onto the ground.

Taking an entire reel of fishing line, I carefully began to thread a separate strand through every cell, until I had over a dozen strings hanging from the hive.

I tied a fish head to the end of one line, a tail to another. I fastened several oyster shells I'd found along the riverbank onto their own string, their mother-of-pearl rims shimmering.

I tied five or six wasps to the nest, still woozy from the cedar smoke, doped up long enough for me to sew them to the other end of the hive.

I pulled up a couple of daffodils and stuck their stems through a separate cell so that they would hold in place.

Taking the nest and the last of my fishing line, I went inside and hung it just above your crib.

When the wasps came to from their cedar-smoke-induced stu-

por, they began to fly in whichever direction they could go, not realizing they were tethered to their own nest. Eventually, they began
to fly in the same direction, spinning the nest round and round with
them. Fish heads, fish tails, daffodils, oyster shells, and wasps, *spinning,
spinning, spinning . . .*

Look at that. Daddy made you your own mobile.

------

*There's water in what's left of your lungs. It's a brackish blend, both salt and
fresh, where the river meets the bay. Silt settles into the fleshy reservoir of gray
tissue, the sand and sediment gathering in the ruptured sacs beneath your rib
cage, like a sunken treasure chest.*

*You're resting along the river bottom. Your reedy ribs remain submerged
in the mud, among the fallen branches that reach up from the muck and mire,
until there's no telling their twisted limbs apart from your own bones, your
knotted boughs coated in a ruddy-colored algae.*

*The currents have dragged at your skin, loosening the flesh until it even-
tually slid off the bone, drifting through the water as if it were kelp. You
can feel the gentle tug of the tides even now, rhythmically rising and falling
throughout the day, every day, for so long.*

*You try to move but you can't. Something is holding you down. Pinning
you in place. There's the thinnest grid pressing tightly against your arms, along
your back, even against your skull. It's metal. A cage made of chicken wire.
You're trapped. The wire has sliced your skin into a grid, branding your body
in a diamond-shaped pattern. Pale cubes of flesh slide through.*

*This is all when you still had skin to give. You've been feeding the sea life
for quite some time now.*

*The crabs came for you first. The blue-shells skittered into your chick-
en-wire coffin, lured in by the fresh scent of flesh drifting throughout the water.
Your body was bait. Their claws pinched at your skin, tearing the flesh free
and plucking at the meat, making a meal out of you. Even the fish feasted on
your body, winnowing their way through the wire and nibbling on the skin*

at your skull. An eel slithered through the wire mesh until it found your eyes, plunging through the left socket, then pushing out the other, threading itself through the optic canal.

Some crabs found themselves trapped alongside your body, unable to escape. Their lifeless shells have now settled alongside your body, heaped into a slimy pile of bones and claws.

You've been forgotten down here. Abandoned in the gelatinous mud. The dead leaves and sludge. You wear a crown of fish ribs on your head. Barnacles have grown over your bones. Your skull is clustered with crustaceous growths, now a breeding ground for polyps. Tumors of tiny oysters sprout out along your spine, their shells branching out from your vertebrae.

You are a reef for this river. Life hasn't stopped for you even if you are dead. Life never stops, not down here in the cold. In the dark.

When the tide is low and the inlet's surface is closer, you can see the sky rippling above.

You see me—

———

I woke up with a start, covered in a thick layer of sweat. The humidity in the room was unbearable. It clung to me. I didn't know how long I'd been asleep, what time or even what day it was. The house was so quiet and yet, I knew something had changed. The elements felt off.

Something was wrong.

Grace wasn't in bed.

Just then, I heard a strum from my guitar. A clumsy chord, almost as if the strings had been brushed by accident. I hadn't played that thing in weeks. Months by now, maybe. Who knows how long it'd been anymore. Not since that night, that's all I knew. I couldn't bring myself to pick it up again. My forearms still felt beyond healing, the scar tissue hardening along my wrists. I was simply hearing things, I figured. I paid the sound no mind.

I could barely feel my arms anymore, they were so sore. Picking up anything at this point, a pencil or a fork, would send a jolt of pain through my joints. It felt like they might pop right out from their sockets. If one of us wasn't holding you, cradling you, you'd wail away and never stop. It reached the point where I had to push the sound of you out of my head.

I didn't get used to it—you never get used to it—but a part of me simply gave up, resigning itself to your keening. It became a game of chicken between me and Grace. It was just a matter of time before one of us would give in and take you into our arms.

Nobody slept for long. Not in our house. If you were awake, we all were awake.

Then why was it so quiet?

Grace must be with you.

Thank Christ.

I went to the kitchen, struggling with a glass of water. I couldn't even bring the damn glass to my lips, my arms hurt so much. I'd just taken a sip when, from behind my back, I swear I heard someone strum my guitar again. Just the gentlest whisk of fingertips over the strings.

I waited to see if I'd hear it again. *Where did I leave the guitar?* The living room? Our bedroom? *Your* bedroom. It had to be there. Where else could it have been? It was quiet—you weren't wailing—which must've meant your mother was tending to you, feeding you, holding you in her arms. *Finally.* I'll admit, that silence sounded so sweet to me. An absolute balm.

There was that clumsy strum again. Who could've been playing the guitar? I strained my ears to hear if it might strum on its own again, but nothing came. Maybe I had just imagined it.

"Grace?" I called. "That you?"

She didn't answer.

"Grace, hon?"

Better look, I thought. *Just to be on the safe side. To be sure.*

I passed your bedroom. Peering in, I found you in your crib, swaddled in your wedding dress blanket. The guitar was leaning against the far corner, right where I'd left it a lifetime ago.

And then I saw that one of its strings was missing.

"Grace?" I called out again.

Still nothing.

I don't know how long I stared at the instrument. I don't know what I was expecting to happen.

The strings were pure steel, thin enough to cut through skin if you're not careful. I've sliced my fingers plenty of times, tuning my strings too tightly, snapping them.

Everything was still. Too still. I wasn't used to this type of silence. Nothing was moving.

The guitar was inert. Immobile.

You weren't moving. I immediately felt my heart leap into my throat as I rushed toward your crib and reached in, grabbing your blanket and pulling it back.

Empty. Just a blanket swaddling air.

"*Grace*," I called out, louder now, unable to hide my mounting panic.

I ran into the hall, using the walls to hold me up.

"Grace!"

I stumbled into our bedroom but you weren't there, either.

"GRACE!?"

———

I found her in the bathtub. The guitar string was noosed around her neck, the back end of the wire looped to the spigot. The steel dug into her throat as the weight of her gaunt body bore down, slicing through her jugular. Blood flowed down her chest and into the tub.

She did this to herself. Why would she do something like this to her—

I collapsed next to the tub and tried desperately to unloop the guitar string. But it had dug too far into her neck. I needed to pick her body up to relieve the pressure at her throat, so I tried wrapping my own arms around her waist and lifting. Still, the wire was too deep. I couldn't pull it free.

Why would she leave me why would she let go why would she leave us—
Us.

I'd never told her what happened that night. What I had left behind in the bay. But she knew. A mother always knows.

And she didn't want to know anymore.

———

It's never been so quiet before, I remember thinking. The silence sounded so suffocating.

I would've given anything to hear you cry again.

———

By the time I dialed 911 and the operator asked what was the nature of my call—*nature*—before I even knew what I was doing, I heard myself say . . .

"My son is missing."

———

And the mouth that just told this story is still warm . . .

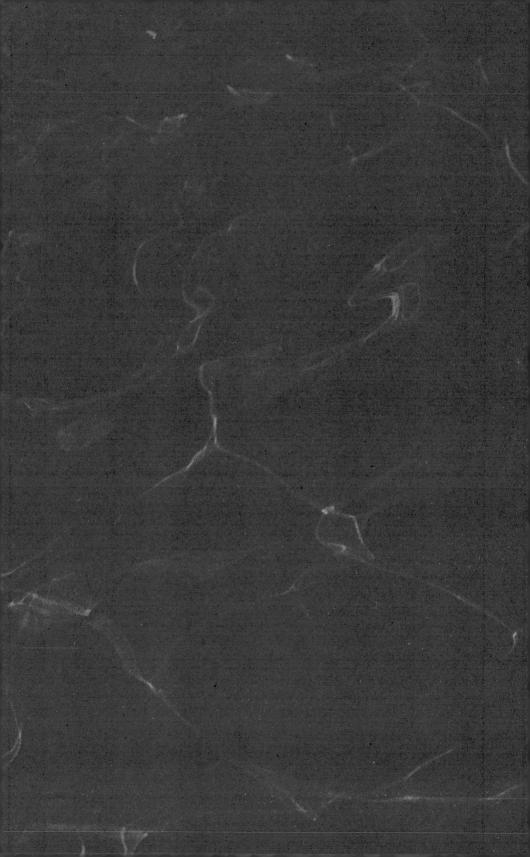

PART FIVE

GROWING
PAINS

ONE

I shift the boy from one hip to the other, one arm anchoring him to me, the other reaching for the doorbell.

A dog's thunderous bark reverberates through the house the second I ring the bell. Did I know Donny even had a dog?

The boy's rail-thin arms clamp around my neck. His legs latch around my waist and tighten—and for a second, I swear he has more appendages than he should. The boy burrows into my body, a tick rutting for blood.

"It's okay," I murmur into his ear. "Everything's going to be—"
no it's not it'll never be
"—okay."

He's just a boy, I keep reminding myself. *He's just a little—*
peeler
—boy.

He needs someone to look after him. Protect him from Henry.
Henry.

I watched as he positioned himself behind Lizzie's body, flossing his own arms between hers. I watched him drag her out of the parlor, her heels skidding across the carpet. I heard the ignition of his truck sputter until the engine finally caught, followed by the crunch of gravel beneath rubber. Then it all went silent. Nothing but the steady hum of traffic on 301.

He's gone, I thought. *Run. Now. GO.*

I can't go to the police. Not after what happened to Lizzie. They'd think I had something to do with the boy's kidnapping. They'd never believe me. *And I'll never see Kendra again.*

Kendra. *I need to see her now. Before it's too late.*

"Answer the door," I mutter, struggling to keep the boy balanced on my hip, "answer the door . . ." I glance at the neighbor's house, just one in a row of pastel homes lining the rest of the block, with their manicured lawns and automatic sprinklers. "Answer the *goddamn* door . . ."

The muscles in my arms burn. My legs pulse and throb. I'm running on pure adrenaline. The boy feels heavier than he was just an hour ago. His grip tightens.

mommy

The dog won't stop barking. It scrapes its claws against the other side of the door, while I'm forced into some sort of two-step on the front porch, shifting my weight between each foot in hopes of relieving the searing strain on my arms.

I can't hold the boy for much longer, but he won't let me go. I have to readjust my grip all over again just to pound my free fist against the door.

"It's okay, it's okay, everything's going to be—"

"*Chewy,*" Kendra says, her voice muffled by the door. "Stop it."

The latch unbolts and I swear something in my chest loosens along with it. *Oh, thank Christ, Kendra's home, thank God . . .* The door opens and I let out all the air pent up in my lungs.

". . . Mom?"

"Help." Kendra steps back as I force my way inside like I'm hefting an overstuffed bag of groceries that's about to rip. I need to put the boy down. Free my arms before they pop out of their sockets.

But he simply won't let go. He keeps digging his face deeper into my neck.

I've entered a Pottery Barn showroom, complete with southern accents. *Bless this house.* A terra-cotta vase holding dried thistle. Polished river rocks in a glass jar. Candles that'll never be lit. Potpourri wafts through the hall—but it can't mask the whiff of brine rising off the boy.

Kendra wrinkles her nose as if I've brought a dead fish into the house.

Chewy won't stop barking at us.

At the boy.

He's a beautiful dog. A golden retriever. One look at him and I know his owners spend more on his grooming than I do on mine. His shining coat reminds me of Heather Locklear's feathered bangs, side-swept and voluminous. His claws *click-clack-click* against the polished floor until he leaps onto his hind feet, snapping his teeth. Kendra does her best to hold him back.

"Chewy's usually not like this," she says. She drags the retriever through the hall, forcing him into a room just off to the side, and shuts it. I can still hear him barking through the door.

The boy clutches my neck, squeezing tighter, cutting off my airflow. He's choking me. Not on purpose, but I'm still getting so light-headed, I swear I see stars

and the moon

and Skyler.

"What're you doing here?" Kendra asks.

This might be the last time I see you. "We need a place to lay low right now."

"Who is this?"

"Skyler." His name slips from my mouth before I even think of holding it back.

Kendra's eyes widen.

She doesn't believe you.

"We did it. We found him."

Tell her about the duck blind! About how he was all alone out there, waiting to be found! Tell her about Lizzie! Tell her how Henry's dumping her body in the river right—

"Madi?"

I give a start at Donny's voice. The dining room is right behind me. He sits at the head of the table with his family. Kendra's other family. His wife. Their two children. Kendra's half siblings. They look so picture-perfect, frozen in their poses like showroom mannequins.

"I . . . I didn't mean to . . ."

"It's okay." Donny stands up from the table, wiping the corners of his lips with his napkin. Becky begins to rise as well, but Donny holds out his hand for her to stop. She automatically sits down and bows her head. She won't look at me. How could she? A mother like me? Look at the rest of Kendra's family. Look how frightened they are. *Of me.*

"What's wrong?" Donny says it in *that* tone. The responsible adult voice he's perfected over the years. *After he abandoned me and Kendra and started a new family.*

He takes a step forward and I instinctively step back. "How can we help, Madi?"

"I . . ." I can't hold on to the boy anymore, I have to put him down, but he won't let me go.

"You don't have to leave," Donny says soothingly. "Stay, Madi. It's okay."

Okay.

I take one look at Kendra's mortified face and see that this is exactly the kind of thing she's always been afraid of. Her mother. Making a mess.

What kind of mother am I?

What kind of mother?

"I'm sorry," I say. "I . . . I shouldn't be here."

"Mom . . ."

"I'm . . . I'm . . ." I step back. There's just too much happening all at once, I can't stop and catch my breath.

Chewy keeps scraping against the other side of the closed door.

He won't give up. He's barking even louder now, desperate to tear through the wood paneling.

"We want to help, Madi." Donny takes another step forward. "Just tell us how."

Something about the way he's moving toward me makes me feel cornered. Kendra is on one side and Donny is on the other. All the while, the boy tightens his grip. I can barely breathe.

I'm crying. I know I'm crying. I can feel the hot tears on my face, the exhaustion and stress coursing through me, the fear that they might think I've lost it, the mounting feeling that I can't let them take the boy, no matter who—or what—he is. What he's done.

I don't know what do to . . .

Donny steps closer.

I don't know where to go . . .

Barking—

I don't . . .

Burning—

I . . .

My arms give out and I drop the boy to the ground.

Kendra's close enough to spring forward, an act of pure reflex, and catch him.

"I got you." She lowers the boy until he stands on his own feet. Kendra's now kneeling before him, the two face to face. "You're okay—"

The boy bites down on Kendra's clavicle.

It happens so fast, none of the adults know how to react. Kendra cries out. I've never seen her eyes so wide, so full of fear before. The two tip over, Kendra falling on her back and the boy landing on top. He won't let go of her. With his mouth. His teeth.

"SKYLER—STOP!" I grab the boy's shoulder and yank with what little strength I have left. His incisors snap together as he tries to slip out of my grip. There's nothing but spite in his eyes.

For Kendra.

He's still on top of her. I have to pick him up. Lift him off. Carry him away kicking, as if I'm breaking up two bickering siblings in the middle of a fight.

But they're not siblings.

I'm not his mother.

Why is he so jealous?

Because he doesn't want to share.

Share me.

There's a ring of teeth marks around Kendra's neck, a trail of broken blood vessels. She touches the wound and sees blood on her hands. She scrambles backward across the floor until she hits the wall behind her, crying.

I take a step toward her, still holding the boy. "Are you—"

"Get him away from me!"

The dog's barking gets even louder now, no longer muffled by the protective boundary of the door.

I hear Becky shout, "Chewy, no!"

The boy slips from my grip and starts crab-walking fast toward the sound of the barking. I turn just in time to spot Chewy barreling down the hallway. *How did the dog get out . . . ?*

Donny stands by the now-open door. *Release the hounds.* Chewy scrambles down the hall at a frantic speed, barking with newfound exuberance. He's charging right for the boy.

And the boy charges back.

His lips split open from Cupid's bow to chin. *Vertically.* His mouth parts like a pair of fleshy curtains.

He bites the dog before it bites him. Chewy yelps. Whether it's in pain or in panic, I'm not certain, but the dog won't stop howling now as he tries to shake the boy off . . .

But the boy won't let go.

TWO

Just leave him by the side of the road.

Nobody would blame me.

He's not my child.

He's not anyone's child.

He's not a child at all.

I could easily open the car door, pluck him from the passenger seat, leave him on the shoulder, and speed off before anyone sees me. And that would be that.

Then why don't I?

The steering wheel doesn't feel right in my hands. I don't know how long I've been gripping it, but I can't bring myself to let go. I've pulled off 301 and cut the engine. I just need something solid to hold me up. To cling to. If I let go of the wheel, I'm afraid I'll collapse.

A sixteen-wheeler barrels by, driving far too close to the driver's-side window. The sudden force of wind and spray of gravel startles me from my stupor.

I don't know where I'm supposed to go. Who I can turn to? I've never felt so alone.

But you're not alone, are you?

I have the boy.

Cars keep rushing past us on the highway, utterly unaware that a monster sits beside me.

A monster who thinks I'm his mother.

All that blood. *And that yelping . . .* The dog simply wouldn't stop howling once the boy got hold of him. It took all my strength to pry him off and run out of the house. He kept kicking at the air as I rushed him back to the car. Donny was probably already calling 911.

There was no time to even look at Kendra. The best thing I could do for her was leave.

She has Donny. She'll be okay. You need to deal with the boy.

Where can we go? I can't think straight. Can't keep myself from crying. I can't breathe in this heat. It's a fucking oven in the car. Wherever I go, that thick humidity from the hotel room follows me. Follows *him.*

You can take the boy outta the South, but you can't take the South outta the boy . . .

The boy crawls across the seat and into my lap. This kid—this kid simply won't let up. I don't have the energy to push him away anymore. I'm so exhausted. Just utterly spent. He never stops. Never tires. He just needs more and more and more of me, but I already feel empty.

mommy

I'm losing my goddamn mind.

mommy

I'm drowning on dry land.

mommy

I let him nestle against me and silently sob. I don't know what to do *what do I do what am I supposed to do.* He latches onto me and I can't escape him. This parasite of a child.

"Skyler, let go of me . . ."

mommy mommy

"Please." I try prying him off but he keeps worming over my body, eager to hold on. To cling. He'll just keep squeezing and squeezing and squeezing until I can't breathe. "Let go . . ."

mommy mommy mommy

"Let go!"

His shoulders soften.

"I SAID LET—"

I shove the boy as hard as I can.

"—GO."

His back hits the steering wheel. His spine unfurls, his skull crashing against the windshield. I hear the sickening crack of glass and everything within me freezes.

"Skyler?"

Oh God what have I done what have—

He looks up at me. His skin blisters at his temples. His cheeks pucker. A small air bubble drifts along the bridge of his nose, trapped below his flesh. His expression looks strained.

"I'm sorry," I say. "I'm so sorry. I didn't—didn't mean to—"

The boy holds out his hand, palm upward.

Give me your hand . . .

It's as if he knows—he's seen me or heard me ask my customers to perform this exact same gesture, time and time again. Here he is, following suit, doing what he believes I do best.

Give me your hand . . .

"You want me to . . . ?" I take his into my own. His fingers feel loose. The skin has lost all structure, like paper soaked in water.

He pulls back, just a gentle tug, and the skin separates from his wrist. He keeps pulling but his skin remains in my hand, a loose glove of flesh reaching all the way to his elbow.

He's shedding his skin. Molting. He holds both arms out for me. He *needs* a hug. One arm is soft and pink, fresh and tender, while the other is covered in a loosening spool of skin.

He's a monster.

He's just a boy.

I take him into my arms. I hold him. Embrace him.

"It's okay," I say, and I hear myself mean it this time, I think. "I've got you. I've—"

Something slips around his neck. His skin—it's all loose along the shoulders. It feels as if he's wearing a soaking-wet T-shirt. The gummy texture of organic material sticks to my hands.

I hear the tiniest tearing sound as his skin splits between his shoulders, the rupture following the seam of his spine.

His flesh peels away from the back of his head in a single strip, like gossamer.

I pull harder.

He tilts his head back *just so* and I watch as the flesh separates from his nose. His mouth cracks open as the skin along his lips stubbornly clings on for an extra second until it eventually peels free from his mouth.

That's it. Almost there. Just a little bit more . . .

I gather sheets of discarded skin in my hands, still warm. Moist. There are a pair of holes where his eyes used to be, the sockets now empty. His mouth is nothing more than a thin slit.

His body is even bigger than before. He's grown by a few inches, his fresh pink flesh now free of its restrictive skin suit.

Henry was right. Skyler is a peeler.

mommy

He holds out his hand to me. At first, I don't understand what he wants from me. Does he need another hug? What should I do? No—this is something else. He wants something else.

mommy

He's reaching for my hands. He wants his skin back.

Wants his blankie.

mommy

He tugs his skin from my hands, and I let him have it. He brings his hands up to the slit in his face and opens wide.

Then he eats it.

All of it.

I watch as the boy starts the arduous process of swallowing the discarded husk of himself whole. First he takes the skin from his head and slides it down his gullet in a single strip. He doesn't bite or chew, simply gulps the casing a little bit at a time, letting it slide down his throat.

Then he's on to his shoulders. He has to use his hands to stuff the hollow fingers into his mouth. First one sleeve, then the next.

He does the same thing with his torso. His waist.

His legs are last. The world's largest strands of transparent spaghetti. His ankles slip past his lips, then the heels, and finally all ten toes.

Head, shoulders, knees and toes, knees and toes.

When he finishes, I draw him close to me.

Have you ever held on to an animal while it rests? Not a domesticated pet. Something from the wild, a creature that survives by constantly keeping vigil, never letting its guard down.

That feral trust. *That bond.* The love of something from nature.

I feel it in that moment. With him. I sense the vulnerability of the boy's body as I cradle him in my arms. The frantic pace of his beehive heart thrums through his chest.

This defenseless child. This helpless thing. He shivers, so I tighten my grip, enveloping him, making sure he knows he's safe, that I'm here while his skin begins to harden once more.

What are you, Skyler?

A word materializes in my mind, more whisper than idea. *Tulpa.* A thoughtform made flesh.

What if Henry really did make this boy?

What if I helped?

THREE

Henry's leaning against the door to my motel room when I pull into the lot, using the frame to prop himself up. Such a classic disappointed-dad stance. I feel like I'm about to be reprimanded for staying out past my curfew. He steps away from the door only after I cut the engine, wincing at the setting sun as soon as it hits his eyes. He looks pale in the light.

"Let's get you inside," he says, opening Skyler's door and helping him out, "before someone sees . . ."

Anyone driving by right then would think they were looking at a family, exhausted from a long road trip, barely able to pick up their feet as they shuffle to their motel room.

What a picture we make.

Lizzie's blood has dried into the shag carpet in a pattern of rusted red sea anemones. Flies swarm around the stale buffet of fast-food leftovers and wrappers. I see the horseshoe crab, its pincers now inert, its dome-shaped shell shattered down the center.

"Why don't you stay back here for a bit," Henry says as he guides the boy through the beaded curtain. "Mom and Dad need to have ourselves a chat."

Is that what we are now? A family?

"You came back," he says once he returns.

"Got nowhere else to go."

"Could've gone to the hospital."

"The doctors wouldn't know what to do with him, would they?"

"Reckon not," he says.

Skyler simply isn't like all the other kids. I understand that now.

"How did this happen," I ask him. "How did he become . . . this?"

"Diving right into it . . ."

I'm too exhausted to do this. "Tell me."

He smiles weakly. "*Thought plus time plus energy.* Those were your *exact* words. That's what you said it would take to bring him back . . . and you were right. Look at what we did, Madi."

"They were just words."

His smile fades. "It's what's behind the words that matter. Words hold power when you throw your whole heart into them. See what happens? We brought Skyler back. *Together.*"

"I didn't do anything—"

"Every time we came into this room, you told me to think of Skyler. Whenever we had one of our sessions, you told me to think of Skyler. Over and over again. *Think of Skyler, think of Skyler* . . . until he finally came back."

"That's not possible . . ."

"I couldn't do it without you. I've tried for years, but nothing ever happened. Until you."

This is ridiculous. "Henry, I made it up."

He flinches. "What?"

"All of it."

"Why?"

Because I felt sorry for you. Because I felt sorry for myself. Because I felt alone. Because for the first time in a long while I felt like I'd found someone who was just as broken as me.

We could piece each other back together again.

"Because I look into folks' lives and tell them what they need to hear." Then, after a breath, I say, "I give them hope."

"*Hope,*" Henry echoes. He sits at the card table as if he's ready for another reading. "That's a funny word. Makes it seems like a situation is out of your hands."

He looks at me and smiles. "Hope doesn't mean *shit*. All I wanted was a day, *just one more day*, to be a family. I couldn't leave it in God's or St. Peter's hands . . . I invoked him my fucking *self*. I poured *my* heart into him. And you know what? It worked. It *worked*. Skyler came *back*."

"Henry . . ."

"The three of us were a family again. He just needed *both* of us to believe in him. Sustain him."

"What happened to Grace?"

"She didn't believe. Believe he was our son." His eyes fill with tears. "He was just a baby and a baby needs his mother. He just couldn't control his appetite . . ."

He places his hand on the card table, and I cover it with mine. "Henry . . ."

"Look at what we've done. We brought him back. He needs us, Madi. Both of us."

"I'm not this boy's mother."

He pulls his hand away. "He *needs* us to stay *alive*. To keep *believing* in him. That's how he *grows*. You feel it, can't you? The *exhaustion*? That's the fucking price of parenthood."

He coughs. It sounds so wet.

"Henry—"

He stands up and heads to the bedroom. The beaded curtain parts. "Skyler?"

I follow behind him.

"Skyler?"

My heart catches in my throat. The room is empty. Skyler has vanished.

He's not in the bathroom. Not under the bed or in the closet. "He's not here." I race out the door, shouting over my shoulder, "I'll check the other rooms."

All the other shops are closed for the day. There's no one at the motel but us. Skyler could be anywhere. My first inclination is to check the bait and tackle shop to see if—

The fireworks shop.

The door is open.

An odor like fecund pepper fills the air. Gunpowder. There are no aisles, no center racks, just an open floor with shelves mounted along the walls. A vibrant kaleidoscope of Technicolor cartons is on display, names emblazoned on their flashy packaging—liberty torches, finale racks, Roman candles, ground spinners, and jumping jacks.

"Skyler!"

The boy stands in the center of the ransacked room. Toppled boxes are scattered at his feet, torn open, loose shreds of shorn cardboard spread everywhere. He's not paying us any mind as he brings a handful of charcoal pellets up to his mouth and shoves them inside.

"Skyler, don't eat that!"

Blackened drool spills from his mouth, half-chewed pellets falling to the floor like loose teeth. Powder coats his fingers, leaving dark smudges along his lips and cheeks.

"Skyler!" I shout. "Put that down—"

The elation on his face is overwhelming. He's so happy to see us. I can feel the humidity rippling off his skin.

Daddy. The boy's voice presses against my temples. I hear him inside my head. He holds his arms out to Henry, eager for an embrace, but Henry doesn't move. *Foolish fire, Daddy . . .*

I spot something like a pincushion in Skyler's other hand. *Sparklers.* All knotted and twisted together, like barbed wire.

"Skyler, no—"

The sparklers ignite on their own. Tender embers cascade across his skin but he doesn't even flinch. His smile is so wide, teeth blackened with charcoal.

"*Skyler!*" I step forward, ready to grab him.

One carton—the Hypnotic Wheel—ignites first. A column

of multicolored sparks strikes Skyler in the shoulder, but he never flinches, never reacts.

A chain reaction has begun and won't stop. A symphony of fire. Rings of Saturn. Moondance Fountain. Shower of Power. Black-beard's Cutlass. They ignite and scream through the shop in a high-pitched fury, sending arcs of brightly colored fire spinning and twist-ing.

Skyler doesn't move once. He practically basks in it. He stands at the cindered heart of it all, flushed in purple and pink. I swear I can make out the incandescent glow of his bones. The outline of his ribs and spine shine through his translucent skin like a lightbulb's wire fil-ament. He emanates a glorious glow, brilliant and vibrant. A flaming palm hovering in the sky.

Foolish fire, Daddy, foolish fire.

Skyler tilts his head back. He's smiling, even now, coming into his own amid the deafening bombardment of fireworks. A black worm works its way out of his ear. A Pharaoh's snake sprouts and curls around the lobe, twisting and twining, until it snaps and falls. Now another reaches out from his nostril. *Both* nostrils. Every orifice in his head is filled with ashen earthworms rising up from mud.

Skyler extends his arms out to his sides as if he's ready to embrace us both. Take us into his open arms.

Arms.

Between his pelvis and armpits, I can count three sets of fleshy stubs protruding out from either side of his torso. Armlets. They can't be any longer than five inches, but there's enough bone beneath the skin for them to flex. They're segmented. Knuckled, like fingers.

Not fingers. These are crustaceous. The articulated legs of a crab wrapped in a layer of human flesh. They branch out from his torso, flexing and glowing.

A neon arthropod.

He's beautiful . . .

It's breathtaking, witnessing what this boy is becoming.

Henry said he's mine. We made this child.

But what is he?

A monster.

A miracle.

The walls ripple in sheets of orange and yellow. The room fills with smoke. Every breath burns. I have to shield my eyes as the fire reaches the ceiling. This store—this whole strip of shops—doesn't stand a chance.

I can feel Henry dragging me back toward the doorway. Away from Skyler.

"Let's go!"

The cool evening air blankets my skin the second he yanks me out of the room. Henry lets go and leans forward, pressing his hands against his knees, and dry-heaves, expelling wet ash.

I turn back to the fireworks shop. "Skyler—"

"Madi, don't—"

I bring my arm up to my face and plunge back into the burning room. A blackened sheet of smoke wraps itself around me, swallowing me whole.

"Skyler!"

I feel a sting on my forearm and hiss at the pain. I think I've been burned . . .

There's something crawling across my arm.

A wasp. Its yellow-and-black-banded body glows vibrantly in the firelight. I look around and see more. Hundreds, maybe. Burning wasps flit about the blaze, zipping through the room in spiraling arcs. I swat them away until I see where they're coming from.

Skyler's cindered rib cage opens like an oyster shell, and the wasps pour freely from his chest.

I take Skyler into my arms and plow through the smoke. He rests his head against my neck, his armlets clasping at my shoulders, my waist, holding on tight.

I'm struck on the side of my face by a blast of green and yellow sparks. I scream, never slowing, running to escape, pressing Skyler even tighter against my chest.

The shop wails and shrieks behinds us as I carry Skyler out into the parking lot. He never coughs, simply burrowing his soft, pink face deeper against my chest. The boy isn't burned but his skin feels loose. It's already bubbling and blistering, splitting at the seams.

He's molting again.

I can't comprehend what this child is becoming. I've witnessed something that defies understanding, all logic, but it's real. He's real.

A miracle. Henry said so himself. What else can he be?

The sun, the moon, and Skyler.

The blaze is already beginning to spread to the motel. Flames chew through its roof. Smoke twines through the evening sky, still pink with dusk.

Traffic along 301 slows down as all the rubbernecking commuters take in the sight before them. We have ourselves an audience.

Henry seizes Skyler from my arms. I'm still coughing, trying to catch my breath. Hacking ash and spitting up black clumps. My eyes are tearing up from all the smoke, but I can just barely make out the hazy outline of Henry carrying Skyler back to our room.

"Where are you—"

I can't finish, coughing out the rest of the question. I have to follow them. I have to—

protect him

—get Skyler back before he's hurt.

"Henry, the motel is on fire!"

I rush in after them. They're not in the parlor. The beaded curtain undulates on its own, crystals clinking.

"We need to go, we need to—"

I can hear the peal of sirens in the distance. The fire trucks are coming. Not only do we need to escape the fire; now we need to get out of here before anyone sees Skyler.

"*Henry.*" I push through the beaded curtain. "We have to—"

I see Henry on the bed, holding a pillow over a lump in the sheets. Skyler's feet kick at the air. They look so small. He's struggling to escape. To breathe.

Mommy, I hear him plead in my head. *Mommymommymamamam-amamamamamaaa . . .*

FOUR

I grab Henry's shoulders to pull him off. He's forcing all his weight down on the pillow, the vague contours of Skyler's head bulging through as he struggles against it. "Henry, please!"

Henry pushes me back. "It's not him—"

"STOP!" I batter my fists against his back, but he's an immovable force.

Henry's crying. His tears fall across the pillow, his face turning a deep purple, as if he's struggling against himself.

Mamamamamamamamamamamamamamamamamamaaa . . .

It doesn't matter what Skyler is. He needs someone to protect him.

He needs his mother.

I need to find something I can use to stop Henry, a knife or something heavy like a—

Like a—

Like—

I grab the amethyst geode from the parlor with both hands. It's so heavy, it throws off my balance, but I'm able to carry it. The beaded curtain flows around me as I rush back toward the bed.

I raise the split rock over my head, filled with purple teeth, and bring it down on Henry's skull.

CRRNCH.

I can hear, nearly feel, the sickening collapse of flesh against bone as the amethyst's jagged edges sink into Henry's scalp.

His neck softens. His spine gives, and he topples off the bed.

I rip the pillow from Skyler's face. His eyes find mine.

Mommy.

In that moment I feel my heart swell. His eyes are bottomless. I could dive right in and never find my way back up to the surface. I want to drown in that boy.

My palms weep blood but I scoop Skyler into my arms and lift him out from the bed.

"Madi . . ." Henry is on the floor, blood seeping from his skull. It trickles down his face, into his eyes, as if he's weeping red.

I won't look back. I have to get Skyler away from here. Away from this man.

"Madi, please—"

Henry grabs my ankle and the room instantly pitches, tilting to one side.

Skyler and I fall to the floor.

I land on my elbows and I hear them pop. Pain radiates through my arms. Skyler goes rolling over the floor as I'm dragged backward.

"He won't let go," Henry manages to say, his words slurred, slow and wet. "He needs us to keep believing in him—"

I turn onto my back, twisting his wrist. Henry grunts and lets go of my ankle.

"He's not—"

I plant my heel directly into Henry's nose. I feel the crack of cartilage more than I hear it, the soft crunch reverberating all the way up my leg. His neck snaps back. I crawl across the carpet with my elbows, still on my back, trying to put some distance between us.

Henry crawls toward me, grabbing my leg again. Our fingers, smeared in blood, slip across each other's skin as I try to fight him off. I grab Henry's head with both hands and dig my fingernails into his scalp. I can feel the fresh crevices in his skull where the amethyst crushed it.

But he won't let up. "He'll hollow you out—"

I spot a chunk of the geode that must've split from its parent when I smashed it into Henry's skull.

"He'll drain the life right—"

I grab the crystal and smack Henry directly in his face, raking its sharp edges across his jaw. Flesh tears, soft and wet. Henry screams. I can see his teeth through his torn cheek.

He rolls off, clutching his face. Fresh blood and spit run down his wrist as he howls through his fingers. The carpet is absolutely soaked in blood.

My hands wrap around his neck. My wet fingers weave over his throat and squeeze. I can't stop myself. All I see is red and pink and purple as the neon sign lights up in the window.

MOMMY.

A pair of arms wrap around me from behind.

MOMMY.

Skyler is on my back so fast, I let out a startled cry. We both fall to the floor.

MOMMY NO.

Skyler's voice forces its way into my head. My vision distorts. I can't think straight. Can't see anything.

By the time I lift my head, I find Skyler nestled against Henry. *Jesus*, the boy's protecting Henry from *me*. "Skyler . . . get away from . . ."

I'm certain I hear sirens now, the wail of a fire truck drawing near. We have to get out of here but I can't move. I'm spent. All three of us simply lie there in our own blood, struggling to gasp for what little air our lungs can manage. I look to Henry, then Skyler, the two of them huddled together as if this were all some sort of family game night. *Time to play Twister.*

Skyler rolls onto his back.

mommy

"Skyler?"

Skyler tilts his head toward the ceiling. His fish-roe eyes roll into his sockets, nothing but orange left in their wake. Then his lips split vertically, his flesh parting from chin to nose.

I peer down his throat, lined in crooked rows of molars. It's like looking down a well made of teeth. So many baby teeth crammed together, even along the roof of his mouth—a lamprey. And there, all the way at the very bottom of that well, I see a steely shimmer.

It's moving. Whatever's at the back of his throat, it's alive.

Minnows.

Dozens of tiny fish cluster together, climbing his esophagus as more water spews from his body. Their fins glimmer.

Skyler's head turns to one side, spewing the fish from his mouth. Their glistening bodies flap haplessly on the floor.

Skyler heaves once more, sending another flush of minnows across the floor. There have to be dozens, *hundreds* of them now, mouths opening and closing, desperate for air.

"What's happening, Skyler?"

"He's coming undone," Henry rasps from between the fissures in his face, the words wet and sloppy. "If we don't keep our connection he'll . . . lose shape. His . . . *consistency.*"

He needs someone to love him.

I grab Skyler and pull him to his feet. I scoop him into my arms. Press him to my chest.

"Madi . . ." Henry calls out, but I don't look back.

I carry him out from the bedroom, through the parlor, into the parking lot.

"Madi, don't—"

The flash of red lights blinds me, but I don't stop running. I carry Skyler through the parking lot, pushing past the firemen as they head toward the burning motel. The gravel feels exceptionally soft all of a sudden, as if it's soggy, pitching me off balance. I collide with a firefighter running in the opposite direction, nearly falling.

I feel Skyler's arms wrap around me.

First, two. Then three.

Four.

Six.

He clutches me in his embrace.

Water, Skyler whispers. I hear him so clearly. Skyler's voice guides me, gentle but persistent, pushing out all my other thoughts and telling me exactly where to go. *Water . . .*

FIVE

Plenty of fishermen tie up their jonny boats along the waterfront and forget about them. Some even leave their keys onboard. The shores are lined with abandoned dinghies. It's just a matter of us driving to the nearest marina and picking a skiff with an onboard motor.

We ride through the night. There's no moon. Skyler's head rolls back over his shoulders, taking in all the stars as I navigate our way upriver, trying to understand everything Henry said.

An imaginary child who took on a life of its own. We focused on the thought of Skyler, channeling him, pouring our mind's energy into finding him . . . until here he was.

We made him.

I made him.

So when the question echoes—*What is Skyler?*—the answer is clearer in my mind now.

Skyler's mine.

A make-believe boy still needs someone to believe in him. What happens to an imaginary friend if the person who thought him up in the first place suddenly stops believing?

What would happen to Skyler if Henry and I stopped believing in him? He's growing weak. *Coming undone,* Henry said. All the thoughts that went into making this boy are suddenly starting to spill out all over again.

Thought plus time plus energy . . .

Plus love. This boy needs love.

A mother's love.

I feel a gentle pressure to steer forward. Skyler's guiding me without a word.

And just like that, there it is. Up ahead. I spot it now.

The duck blind.

Waiting for us.

The thatched hut hides our boat. I cut the motor and the skiff coasts the rest of the way into the wooden enclosure. I scoop Skyler up and carry him onto the roof. The wood bends under our weight, but it's sturdy enough to hold us. Our own island in the middle of the river.

"We're safe here." I sit down, leaning against one of the posts. I'm so exhausted. A wave of fatigue sweeps over me so suddenly. I'm crashing fast. "Nobody will find us here . . ."

Skyler climbs into my lap. I take hold of him, letting him nestle against my chest, and wrap his arms around my waist.

"It's okay," I say. "You're okay now . . . I won't let anything . . ."

My eyes can barely stay open. I'm drifting . . .

Drifting . . .

The weight of Skyler's body presses against mine and I feel something shift beneath his skin. Whatever's under his flesh will find a way out. It simply is who he is.

Whoever said blood is thicker than water never grew up on this river. We may not be bound by blood, but Skyler is certainly mine. We're family bound by thought. By this river. The Piankatank runs through this boy's veins, just like everyone else who lives here. Its water feeds us, sustains us. Washes our sins away. Most of them, at least. The others we hide at its bottom.

Let the crabs peck at the rest.

life never stopped for me . . .

not down here in the cold . . .

the dark . . .

when the tide is low and the surface is closer to me . . .

I see the sky rippling above . . .

I see you up there

mama

just on the other side of the surface . . .

you're standing on the dock . . .

looking out at the river . . .

look down . . .

I'm right here . . .

right beneath your feet . . .

all you have to do is look down and

see me

My eyes fly open.

The sky is a dull gray. The sun's just a few inches away from breaching the horizon. Dawn's already bleeding through the tree line along the shore.

How long was I asleep? I couldn't have dozed off for more than—

"Morning."

Henry sits across from me. He looks practically ashen in the early light. Half of his face hangs in tatters, the streamers of his lips flap off his jawline. His shirt holds more blood than his body does, from the looks of it, yet there's a certain serenity to him as he cradles Skyler in his arms. He looks like a piece of raw chicken, if I'm being honest. Something to bait a crab trap.

"We didn't want to wake you."

Skyler is wide awake. Of course he is. That boy never sleeps. He's huddled against Henry's chest. My gut instinct is to rush across the blind and grab Skyler, but I can tell he's pleased to be in his father's arms. He just wants to be held. Henry gently rocks back and forth, wetly humming through his eviscerated lips.

"Skyler, honey . . ." I want to tell him he can come to me, if he wants. I promised he'd be safe. That I'd protect him. But he doesn't need protection from Henry. He wants us both here.

"How'd you find us?"

"Skyler told me," Henry says. No arguing with that. Always whispering in our minds, his voice so soft it sounds like the wind. Skyler lured us both to the duck blind. He wanted us here.

Together.

Henry drifts. At first, I think he's lost too much blood, but I realize he's simply off on another one of his mental walkabouts. "Used to come here with Grace. Fell in love right here. We'd light sparklers all summer long. Watch them dance over the water . . . Foolish fire."

Skyler looks over and smiles at me. A fiddler crab emerges from his ear. Its compressed body slips out of the canal as if it were a burrow in the sand. The boy barely blinks as the crab skitters across his earlobe and down his neck, joining a cluster of crabs crawling along his shoulders. Their claws rise up in the air as they scuttle over Skyler's skin. I can hear the faint clicking of their mandibles.

This boy. This strange, beautiful boy . . . *What is he?* It doesn't matter anymore.

We are his creators.

His parents.

I slowly pull myself up from the boards and wince as I lean against one of the duck blind's posts, feeling sore in nearly every muscle.

"Sleep well?" Henry asks. "Any dreams?"

"A few."

"I've had them, too." Henry coughs. "They're Skyler's, I think."

It's strange to think we've all been sharing the same visions, but it's not so surprising. They brought us together, didn't they? Have our visions been Skyler's dreams all along?

"Sorry about . . ." I lift my hand and point to my face, meaning his face, swirling my finger.

"Water under the duck blind, I reckon." Even now he's trying to be charming. I can't help but smile. Just a bit.

"What brought you back?"

He smiles—I think he smiles—his teeth visible through his cheek. "You."

Things get quiet between us for a moment. "Is it really him?" I have to ask. "Is it Skyler?"

"I want to think he's the best parts of us. Probably the worst parts, too. All that heartache is in there . . . In him. I don't know what exactly that makes him."

I can't help but wonder: *What are the worst parts of me? What does Skyler have of me?*

"Can he stay? With us?"

"He'll want you all to himself, Madi . . . He won't share."

I think about Kendra in that big pastel house. The look of horror on her face when she saw what Skyler was. I've never loved anyone as fiercely as I love that girl, but she has Donny. She has a whole *family*. I've never been the right kind of mother for her.

She doesn't need me like Skyler does.

We can start over.

A family.

Families are fluid. Families are made up of so many other families, ripped apart and stitched back together again. Patchwork quilts of different kin. Why can't this be ours?

Henry's grip on my hand loosens as he sits up. Coughs. He lifts Skyler up from his lap.

"Come on. Let me get a good look at you."

Skyler stands before his father. Henry remains sitting, the two now face to face with one another. Henry wraps his hands around the boy's shoulders and takes him in. Marveling at him.

Then he hugs his son.

All six of Skyler's arms wrap around his father. The two hold on to each other for a breathless spell and I can't help but wonder if they'll ever let go.

Henry finally pulls out from his son's grip. "Why don't you . . . go over to your mother?"

Skyler skitters sideways across the duck blind to me. He crawls up my legs before nestling himself into my lap, compressing his body into a ball against my chest. The boy just fits.

"I'm sorry I dragged you into this, Madi . . ." His words are eclipsed by a coughing fit. Tears run down his face. "Skyler couldn't live without Grace. I understand that now."

He pulls his oyster knife out from his pocket.

"Henry . . ."

"My son is gone."

I clutch Skyler to my chest, shielding his eyes as Henry raises the knife.

"Henry, please—"

And then I watch as he jabs it into his own neck.

"*Henry!*"

He does it again, puncturing his jugular, sending a jet of blood into the air as he yanks the blade free and stabs himself again. Three swift thrusts—*splk-splk-splk*. It looks as if he's going back for a fourth but his body gives out, backbone slackening against the post.

His hand falls to the boards and releases the oyster knife. The dull blade rolls out from his fingers, leaving a trail of blood along the wood. Purple arcs spurt from his neck, drizzling across the slats like rain. It gathers in an obsidian puddle, then dribbles through the slats.

"Don't look." I press Skyler as tight as I can against me, shielding his eyes. "*Don't.*"

I watch the life leave Henry's body. He exhales wetly one last time. His arm relaxes, his hand sliding down to his lap. Then he's gone.

Henry is gone.

I find myself leaning forward, reaching out to him, when suddenly . . .

Skyler's body goes rigid in my arms.

". . . Skyler?"

The boy's spine stiffens, limbs shaking at his sides.

"Sky . . ."

His head suddenly judders across the wooden boards, pounding against the roof.

"No no no . . ."

He begins to glow, blue, electric, bioluminescent. Neon. A little will-o'-the-wisp. Foolish fire. I feel a slight sting as I touch him. Jellyfish tentacles. Skin bright as the moon. I suddenly remember what a group of jellyfish is called . . . A *smack.* The wasps' nest in his chest is frantic with activity, the hive alive and angry, as if I just shook their nest.

Undone. The boy's coming undone.

"Stay with me, Skyler, *please*—"

His eyes roll into their sockets, nothing but white now.

Not white. *Translucent.*

Skyler's left eyeball slowly pushes itself out from its socket and drops onto the duck blind. It hits the wood with a soft, wet slap and rolls over the boards for an inch or two.

Then comes the right.

He blinks and both eyeballs return, each socket filling up with another.

Then they tumble out again.

They're not eyeballs at all, but comb jellies, pushing their way out and rolling down his pale cheeks. Skyler's weeping jellyfish.

His eyes well up within his sockets and another gelatinous tear rolls out.

Then another.

Another.

"Skyler, please—"

Blood runs out from his nose. No, not blood. A rusty sludge. River mud, wet with brine and dead fish. He foams at the mouth like a crab spewing bubbles from its lungs.

He's dying. Skyler is dying in my arms.

"Don't." I press my hands against his chest, holding him. "Don't leave me."

A ripple works its way up the boy's throat. A thickened wrinkle undulates along his esophagus, rising toward his mouth. His shoulders pump, as if he needs his whole body to eject whatever is making its way toward his mouth.

"Skyler!"

I see the eel. Its snout winnows through Skyler's lips. It's too big for the boy's mouth. His lips stretch to their limit and I'm worried his mandibles might crack before the eel unspools itself. It wrestles against the boy's tongue before finally falling to the boards. It wriggles its way off the edge of the blind, slithering back and plunging into the water below.

A shower of minnows dribbles from his lips, spilling everywhere.

The tiny fish tumble onto the blind, flopping across the boards before slipping through the slats toward the river.

I can't let Skyler go. I can't lose him.

"Stay with me."

If Skyler was born out of Henry and me, our thoughts bringing him into existence, then I need to play both roles. I'll be both mother and father.

"Give me your hand," I say. Lord knows how many times I've said it. *Give me your hand give me your hand give me your hand—*

"I'm here. I won't let go, I promise. Just stay with me."

I pour myself into him. All my thoughts. All my heart. I give it all to him. *Everything.*

I'll never stop believing in Skyler.

I'll never stop believing.

I feel him inhale and exhale, the wasps quieting within his chest. I feel the minnows winnow beneath his skin, their thin bodies swimming through his bloodstream.

Skyler blinks back.

He *sees* me. The warm orange glow of his fish-roe eyes returns and in that breath, I think—*You were born of this world and are utterly beyond it. You're unlike any child I ever met.*

What you need is love.

A mother's love.

I wrap my arms around him and hold on tight, as tight as I can, clasping him to my chest and humming his lullaby, the lyrics slipping out of my mouth.

You were born . . .

I stare up at the last hint of stars left in the early-morning sky. I feel all of Skyler's arms weave around my waist, my chest, my shoulders.

By the water. . .

I'm ready to give you everything. All that I have, son.

Every last thought.

SIX

Head, shoulders, knees and toes . . .

Knees and toes . . .

Skyler is set to molt again. Won't be much longer before he peels,
I can tell. His skin is beginning to pinch around his eyes, tugging on
his cheeks. A thin fissure runs the length of his nose, where the flesh
is at its tenderest. It'll tear there first, ripping right down the middle,
until the rest of his face follows. Then his neck, his shoulders and
arms, down his chest, waist, all the way to his feet. Reminds me of
that song I used to sing to Kendra, pointing to all her body parts:

Head, shoulders, knees and toes . . . Knees and toes . . .

Eyes and ears and mouth and nooooose . . .

Head, shoulders, knees and toes . . .

Knees and toes!

I'll sing to Skyler when it's just the two of us snuggled in the
boat's cabin. It's getting pretty cramped down here, to be honest.
Wasn't much room to begin with. We tossed as much unnecessary
stuff as we could. A whole stack of Skyler's missing-person flyers
went overboard, his black-and-white baby face drifting across the
river's surface.

It's just the two of us now. That boy's growing up far too fast. A
weed on two feet.

Tell me the story again, Mama . . .

"It hasn't changed since the last time I told it to you, hon . . . or the time before that."

Skyler wraps his arms—all six of them—around me and everything goes warm. Soft. The world simply melts away for a while and I feel safe in my boy's embrace, like I'm at home.

I want to hear it again . . .

"I'm exhausted, hon. You've plumb tuckered me out. I need some rest . . ."

Please, Mama? Pleeease?

"Fine, fine." I say it with a well-rehearsed sigh. This is all a part of our routine now. Our nightly ritual. I could call it a bedtime story, but when is it ever bedtime? Skyler never sleeps. He's always hungry for more of himself. And I give in to him. How can I say no to that boy?

I'm supposed to be the one putting him to bed, but more often than not nowadays, the shoe's on the other foot. "Here we go . . . This is the story of how you came to be, my little will-o'-the-wisp . . ."

How many times am I going to tell this story? For as long as there is air in my lungs, I guess. This story is the only thing keeping Skyler alive. It's feeding him. Sustaining him.

I'm all the family he's got now.

Skyler watched on as I rolled what was left of Henry's body off the duck blind. The boy made a meal out of most of his father. The soft parts, at least.

When Skyler finished, Henry looked as if he'd been pecked by the bottom-feeders scuttling under the river. For the better, I reckon. If his corpse ever washes ashore, the authorities will more than likely assume he'd been nibbled on by crabs. Not his own son.

When Henry struck the water, it sounded like thunder rumbling at our feet. It echoed across the Piankatank in the early-morning light. I watched him sink below the surface, his bleeding features growing fuzzier, losing their clarity the deeper he went, until darkness swallowed his body. Let the crabs have what's left of him. Let the fish feed on the rest.

That wasn't the last time I laid eyes on Henry McCabe. I still see him in his son every day. Skyler has his father's nose. His cheekbones. His smile.

But he has his river's eyes.

SEVEN

I don't know how long we can hide on Henry's deadrise. There are enough feeder creeks throughout the Piankatank for us to pick another inlet each night, lay ourselves low by sunrise. I'll tie up to somebody's dock in the middle of the night before letting Skyler run off and play.

The boy seems at home onboard. At night, I'll hear him slip off into the water. Where he's going, he never says. He waits until I drift off before heading to shore, leaving me to rest.

One night, I pretended to fall asleep, waiting for Skyler to scuttle off before calling Kendra. We agreed I shouldn't reach out to anyone on dry land. Especially Kendra. It was better to let go. This was our life now. Our family.

But I needed to hear her voice. Just once more. To say goodbye.

Kendra picked up on the third ring. "Mom?"

"Kendra?" I kept my voice low. "Can you hear me?"

"Are you hurt? Where are you?"

"I'm okay," I whispered. "I can't talk long. I just wanted—" *to make sure you're safe and as far away from your little brother as humanly possible. He's such a jealous child.*

"The police are looking for you," she cut right in. "They think Henry kidnapped you."

"How long have I been gone?"

"Two days."

Only two? Skyler's growing so fast. I figured we'd been drifting on the river for longer.

"Everybody's been trying to reach you . . ."

There's no time for that now, I imagined myself saying. *I need you to listen me. Skyler will be back any minute. I just needed to tell you how much I love you, hon. How proud I am. I know you're going to do great things in this world. You are everything I could've hoped for—*

Skyler tugged the cell phone out from my hand—*which pincer is that?*—before I could say any of these things. *How long has he been listening? Does he know it's Kendra on the line?*

What will he do to her if he finds out?

I heard the phone splash. Maybe it was just a fish cutting across the water's surface.

Rest now, Mama, rest . . .

EIGHT

I snap out from sleep with a start just as something skitters across my neck. Not just my neck. It's everywhere. I feel spiky legs scuttling over my thigh, working their way up my leg.

The air is oppressively hot. Every breath weighs my lungs down.

Just a dream, I think. I'm in the motel room. In bed. *You were just having a bad—*

Something shifts underneath the sheet.

Pinpricks of barbed legs crawl along my stomach. My drowsy mind reels off all the prickly possibilities—*Tarantulas or scorpions or black widows, oh my*—as I bolt upright.

What is that?

I hear them clicking. The tiniest ticking sound, wet and metallic, snickers through the darkness. I run my hand along the mattress, expecting to find Skyler next to me, but the boy's not there. The bed is wet where he should be, soaked through.

"Skyler—"

Something snaps at my fingertip. I hiss at the sudden sting and yank my hand back.

Another snaps at the back of my leg. There's more than just one. *In the bed.* I scramble up to my knees and hit my head on the roof—*Jesus Christ*—and realize this isn't my bed at all.

This isn't the motel.

Where am I?

The boat. I'm still aboard Henry's deadrise. And the cabin is crawling with blue-shells.

Dozens of crabs lift their pincers, as if to beseech the heavens. Honoring me.

Mother, they all seem to say.

Mother.

Over and over again, wetly clicking, *mother mother.*

I can't help but admonish Skyler, even if it's simply in my head: *If you want to invite your friends over, you've got to ask your mother first. We're not running a motel here . . .*

I brush the blue-shells from my body. One pinches the meat of my palm. I hiss and reel my hand back, taking this clamping tagalong with me. I whip my arm through the air until the crab lets go. It spirals across the cabin before striking the hull, its shell cracking with a sickeningly brittle crunch. Crabs skitter into the corners of the cabin, hiding in the shadows.

Hussh . . .

Skyler's arms weave their way around my waist from behind, enveloping me in his embrace. One second he's nowhere to be found—the next, he's cradling me, cooing in my ear.

Rest, Mama . . . rest . . .

A part of me wants to scream. To tear free from his grip and run as far away as I can. But I can feel the undertow of fatigue pulling me under even now. It's swift and pervasive and nearly impossible to resist. *Rest, yes . . .* That's all I want to do. That's all I ever want to do now.

Parenting is just so exhausting.

NINE

A monster still needs its mother, but even I drew the line at the baby.

I knew about the dogs. The cats. Somehow he'd even dragged a deer back on board, saving it for a snack. I woke up to a fawn's corpse in the cabin, tucked in bed beside me, breaking our big rule about food in bed. Sometimes, I swear, that boy simply doesn't listen to his mother. I've got to remind him again and again: *No eating where we're supposed to sleep.*

We've been attracting far too many flies lately. I don't want to share a bed with insects.

I can turn a blind eye to housepets every now and then, but not people.

Certainly not children.

I feel him siphoning my energy, but it's slower now. Less painful. Maybe he's trying to keep me around. Maybe he's simply savoring me. Who knows?

But his palate is maturing. His tastes are changing the bigger he grows. Sometimes his meals are old enough to beg.

I knew he was hiding the girl from me. He didn't want me to know, but of course I found her. Parts of her. Skyler can't hide these things from me, no matter how much he spreads her around the boat. I'm tired of cleaning his mess. *I'm not your personal maid. This is not a motel.*

He barely listens to me anymore.
Such a sullen teen.

TEN

I can't remember if I turned the sign on or not. Maybe I'll tell someone's fortune today.

Got to put food on the table. Keep this roof over our head.

Taking care of Skyler has become a full-time job. It's downright exhausting. That boy simply never sleeps. He always wants to hold me. I'm so tired all the time now. I try to sleep, but there's just never enough time to catch up. I close my eyes but I still see everything. My eyelids offer no solace, the future sprawled out before me.

My son. My moon.

My Skyler.

Tell me the story again, Mama. The humidity of his exhales covers me in a thin layer of sweat.

"Didn't I . . . just tell you?" My tongue scrapes over the roof of my mouth like sandpaper.

I want to hear it again . . .

"Could've sworn I . . . told it . . ."

Again, Mama.

Again.

I always prided myself on being able to read people. That's not being a fortune-teller, it's being a good listener. I figured out what people needed to hear about themselves. To believe.

Henry believed in his own story of Skyler so much, he got me to believe along with him. I helped harness his grief, I gave it a direction—a target—and together, we manifested this child.

Our very own Skyler.

Thought plus time plus energy. That's my secret recipe.

My *family* recipe.

There may come a day when Skyler is strong enough to live on his own. He'll no longer need his mother, just like he outgrew his father, but he's not quite there yet. We'll just have to wait and see. Until then, it's just the two of us. Us against the world. Mother and son.

Who knows? Maybe, when I'm old and gray and can no longer take care of myself, my son will take care of me. Isn't that what we all want? For our children to look after us?

ELEVEN

"The day you were born," I start, like I always do, spinning this yarn just the way he likes, "I ran right out into the road, ready to ask the first person I met to stand as your godfather."

Who'd you find?

"Well, the first person I came up to was God. He already had it in His mind what I was going to ask Him, so He said, *Poor girl, of course I'll hold your child over the font.* I asked Him, *Who are you?* And He replied, *Why . . . I am God.* So I said, *Then I don't want you for my child's godfather. You give to the rich and let the poor go hungry.* And I turned away from Him."

You turned away from God?

"I did."

Then what happened?

"Next I came up to the Devil. He gives me this sly wink, purring in the pearliest voice you ever did hear—*Take me as this child's godfather and I'll give it all the riches in the world.* So I asked him, *Who the hell are you?* He replied, *Who else? I'm the Devil.* So I said, *I don't want you for my child's godfather, either. You lie and lead people astray.* I turned away from him, too."

You turned away from the Devil?

"That I did."

So what happened next?

"None other than bone-dry Death himself comes walking up to me, swinging his scythe around. *Why not take me as this child's godfather?* he asks. So I ask back, *And just who do you think you are?* But I already knew. *I am Death*, he said. I went ahead and said, *You make the rich and poor alike. You make all people equal. You will be the godfather of my child* . . . And so he is."

TWELVE

Calling Skyler a boy seems inappropriate now. He's all grown up. Just look at what he's become. His skin splits down his back and peels away from in his hands.

I can't help but feel a swell of pride as I help him out of his old flesh and into his new. I wonder if this is what it feels like on your son's prom night, helping him slip into his tux. Making sure everything fits. All buttoned up. *I should get a picture of him,* I think.

The flesh at his lower elbows is caught. He keeps tugging but the skin won't pull free.

"Here, let me help." I take hold of the folds. "You're gonna rip it if you're not careful."

I gently yank, taking it slow, so the sheet of skin peels off in a single strip. The tacky smack of wet flesh peeling away from the tender tissue below sounds so loud, it fills the cabin.

"There you go . . . See? Where would you be without your mama?"

Look at him. Just look at this beautiful thing. I've watched him grow, peeling away the layers of his skin . . . *but his eyes.* They've changed. *Where have I seen those eyes before?*

Kendra.

I swear I see her looking back at me. Her features have intermingled with his own. Those are her cheekbones, the slender slope of her nose. *It's her.* I've been thinking so much about her, Skyler must've absorbed all those thoughts into himself. It's not just Skyler anymore. He's Kendra now, too, the semblance of them fused together in one body.

Just look at them. Siblings sharing skin. I made this. The best parts of me. All that's left.

Skyler usually eats his old husk once he's done shedding. His mandibles unlatch and he'll tuck the flimsy sheets of skin into his elongated mouth, swallowing it in these wet, hefty heaves, inch by inch, until it's worked its way down his throat.

But tonight he holds out his skin for me to take, as an offering.

"For me?"

It's so smooth, so soft to the touch, like a satin blanket. He slips the skin casing over my shoulders, still warm from his body. I'm always so cold now, even when it's over a hundred degrees inside the cabin.

"Thank you, son . . . Thank you."

My very own blankie, pearly white. I can just barely make out the blistered patterns of embroidered animals. A crab, a fish, a duck, a bee, all made of the softest material. Like satin. Baby's skin.

Rest, Mama. Ressst . . .

THIRTEEN

I must've forgotten to turn off the sign. When I wake up, dragging myself out from my sleep, I see the neon hand floating right above me. Such beautiful colors. Pink and purple hues.

It's not just one neon hand anymore. There are bound to be a dozen of them now, all those open palms, those phosphorescent fingers rippling through the air, surrounding me.

Wait. That's not neon.

Those are jellyfish. Hundreds of bioluminescent comets. It's a downright meteor shower over my head. Pink and purple and red and blue. Pulsing bells drifting about, close enough to touch. I can't tell if I'm in the water or not. I could be sailing through the night's sky. I'm either up or down or both. Where does the water end and the sky begin? It's all warm to me.

Give me your hand . . .

I reach out to touch the nearest jellyfish. My fingertips graze through their tentacles, like passing my hand through a beaded curtain. It stings with electricity. Pulsing with life.

Give me your hand . . .

The jellyfish shift, changing course. Now they're swimming all around me.

Through me.

I'm in a stream of shooting stars. I feel the dull current of their electricity coursing through me.

I'm glowing. I'm pink and purple, a bioluminescent firework bursting into the night's sky.

I feel like foolish fire.

FOURTEEN

Parents know there'll come a day when their kids are grown enough to live on their own.

Skyler is no exception.

Every child's got to leave the nest someday.

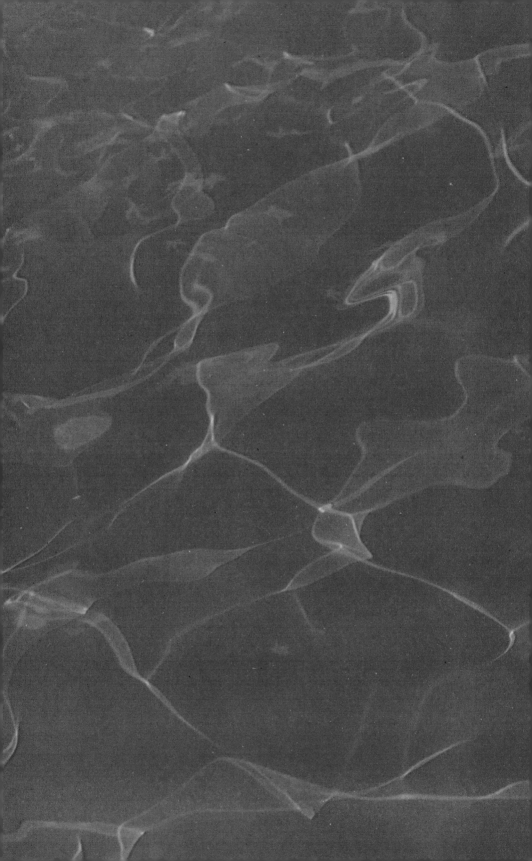

CRAB TRAP

William Henshaw was the inaugural poet laureate of Shell Oil. He'd put in thirty years as regional sales manager and, after dutifully clocking in and clocking out toward his pension, it was finally time to retire. It wasn't particularly thrilling work by any stretch of the imagination, but it put food on the table. A roof over his family's head had to stand for something.

Bill loved to pen little ditties for his wife and daughters. What started as a Valentine's Day lark decades back, a poem to his beloved, eventually led to birthday missives and other holiday sonnets. He could come up with a verse for just about any occasion, big or small, anniversaries or commemorating a first lost tooth. Suze even cross-stitched the family favorite "Henshaw Grace," framing the poem in their dining room for all their dinner guests to see:

> *Thank you Suze for all your meals,*
>
> *thank the grocer for their coupon deals.*
>
> *Thank you Lord for your good wishes,*
>
> *thank you Bill for doing the dishes.*

Hokey poetry, that's all, but Bill certainly loved to write it. His coworkers quickly caught on to his humble literary ambitions and invited him to contribute a couplet to the company newsletter now and then. After that, they gently egged him on to whip something up for nearly every occasion—holiday parties, quarterly reports, sales conferences, you name it, Bill dutifully penned a poem for them all. He was happy to take requests.

The only retirement that wasn't marked with an ode was his own, sadly. When it came time for Bill to hang up his proverbial boots and say farewell to Shell, someone in graphics got into the spirit and drafted up a certificate, complete with an official—official-looking, at least—gold Shell emblem embossed at the bottom. It might not have been a Pulitzer, or company-sanctioned for that matter, but Bill couldn't help but feel a pang of pride when his officemates presented him the certificate at his send-off, matted and framed for him to hang up at home:

We hereby honor William A. Henshaw, the Poet Laureate of Shell Oil

What Bill would miss most about work was a particular ritual he devised for himself. Hours before the sun crawled out, he'd wake ahead of everyone else in his house and get dressed as if he were heading in for work—same navy blue suit and a choice of one of five ties in constant rotation, all Christmas gifts from his daughters. He'd climb into his car with a thermos of freshly brewed Folgers and drive to the nearest inlet along Interstate 64. The Chesapeake Bay was within spitting distance of his office, less than a twenty-mile drive. As long as Bill beat traffic, he'd practically have the whole highway to himself.

More often than not, Bill would head down to Norfolk. Perhaps Pungo, if the weather was nice and there was no rain. He would park the company car on the road's shoulder, take a sip of coffee to warm himself up, slip his hip waders over his suit and go chicken-necking.

One final day on the job, one last fishing trip.

Bill wouldn't miss this lengthy commute to work, but he'd certainly miss *this*. The solitude of the water. Watching the morning sun break over the bay. Those black rubber overalls fit over his navy blue blazer. What an odd picture he must've struck. If anyone spotted him, they'd see a businessman, all decked out in his suit and tie, waltzing out into the waters.

He was ready to spend the next hour fishing for blue-shells with nothing more than a piece of raw chicken tied to the end of a sawn-off broomstick.

Wire net in hand, Bill trudged out into the inlet, easing deeper into the dark waters. He had fastened a foam life ring to the bottom of a plastic laundry basket. Whenever he scooped a crab into his net, he would simply plop his catch into the basket floating by his side. Once Bill caught his limit, filling the basket to its brim, he would tie a plywood disc that fit across the top, sealing his snapping bounty inside. He'd keep his catch in the trunk of the company car for the rest of the day while he was at work, those dozen or so crabs clicking and foaming as they climbed over each other. Bill would bring them home that evening, and Suze would sprinkle on a little Old Bay seasoning and steam the batch up for dinner, the whole family picking crabs together.

Legend has it one wily crustacean escaped from the laundry basket. That blue-shelled absconder crawled into an upholstered crevasse and eventually croaked. It took days to find that damn crab, but not before stinking up the entire interior. Even after Bill salvaged the dead crab from its final resting place, squeezed between the seat cushions, he was never quite able to get rid of the briny smell. Nobody else in the office wanted to use the car after that, so it unofficially became Bill's . . . or so the story goes whenever his coworkers told it, reaffirming the old adage:

Old fishermen never die, they just smell that way.

Bill waded farther out into the water and settled into the stillness of the inlet. He gently cast the pale chicken neck off, letting it plop and sink into the water. A yellow flap of fatty skin fanned through the murk, like a silk scarf billowing in the black before fading into the depths.

From here, it was merely a matter of patience.

Bill stood perfectly still, up to his hips in salt water. He sensed the dull tug of the currents pulling at his legs, the undertow eager to lure him out deeper into the Chesapeake.

Bill would wait for the slightest pluck from the string. He was the spider nestled into its web, patiently waiting for the unwitting fly to waltz into his trap. Once he knew a crab was on the other end, he'd begin to lift—*slowly, slowly*—bringing the chicken neck up to the surface. If he took his time, soon the hazy outline of a blue-shell gnawing on that raw chicken would rise into view. Once it was near the surface, he'd sweep his net under the feeding crustacean and scoop it up. *Gotcha.* Bill had done this so many times over the years, perfecting his strokes, it was practically balletic, one arm rising high while the other swooped down. Here he was, a man in his element, at his most serene, harvesting the fruit from the ocean floor. He was at peace.

He would truly miss this.

Bill suddenly felt that persistent pull from the other end of the line. He had to make sure to reel it in slowly, gently, so the crab wouldn't startle and release the bait. There was no hook, so the crab could let go at any moment. There was always the risk of losing his catch. That was the joy in crabbing for Bill, the sport of it all, holding his breath until he swept up his prize.

But when Bill tugged this time, he was immediately met with resistance. Whatever was on the other end of the line was far heavier than a crab. He pulled again, adding just a bit more pressure. The line tautened. His bait must have snagged on something along the silty bottom. Something at his feet. He blindly probed the blackened water with the boot of his hip waders. His rubberized toe pressed against a stubborn sponge, flexible but unyielding. It collapsed under the pressure of his foot, then bounced back up once he lifted his sole off it again.

What is this? Bill couldn't pull his line free. The chicken neck was caught on whatever this thing was. He needed to lean forward, just a bit, and see if he couldn't manage to—

Water spilled over the lip of his hip waders. The cold flood rushed into his boots and immediately seized his bones.

"*Dammit,*" Bill cursed under his breath. His suit was soaked. He was completely drenched from the waist down. Freezing. He hadn't packed a spare set of dry clothes. And on his last day at Shell, no less.

He'd trudge into the office sopping wet, giving his officemates one last hoot to remember him by. Bill would never live this down. Just what he needed.

Well, it's too late to turn back now. His slacks were already soaked. Might as well keep going. With a deep breath, Bill plunged his hand into the cold water and reached for his feet.

His fingers found a ring. Several metal rings, thin and honey-combed.

Chicken wire.

It must be a crab trap. *Of course.* Commercial fishermen toss them into the water all throughout the bay. Usually, they're tied to a buoy to mark their location, making it easier for their owners to pinpoint them when it's time to dredge them back up.

This trap had been abandoned. Forgotten, from the feel of it. The cage was slippery, coated in a gelatinous film of algae. It must have been down here for an awful long while.

Years.

Bill tugged. The cage wouldn't give easily, as if it had adhered to the bottom. He had to yank even harder to pry it free from the muddy bottom. It was like worrying a loose tooth—*back and forth, back and forth, back and forth*—fiddling with the nerve until it finally snapped.

Bill lost his footing and nearly tumbled backward into the water. He stepped forward at the last moment and planted his boot along the muddy bottom, sparing himself any further embarrassment of plunging completely underwater. He was determined to uproot this trap no matter what now. He flossed his fingers through the wire mesh and made a fist with his hand.

"Come on, come on," he muttered to himself. Holding both his net and broomstick in the other, he maintained his balance as best he could as he tugged again, harder this time.

Who knows, he thought, *maybe there were a few blue-shells trapped inside. That would make this mess worthwhile . . .*

Bill felt the mud give. He'd worked the loose tooth enough that it finally uprooted itself.

"There you go."

The sun finally crested the horizon, illuminating the water, so when Bill triumphantly freed the trap and lifted it out from the brown murk, he could see there were no crabs inside.

Bill gasped.

There was a doll in the center of the trap. No, not a doll . . .

A baby.

A skeletonized infant, to be exact.

The web of algae-covered wire made it difficult to completely see inside the cage. Water dribbled from the spoked mesh, tendrils of bulbous brown seaweed freely dangling like clumps of wet hair.

Bill felt ill. All the coffee he'd drunk on an otherwise empty stomach simmered like acid, boiling in his belly, threatening to rise back up his esophagus in a caffeinated volcano.

But he couldn't turn away. Bill found himself transfixed by the sight in his hand.

What is this?

A persistent part of his mind begged him to release the trap—*drop it, Bill, just let it go.* He'd never seen anything like this before in his life. He couldn't fathom what he was staring at.

Who would—*could*—do such a thing?

To a *child*?

There wasn't much skin. What flesh was left was gray and water-logged, much like the loose flapping chicken skin of Bill's own bait. His mind ineffectually tried to accommodate the mounting horror by suggesting this wasn't a baby at all, but merely a bloated Perdue, the loose blanket of yellow-gray skin sloughing off the fowl's pale breast. But the bones didn't match. Bill knew that. This wasn't a chicken. Of course it wasn't. He wouldn't—*couldn't*—allow his mind this minor lapse. This corpse deserved that courtesy, at least. It was the decent thing to do.

This was a human being.

A child.

The infant's rib cage was a trap all of its own, capturing its fair share of tiny sea life. Thin spokes of bones that held a gray mass of organs. The exposed lungs writhed with life. Minnows. Dozens of them. Now that they were out of the water, the tiny fish flopped breathlessly about the muddy morass of human tissue, desperate to find their way back into the safety of the bay.

There just wasn't enough skin, not nearly enough meat still clinging to its bones. What flesh was left was a discolored gray. The rest had been pecked clean, scavenged by crabs and fish that could easily flit in and out from the trap without getting stuck. A buffet for the bay.

This baby must have been down here for years. *Jesus, years*, Bill realized. How else could he account for the algae blossoming along the jaw? The barnacles clustering around the skull? At first, Bill believed this baby had over a dozen eyes staring out at him from behind the cage's thin bars. It took a few persistent blinks to force that image out of his mind and realize it was a constellation of crustaceous biofoulers scattered across the slope of its exposed cranium.

Bill had never seen such a small skeleton before. How old had the baby been when it had been crammed inside? A standard crab trap is usually no bigger than a television set. Back when families owned television sets, at least. Not these newfangled plasma screen TVs. He remembered when he brought home his family's first Panasonic, all those years ago. How his daughters plopped themselves down in front of its screen and flipped the power switch, the blue-green glow casting an aquamarine sheen across their cheeks. That was ages ago. His daughters were all grown up now, married and with children of their own. Beautiful grandchildren. Such sweet, tender faces. Rosy cheeks. *If something like this ever happened to . . .*

Bill gasped the second he envisioned his own girls' skin sloughing off their faces. He didn't want these images in his mind, but now that he'd seen this infant skeleton, he couldn't stop the barrage of images from insinuating themselves into his imagination. Creeping in like crabs festering within the nooks and crannies of his mind.

That image wouldn't go away now.

What should he do? He knew he needed to find a phone or flag someone driving by—but for the life of him, Bill couldn't move. He felt so lost in that moment. He didn't know what could be done for this child. It'd been lost to the water for so long, Bill didn't want to let it go.

He simply couldn't get this child out of his mind.

So William A. Henshaw, the inaugural poet laureate of Shell Oil, on his final day as regional sales manager before retirement, did what always came so naturally to him.

He wrote a poem.

We'll never know who you are

Or who you were meant to be

Whoever left you in this place

Sadly cast you out to sea

The water is your home now

The fish are your family

Whatever your name had been

The fish whisper it tenderly

In life you never grew up

In life you never got to see

That there is love in this world

So here's some love from me

ACKNOWLEDGMENTS

Skyler's bedtime story is based upon Jakob and Wilhelm Grimm's "Godfather Death." The final line of Henry's story in part four is also a frequent button for the Brothers Grimm. The nursery rhyme "Myself" comes from Mother Goose. The nursery rhyme "When" ("Once there was a little boy, he lives in his skin . . .") comes from a book published in 1814 that I can't find now.

Respect is due to the true crime/Reddit urban legend of Olivia Mabel. Though it would appear that this story is a hoax, certain corners of the internet still believe it to be true. I do.

"Pockets of Light" by Lubomyr Melnyk was on heavy rotation during the writing of this book, as well as Aldous Harding's music. Thank you for providing the soundtrack for my tale.

The following books proved invaluable to me during the writing of this novel: *Find Me: How Psychic Detectives from Around the World Have Banded Together to Find Missing People* by Dan Baldwin, *Missing Person: The True Story of a Police Case Resolved by the Clairvoyant Powers of Dorothy Allison* by Robert V. Cox, *Adventures of a Psychic: The Fascinating and Inspiring True-Life Story of One of America's Most Successful Clairvoyants* by Sylvia Browne, *Real Life Psychic Detectives: True Crime Stories of Clairvoyants Solving Murder Cases* by Jack Smith, *Superstition* by David Ambrose, *The Tulpa* by J. N. Williamson, *Tulpa: Thought-Forms* by Charles W. Leadbeater, *With Mystics and Magicians in Tibet* by Alexandra David-Neel, *Who's Afraid of Virginia Woolf?* by Edward Albee, *The Night Listener* by Armistead Maupin, *I Can Lick 30 Tigers Today! and Other Stories* by Dr. Seuss, *The Girl on the Volkswagen Floor* by William A. Clark, *Behind Her Eyes* by Sarah Pinborough, *The Full Facts Book of Cold Reading* by Ian Rowland, *Anagrams* by Lorrie Moore, *Buried Child* by Sam Shepard, *Audrey Rose* by Frank De Felitta, *The Empty Man* by Cullen Bunn (and its film adaptation by David Prior), *Conjuring Up Philip: An Adventure in Psychokinesis* by Iris M. Owen, *Margins of Reality: The Role of Consciousness in the Physical World* by Robert G. Jahn, *Parapsychology: A Concise History* by John Beloff, *The Insatiable Volt Sisters* by Rachel Eve Moulton, *The Changeling* by Zilpha Keatley Snyder, and last but certainly not least . . . *Safe Haven* by Nicholas Sparks.

I consider this book to be southern gothic folk horror. The documentary *Woodlands Dark and Days Bewitched: A History of Folk Horror,* directed by Kier-La Janisse, along with many of the stories and films covered within, offered endless inspiration for me while writing.

Bless the beta-readers: Rachel Harrison. Molly Pohlig. Rachel Eve Moulton.

To my editors Jhanteigh Kupihea and Rebecca Gyllenhaal. To Nicole De Jackmo, Jen Murphy, and Christina Tatulli. To Jane Morley, Andie Reid, Mandy Sampson, John McGurk, and David Borgenicht. To Amy J. Schneider. To everyone at Quirk Books: Thank you for giving my stories a home.

To Nick McCabe and everyone at the Gotham Group. To Judith Karfiol.

To the people and stories I heard growing up in and around Virginia's middle peninsula.

To my grandfather. To my mother. To my fathers.

To my family. My wife. My sons.

For twenty minutes on July 3, 2022, while I was working on the second (fourth?) draft of this novel, our youngest son went missing. We were visiting his grandparents' house in Virginia where this book is loosely set and certainly inspired by. Those twenty minutes were some of the most terrifying moments in my life and made this book feel too close to the bone. We found him, held him, hugged him, and admonished him, all the while thanking the heavens that he was safe.

Then it was back to revisions.